little black dress
· IT'S A GIRL THING ·

Dear Little Black Dress Reader,

Thanks for picking up this Little Black Dress book, one of the great new titles from our series of fun, page-turning romance novels. Lucky you — you're about to have a fantastic romantic read that we know you won't be able to put down!

Why don't you make your Little Black Dress experience even better by logging on to

www.littleblackdressbooks.com

where you can:

- ♥ Enter our **monthly competitions** to win **gorgeous** prizes
- ♥ Get **hot-off-the-press** news about our latest titles
- ♥ Read **exclusive** preview chapters both from your **favourite** authors and from brilliant new writing talent
- ♥ Buy **up-and-coming** books online
- ♥ Sign up for an essential slice of romance via our **fortnightly email** newsletter

We love nothing more than to curl up and indulge in an addictive romance, and so we're delighted to welcome you into the Little Black Dress club!

With love from,

The *little black dress* team

D0993377

Five interesting things about Rachel Gibson:

1. Growing up, I didn't like to read. I liked to play tetherball and wanted to be a tetherball champion.

2. I have a deadly fear of grasshoppers.

3. I am a shoe-aholic. I think ugly shoes are an abomination of biblical proportion.

4. I love to read the tabloids. Especially the ones featuring stories such as Bat Boy and women having Big Foot's baby.

5. I write romance novels, but I hate overly sentimental movies and sappy love songs.

Also by Rachel Gibson

Daisy's Back in Town
Sex, Lies and Online Dating
I'm in No Mood for Love
The Trouble with Valentine's Day
Simply Irresistible
Tangled Up in You
It Must Be Love
True Confessions
Lola Carlyle Reveals All
Truly Madly Yours
See Jane Score

Not Another Bad Date

Rachel Gibson

little
black
dress

First published in 2008
by AVON BOOKS
An imprint of HARPERCOLLINS PUBLISHERS, USA

First published in Great Britain in 2008
by LITTLE BLACK DRESS
An imprint of HEADLINE PUBLISHING GROUP

A LITTLE BLACK DRESS paperback

4

ISBN 978 0 7553 4597 7

Typeset in Transit511BT by Avon DataSet Ltd,
Bidford-on-Avon, Warwickshire

Printed and bound in Great Britain by Clays Ltd, St Ives plc

Headline's policy is to use papers that are natural, renewable and
recyclable products and made from wood grown in sustainable forests.
The logging and manufacturing processes are expected to conform to
the environmental regulations of the country of origin.

HEADLINE PUBLISHING GROUP
An Hachette Livre UK Company
338 Euston Road
London NW1 3BH

www.littleblackdressbooks.com
www.headline.co.uk
www.hachettelivre.co.uk

Prologue

Devon Hamilton-Zemaitis was a beautiful woman. Being dead didn't change that.

On a dreary Friday afternoon, beneath a steel gray sky, everyone inside the Grace Baptist Church on Thirty-first and Elm agreed that Devon made a fine-looking corpse. Even in death, she was everything her mother had raised her to be: gorgeous, stylish, and envied. She lay in perfect repose within the pale pink satin of her mahogany casket. The muted lights shone in her ash blond hair and caressed her smooth face, made flawless from years of strict skincare regimes and Botox. Subtle tattooing lined her eyes and shaded her lips and Oscar Seinger, of Seinger and Sons Funeral Home, had done an excellent job concealing the gash on the left side of her forehead and the dent in her skull.

As her friends and fellow members of the Junior League filed past her casket, they wept delicate tears into monogrammed handkerchiefs and secretly thanked the Lord that it had been Devon, and not one of them, who'd run the stop sign at Vine and Sixth and t-boned a Wilson Brothers garbage truck.

A garbage truck, Meme Sanders thought as she

stared down at her friend since first grade. That wasn't a very dignified end to one's life, but leave it to Devon to go out looking good in her Chanel bouclé tweed and Mikimoto pearls.

A garbage truck. Genevieve Brooks dabbed at the corner of her eye and hid a slight smile behind her handkerchief. On the same day that Devon had voted to keep Lee Ann Wilson out of the Junior League, a Wilson Brothers garbage truck had taken out Devon. Genevieve wondered if anyone but her appreciated that particularly delicious twist of irony. Of course Devon looked beautiful, Genevieve acknowledged as she gazed down at the woman she'd known since her first Little Miss Sparkle Pageant. Devon would not have been caught dead looking – well, dead – and Genevieve wondered if Devon wore the matching two-toned Chanel pumps or if people really were buried without shoes.

A garbage truck. Cecilia Blackworth Hamilton Taylor Marks-Davis wept into the lapels of her latest husband's Brooks Brothers suit. Her baby girl had been killed by a garbage truck. How horrifying. Only thirty-two and now gone. What a waste of a beautiful woman and a beautiful life. At least that husband of hers had seen to it that she looked good, although really, the white bouclé was so last-season.

Cecilia glanced over her shoulder at her son-in-law and granddaughter. The poor girl clung to her daddy and buried her face in his tailored black suit. Cecilia had never liked Zachary Zemaitis. Had never understood why Devon had been so set on having him. Lord knew he was handsome, but he was just so . . . male. With his big arms and shoulders and chest,

and Cecilia had always been uncomfortable around
men with hundred-proof testosterone flowing through
their veins.

A garbage truck. Jesus, Joseph, and Mary. Zach
Zemaitis sat in the front pew with his arm around his
ten-year-old daughter. Devon would have hated that,
and wherever she was, Zach was sure his wife was
raising hell . . .

'. . . A garbage truck,' Devon Hamilton-Zemaitis
complained to the dead guy behind her in line. He was
bad-mannered enough to roll his eyes.

'Lady, we all have problems,' he said. From what
Devon could see, the man's biggest problem was that
his family had buried him in a cheap suit. Probably JC
Penney.

Devon shuddered delicately. At least Zach had sent
her to heaven in her Chanel and her best pearls.
Although the bouclé was so last-season, and she *was*
missing her matching two-toned pumps. She looked
down at her bare feet, covered by white wispy clouds.
She hoped to God Zach didn't donate her things to the
Junior League auction, or it was likely Genevieve
Brooks would end up with the Chanel pumps.
Genevieve had been jealous of Devon since their Little
Miss pageant days, and Devon hated the thought of
Genevieve forcing her big bony feet inside those
beautiful shoes.

Without taking a step, Devon moved forward in
line. It was an odd sensation, moving about as if she
stood on some invisible conveyor belt. But then, being
dead was odd. One moment she'd been speeding home
to have it out with Zach, and the next she'd been
sucked up by a white light and landed in a place

without walls or substance. She thought maybe she'd been in line for an hour, maybe two, but that couldn't be right. On a subconscious level, she knew there'd been a funeral, and she had been buried in her white suit. Four or five *days* must have passed since the accident, but how was that possible?

She thought of her little girl and got a weird feeling in her chest. It wasn't really an ache, like when she'd been alive. It was more like a nice warm tingle that was filled with love and longing. What would become of her poor little Tiffany? Zach was a good father, when he was home. Which wasn't often, and a girl needed her mother.

She moved once more and stood before a towering white desk in front of a pair of massive golden gates. 'Finally,' she said through a sigh.

'Devon Zemaitis,' the man behind the desk spoke without opening his mouth or looking up from the scroll before him.

'Devon *Hamilton*-Zemaitis,' she corrected him.

He finally glanced up, and the white wispy clouds reflected in his blue eyes. Without expression he waved a hand, and an older woman appeared. She wore a severe bun and a lavender suit with gold buttons.

'Mrs Highbanger?'

'High*barger*,' her sixth-grade teacher corrected.

'When did you die?'

'Five years ago in man's time, but one day with the Lord is as a thousand years, and a thousand years as one day.'

Devon felt like she was in school again listening to Mrs Highbarger rattle on about fractions. 'Huh?'

'God does not mark the days as man on Earth.'

'Oh.' She guessed that explained why it felt like she'd been dead about an hour. 'So are you here to take me to heaven?' she asked, all prepared for her meeting with God. She had a few things she wanted to ask him. Important things, like why he'd allowed catastrophes like cellulite, bunions, and bad hair to exist. Then she'd want God to answer some of life's biggest mysteries, like who shot J.F.K. and—

'Not quite,' Mrs Highbarger interrupted Devon's running list of God Q and A.

'What?' She was sure she hadn't heard right. 'I'm going to heaven now. Right?'

'While on Earth, you did not earn your place in heaven.'

'Is this a joke?'

Instead of answering, Mrs Highbarger moved without moving, and Devon was pulled along behind her.

'I *earned* plenty! I raised more money than anyone else in the Junior League. My benefits were always the most fabulous.'

'You only helped others to help yourself, to get your picture on the society page and to lord it over your friends.'

Who cares, Devon thought.

'God cares,' her old teacher answered.

'You can read my thoughts?'

'Yes.'

Crap.

Exactly.

They moved downward as if on an invisible escalator, and Devon felt her first hint of panic. 'I'm not going to hell? Like with Satan and a burning pit of fire?'

'No.' Mrs Highbarger shuddered. 'You're going someplace in between, where everyone's version of hell is different.'

Devon thought of Genevieve Brooks reading the minutes of Junior League meetings and felt a stab to her brain. Listening to Genevieve for eternity would be hell.

'Because God is a loving God, you will be given a chance to earn your way up.'

That was a relief, and Devon began to feel a bit optimistic. She'd earned a place on the University of Texas cheerleading squad. Compared to that, this was going to be a breeze. 'How?'

'You start by righting those you have wronged.'

Devon thought hard. She was a good person. Practically perfect. 'I've never wronged anyone.'

Mrs Highbarger looked over her shoulder at Devon, and a memory floated in front of her face. A memory of blond curly hair, turquoise-colored eyes, and unicorns. 'Oh.' With a swipe of her hand, she waved away the memory. 'She was all wrong for him. He didn't love her. Not really. He loved me. I did both of them a favor. She's probably married with a bunch of weird kids.'

'She never found love again.'

Devon figured God wanted her to feel bad about that, but she didn't. That girl had almost stolen Zach, and everyone knew that Zach belonged to Devon. The girl had been out of her league and gotten exactly what she deserved.

They continued downward, and Devon's optimism popped like a soap bubble. 'What do I have to do?'

'Make it right.'

'Like give her three wishes?' They reached the

bottom of wherever they were going and stood in the middle of slightly darker clouds.

'More like a gift.' Mrs Highbarger held up one finger. 'You get one chance to make it right. If you don't mess it up, you move to the next level closer to heaven, where you will receive one more chance and so forth.'

So she had to make things right with what's-her-name with the curly hair. The girl she'd hated since grade school. That really did bite. Hard.

'You don't have an eternity,' the old teacher warned. 'If she finds someone to love before you've fixed the past, your chance of moving up is over.'

Devon smiled and thought of the perfect gift. 'There,' she said, as Mrs Highbarger shook her head.

'You just don't learn.' The teacher took a step back through sliding glass doors that suddenly appeared. The doors whooshed closed, and the gray mist formed solid walls, and for one terrifying moment, Devon thought she might be in some sort of prison. Her skin tingled, and she looked down at herself as her beautiful Chanel suit wafted and shimmered and turned into a horrible gray sweatsuit with Tweety on the front. 'Where am I?' she called out, as Mrs Highbarger was swallowed up by the mist.

She turned and gazed at rows of shopping carts and endless sales signs. A little old lady in a pink housecoat and a blue smock with a yellow smiley stood before her.

'Welcome to Walmart.'

'**K**iss me, babe.'

'No, really.' Beneath the light of a sixty-watt bulb on her porch, Adele Harris placed a hand on the chest of her latest date. 'I've had enough excitement for one night.'

Investment banker and former nerd turned world-class jerk, Sam King mistook the hand on his chest for a caress and took a step forward, backing Adele against the front door. Cool October air slipped across her cheeks and between the lapels of her coat, and she watched horrified as Sam lowered his face to her. 'Baby, you don't know excitement until I fire you up with a kiss.'

'I'll pass. I don't thi— urggg—' Sam smashed his lips against Adele's and silenced her protest. He shoved his tongue into her mouth and did some sort of weird swirly thing. Three quick circles to the left. Three to the right. Repeat. She hadn't been kissed like that since Carl Wilson in the sixth grade.

She forced her free hand between them and shoved. 'Stop!' she gasped as she reached into the small purse hanging from her shoulder and pulled out her keys. 'Good night, Sam.'

His jaw dropped and his brows lowered. 'You're not inviting me in?'

'No.' She turned and unlocked her front door.

'What the hell? I just spent a hundred and twenty bucks on dinner and I don't get laid?'

She pushed the door open and looked over her shoulder at the moron standing on her porch. The evening had started out okay, but had begun a downward descent with the salad course. 'I'm not a prostitute. If you'd wanted a sure thing, you should have called an escort service.'

'Women love me! I don't have to pay a prostitute,' he protested a bit too much. 'Women are dying to get some Sammy.'

By the time the dinner plates had been cleared, the date had nosedived into the third level of hell, and for the past hour Adele had tried to be nice. 'Of course they are,' she said, but failed to keep a bite of sarcasm from her voice. She stepped into her house and turned to face him.

'No wonder you're thirty-five and alone,' he sneered. 'You need to learn how to treat a man.'

For the past hour she'd pretended interest in his narcissistic ramblings. His nonstop bragging and his presumption that he was quite the catch and she was *very* lucky. She tried to tell herself that it wasn't his fault. That lately she'd begun to suspect there was something about her that made men insane, but he'd just crossed the line. Poked at a very sore spot. 'And *you* need to learn to kiss like a man,' she said, and slammed the front door in his stunned face.

'What the hell is going on in my life?' She pushed one side of her thick curly hair behind her ear and leaned her back against the door. This was getting ridiculous. Every man she'd dated for the past . . . what? . . . two or three *years* had been a jerk. If they hadn't started out as jerks, they'd quickly turned into jerks. At first she'd thought she was just a jerk magnet. That she attracted idiots, but lately she'd begun to wonder if there was something else going on. That there was something about her that turned otherwise-okay men into morons. Because really, how many jerks and idiots were there in this world? And how likely was it that she just happened to date every last one of them? Repeatedly? Without a break?

Not likely. Adele flipped the dead bolt and pushed away from the door. For the past few months, she'd begun to think that she was cursed. Cursed with perpetually bad dates.

She hung her coat in the front closet and moved into the living room. She tossed her purse onto the green sofa and reached for the remote control on the glass-and-iron coffee table. A couple of months ago, she'd mentioned to her friend Maddie that she thought she might be cursed, but Maddie had laughed it off and Adele hadn't brought it up again.

There were some people who thought she was a little different – maybe *a lot* different. Growing up she'd believed in magic; in fairy dust and unicorns and pots of gold. As a child, she'd believed in cracks in time and life on distant planets. Ghosts and alternative realities. In endless possibilities. As an adult, though she never ruled out anything completely, she no longer believed in endless anything anymore.

She turned on the television and sat on the arm of the couch. These days, she might not believe in endless anything, but she did make a good living off her imagination and the possibilities she'd believed in as a child. To date, she'd published ten science-fiction and fantasy novels. Researching those books had taken her to some truly bizarre places, and she'd personally witnessed too many instances of paranormal phenomena that could not be explained away by science to casually dismiss anything out of hand.

She flipped through the TV channels and paused on the ten o'clock news. Out of the many books she'd written, she'd never researched curses, and she didn't know a lot about them. She didn't know how curses worked, if they had to be cast by means of witchcraft or black magic. If just anyone could curse anyone else, or if there had to be a certain knowledge of curses, spells, and hexes?

I'm crazy. Adele felt her brain squeeze, and she dropped the remote onto the sofa. As crazy as people sometimes thought she was. She rose and moved through her living room to her bathroom. Because really, what kind of person thought she was cursed?

A crazy person, that's who.

She pushed her long sleeves up her arms, turned on the water above the sink, and reached for the soap. A crazy woman who hadn't had a good date or decent sex in years. A perpetual bridesmaid but never a bride. In the past two years, she'd been in the weddings of two of her close friends, while a third friend, Maddie, had just announced that she was getting married in the spring. Maddie, who thought all men were potential serial killers. Maddie, who was so paranoid she carried an arsenal of pepper spray, brass knuckles, and stun guns, had found someone to love her. Crazy Maddie had found someone who wanted to spend his life with her, and Adele couldn't find someone who wanted a relationship past midnight.

The soap slipped out of her hands as she worked up a good lather. She looked up into the mirror and washed her face with her fingertips. It was really depressing. A couple of years ago, the four friends had all been single and meeting for lunch and going on vacations to the Bahamas together. They were all writers and shared a lot in common. Then one by one they'd all gotten married, or were getting married, and Adele was the only one left single and alone. She could no longer pick up the telephone anytime she felt like it and discuss book plots, man problems, or the latest episode of *CSI*. After years of having an active social life, she now felt alone and lonely. She felt cut off and sorry for herself. She *hated* feeling sorry for herself almost as much as she *hated* all the time she spent wondering what was wrong with her.

She reached for a washcloth, ran it under the warm water, and rinsed the soap from her face. She'd been in love twice. The last time had been three years ago. His name had been Dwayne Larkin and he'd been tall, blond, and very hot. He hadn't been perfect, but she'd overlooked his annoying habit of smelling the armpits of his shirts and playing air guitar on the zipper of his jeans. Despite his faults, they'd shared some things in common. They both loved old science-fiction movies, being lazy on a Saturday afternoon, and they knew what it was like to lose a parent at a young age. Dwayne had been nice and funny, and she thought she just might want to spend the rest of her life as Mrs Larkin. She'd even mentally started to pick out a china pattern. Right up until the day three years ago that he'd stood in her kitchen and called her a fat ass. One second he'd been telling her about his day at work, then in the next, he just stopped in midsentence, turned his head to one side like some sort of android, and said, 'You're a fat ass.'

She'd been so stunned, she'd asked him what he'd just said. Unfortunately, he repeated it.

'Adele, you have a big fat ass.' He'd set down his beer and spread his hands really far apart. 'About three ax handles.'

Out of all the hurtful things he could have said to her, that was the most hurtful. He could have called her stupid or ugly, and it would not have wounded her so deeply. Not only because it was her biggest fear, but because he'd known how deeply it would hurt her. He'd known she'd inherited her grandmother Sally's bubble butt and that she jogged five miles a day, every damn day, to keep it from taking over the lower half of her body. Before that night, he'd always said he loved the way her bottom fit in his hands. Apparently he was a liar. Worse, he was a mean liar.

Adele had kicked him out of her life, but for some reason, Dwayne just wouldn't go completely. Every month or so she'd open her front door and find random stuff on her porch. One sock, a scrubby, or a headless Darth Vader, all the things she'd forgotten and left at Dwayne's house after the breakup.

She turned off the water and dried her face. Her friends thought she should have Dwayne arrested or hire someone to beat him up. Yeah, he was a bit of a stalker, she thought as she moved to her bedroom, but she wasn't frightened or creeped out by Dwayne.

A pile of scrunchies sat on her oak dresser and she pulled her long, curly hair into a thick ponytail. If anything, she was more annoyed with Dwayne than scared, and wished he'd just move on. It hadn't been easy, but she'd moved on.

She changed into a plain white T-shirt and returned to the living room. She'd stopping buying and wearing nice lingerie about the second year of the curse. Sexy undies were a waste, and plain T-shirts were comfy to sleep in.

After every loss and setback in her life, she'd moved on. She'd recovered from the death of her mother when she'd been ten, and her broken heart had eventually healed after getting shattered by her first love. Not that she equated the death of her mother with getting dumped by the first boy she'd ever loved, but each loss had been devastating in its own ways and had changed her life. Losing her mother had taught her how to be independent. Losing her first love had taught her not to give her heart away so easily.

The Tonight Show replaced the news, and Adele changed the channel. She hadn't thought of her first love in years, but even after all this time, she still felt embarrassed over how fast and hard she'd fallen for him. She'd loved everything about Zach Zemaitis. She'd loved his easy smile and the sound of his deep laughter. She'd loved the weight of his arm across her shoulders and the smell of his T-shirts and warm skin. The first time he'd kissed her, she'd felt it *everywhere*. Heart. Stomach. Backs of her knees.

She'd met him in her senior year at the University of Texas, but she'd known who he was the first day she'd set foot on campus in her freshman year. Everyone knew who Zach Zemaitis was. Longhorn football was huge, and with his golden boy good looks, and impressive stats, everyone in Texas knew of UT's star quarterback. Everyone knew he was destined for the pros just as everyone knew he dated UT's head cheerleader, Devon Hamilton.

Adele might not have known Zach until they met in college, but she'd known Devon for most of her life. The two had come to UT from the same small Texas town. They'd attended twelve years of the same public schools, but the two hadn't exactly been friends. Not even close. Devon's family had been wealthy, while Adele's father had barely scratched out a middle-class existence for himself and his two daughters. Devon did not associate with girls whose families didn't belong to the Cedar Creek Country Club and whose mothers weren't members of the Junior League. Adele had always been beneath Devon's notice – until the sixth grade, when Adele had committed an unpardonable transgression. The two girls had been up for the role of Tinkerbell in their school's production of *Peter Pan*, and Adele had won. After that, Devon had taken it upon herself to periodically make Adele's life hell. The last time had been their senior year at UT when they'd both been up for the role of Zach's girlfriend.

Adele paused on the Sci Fi Channel and *The Dresden Files*. She sat on the couch and figured there were worse things to do on a Saturday night than watch Paul Blackthorne, in his leather coat and perpetual five o'clock shadow, solve paranormal crime and save Chicago from power-mad vampires, werewolves, and assorted badasses. Worse things like suffering her way through another bad date.

But tonight, Paul didn't capture her attention, and her mind returned to Zach Zemaitis and the way he'd looked in a pair of worn Levi's and a soft old T-shirt.

They'd been in the same communications studies class, back when she'd thought she just might be a journalist. For the first few weeks of that semester, she'd sat in the back row, trying not to notice the short commas of blond hair touching the tops of his ears and the back of his long, thick neck. Like all the other females in the class, she'd tried not to let his wide shoulders and big arms distract her, and like the other girls, she'd failed.

Zach had been blessed with looks and talent. He'd been treated like a rock star, yet everyone on campus genuinely seemed to like him. While Adele could appreciate his hard body and gorgeous face, she'd always figured there had to be something wrong with his brains. He had to have a mental defect, perhaps the result of too many hits to the helmet that made all that physical perfection a total waste and a damn shame. Why else would a guy like Zach date a heinous bitch like Devon Hamilton? Sure, Devon was gorgeous, but there were a lot of gorgeous girls at UT. Obviously, he was retarded or just superficial. Maybe both.

Then one day he plopped down in front of her and turned in his chair. If suddenly looking into Zach's dark brown eyes surrounded by long, thick lashes hadn't been shocking enough, he'd said in an easy drawl, 'I've been wonderin' how you get your hair to do that.'

'What?' She'd been so stunned, she'd actually looked behind her to see whom he was talking to. There hadn't been anyone but her, and she'd turned back, and asked, 'Are you talking to me?' Because jocks like Zach, with beautiful cheerleader girlfriends, didn't talk to girls like Adele. She was into theater and hung out with people who debated interplanetary teleportation.

Not that she thought she wasn't good enough or pretty enough, she just didn't live in the same privileged sphere, where everyone kissed your ass because you could throw a football or execute a perfect back handspring into an equally perfect herkey jump.

His soft laughter had filled the silence between them. 'Yeah, I'm talkin' to you. Do you get it permed?'

Was he making fun of her? Before the days of Carrie Bradshaw and Shakira, she'd always hated her hair and had never understood why anyone would get a perm when they could have straight hair. 'I don't do anything to it,' she'd answered, waiting for the punch line. Back in junior high, she'd been called pube head. Usually by his cheerleader girlfriend.

'It's just naturally like that?' His gaze moved across her face and touched her hair.

'Yes.' He had the longest lashes of any guy she'd ever seen, and yet he was the most masculine guy she'd ever seen.

'Hmm. It's really pretty. I like it.' He looked back into her eyes, and said, through a flash of white teeth and perfect smile, 'I'm Zach.'

Had he just said her hair was pretty? *Shocking.* 'Adele.'

'I know.'

Shock number two. 'You do?'

'Sure.'

Then he'd turned back toward the front of the class, tossed a notebook and pencil on the desk in front of him, and she'd been left staring at the back of his football player's neck and wondering what the hell had just happened.

The next scheduled class day, he'd sat in front of her again. And once again, he'd turned around. This time he asked about her silver cuff bracelet engraved with three Celtic knots.

'This symbolizes the interdependency of nature,' she'd explained, while wondering why he was talking to her again. She didn't even go to football games. 'This, the relationship of man and Earth. This, the unity knot of lovers.'

He looked up from her wrist and grinned. 'Unity of lovers, huh?'

She pulled her hand back and shrugged. 'That's what some archaeologists believe. The Celts left very few records, so no one really knows for sure.'

He reached across the desk, grasped her fingers in his warm palm, and lightly tugged her hand toward him. 'I've never seen a knot of lovers that look quite like this.'

She tried to pull her hand free, but he'd tightened his grip. 'You won't find it in *Penthouse* or *Hustler*.'

He chuckled deep in his chest and let go. 'I guess that explains it.' He looked into her eyes for several long seconds, then turned around as class had begun.

Her fingers still warm from his touch, she'd grabbed her pen and pretended an interest in the professor at the front of the room. But in order to see the teacher, she had to look past Zach's wide shoulders in the T-shirt that hugged his muscles and fit tight around the bulge of his biceps. She gave up and studied the back of his head and his golden hair.

Zach didn't seem slow, like he'd taken too many hits

to the head. He seemed kind of nice, but there had to be something wrong with him. Some *thing*. Some reason why a nice guy would date Devon Hamilton.

She was still wondering about it five hours later when Zach walked into the restaurant where she worked five nights a week serving pizza. He came in with three of his football friends, but he'd hung around until she got off work.

'Where's your girlfriend?' she'd asked, as he opened the door for her.

'What girlfriend?'

Adele walked out into the crisp autumn night and shoved an arm into her sweater. 'You know what girlfriend.'

He moved behind her and held her sweater while she threaded her other arm inside. 'Describe her for me.'

'Blond. Skinny. Jumps around a lot in a cheer-leader's skirt.'

'Oh, that girlfriend.' He pulled her hair from the back of her sweater, and the tips of his warm fingers brushed her neck. 'She isn't my girlfriend.'

Adele looked up into the shadows of his face. 'Since when?'

'You ask too many questions.'

It really wasn't her business anyway. It wasn't like he was asking *her* out. 'Aren't you cold?'

'I'm like a furnace. I don't get cold.'

She supposed it had to do with all those muscles. He walked her back to her dorm room and left her at the door with no more than a handshake. But the next night when he walked her to her door, he backed her against the wall and kissed the air from her lungs. He'd told her he couldn't stop thinking about her, and within two very short months, he'd made her love him so completely that she'd found it hard to breathe around him. Hard to do anything but think about him. She fell so fast and hard and completely, she hadn't thought twice about giving herself to him, body and soul.

Adele had never planned to save herself for marriage, but she had wanted her first sexual experience to be with someone she loved. She'd thought that person was Zach, but once she'd given him everything she'd had to give, he'd crushed her heart like a can of Lone Star. He'd dumped her flat and returned to Devon, and Adele had been so devastated that she'd left the University of Texas at midterm and moved more than a thousand miles away to live with her grandmother in Boise, Idaho. A few months after she'd moved in with her grandmother, she'd received an invitation in the mail. Cecilia Blackworth Hamilton Taylor-Marks and Charla May and James Zemaitis requested the honor of Adele's presence at the wedding of their children, Devon Lynn Hamilton and Zachary James Zemaitis. There had been no return address, but Adele had known who'd sent it.

Adele had known that Zach would marry Devon, but apparently it hadn't been enough for Devon to have Zach. She'd wanted to rub Adele's face in it.

She'd never told anyone about her relationship with Zach. Not her friends and not her sister. Looking back on it, she wondered how she could have been so foolish. Not only had she given her heart away easily, she'd given it to a jock.

The last she'd heard, Zach was playing pro ball for Denver, not that she kept up on sports. But occasionally she had heard his name mentioned in the sports segment of the nightly news or seen his face selling Gatorade or Right Guard or jock itch cream on television. Okay, so she'd never seen him selling jock itch cream.

She didn't know if he was still playing for Denver or had been traded. She didn't know where he was or what he was doing, and she didn't give a damn. Hopefully, he was still married to Devon, and his wife was making his life hell.

Adele leaned her head back against a cushion and let out a breath. She was getting a little bitter. About her life and men, and she really didn't want to live that way. She loved her life, mostly, and despite her rash of bad dates and her first heartbreak, she loved men.

Don't I?

She sat up and looked across the room. What if all the bad dates had more to do with hidden anger and resentment? Adele shook her head. No, she didn't have hidden anger and resentment. Or at least she didn't think she did, but . . . if it was hidden, how would she know?

'Oh God,' she groaned. She *was* crazy.

The telephone rang and saved her more mental torment. She rose and moved to the kitchen to pick up the cordless receiver. She glanced at the area code and groaned. Apparently her mental torment was not over. She really wasn't in the mood to talk to her older sister, Sherilyn. The responsible one. The one with the perfect life. The one happily married to a dentist and happily raising a perfect teenage daughter in Fort Worth. The perfect sister due to have a perfect baby boy in four months. The one who wasn't cursed or crazy.

She thought about letting it go to voice mail, but in the end she answered because it might be important.

'Hey, Sheri. How're things?'

'William left.'

Adele felt her brows go up and her eyes widen. 'Where did he go?'

'He's moved in with his twenty-one-year-old assistant.'

'No.' Adele pulled out a kitchen chair and sat. She'd never liked William, but she'd never suspected he was so low as to abandon his pregnant wife.

'Yes. Her name is Stormy Winter.'

Adele supposed there were more important questions, but the one she asked was, 'Is she a stripper?'

'He says no.'

Which meant she'd asked. 'How's Kendra?' Adele asked, referring to her thirteen-year-old niece.

'Mad. At me. At William. At the world. She's embarrassed that I'm pregnant and that her father's moved in with somebody eight years older than she is.'

Wow. Sherilyn's life was more messed up than Adele's. That was a first.

'My life is a wreck.' Sherilyn's voice broke, and she started to cry. 'I don't know how this happened. One day everything was per-perfect, then the next William's run off.'

Adele suspected there'd been signs that Sherilyn had chosen to ignore. 'How can I help?' she asked, figuring there was really nothing she could do but listen.

'I'm moving back to Cedar Creek. Come home with me.'

Adele was home.

'I need you, Dele.'

Adele hadn't been back to Cedar Creek since her father's funeral seven years ago.

Sherilyn burst into another round of sobbing before she pulled herself together and managed, 'I nee-need my family in my time of cris-sis.' By the sounds of it, Sherilyn was beyond crisis and rushing headlong into a breakdown. 'Please. I have to go home. I can't stan-nd it here without William. All our friends kn-ow, and they pity me. My life is falling ap-part.'

Sherilyn was the most capable woman Adele knew, and she knew a lot of very capable women. For that reason and many others, she and Sherilyn had never really gotten along for more than five minutes at a time. 'Oh, Sheri . . .' For the first time ever, Sherilyn needed her, and Adele was the only real family she had left. But . . . Adele's life was in Boise. She'd bought a house and planned on painting her office. She was thinking about getting a Pug.

'Just for a little while. Until Kendra and I get settled in our new pl-ace.'

She'd made a life for herself, and she had friends here. Good friends . . . who were married or getting married and had lives different from hers now. She was quite possibly cursed with bad dates and was very likely crazy. Maybe she needed a break. To get away from her life.

Just for a few weeks. 'When do you need me?'

Texans loved God, family, and football, though not always in that order. It all depended on the time of the year and your brother's latest wife.

Bless her heart.

Sunday belonged to the Lord, and he ruled the pews of the Bible Belt. His word whipped the faithful into a religious frenzy with sermons of sin and redemption and charged the air with the electric buzz of his spirit.

Can I get an Amen?

God could have Sundays. Friday nights were devoted to high-school football. Across the Longhorn State, high-school ball ruled the stands, whipping the faithful into a gridiron frenzy and charging the air with the electric buzz of twenty-five thousand cheering fans.

Can I get a Glory Hallelujah?

As the sun set over the flat plains of Cedar Creek, stacks of fifteen-hundred-watt lights flooded the green turf of Warren P. Bradshaw Stadium. Armed with felt pendants, bright pom-poms, and stadium blankets, half the population of Cedar Creek turned out to watch the Cedar Creek Cougars battle their crosstown rivals, the Lincoln Panthers. With a shot at State on the line, the buildup to the game was intense.

From the moment of the kickoff, a bruising back-and-forth brought the fans to their feet and the Panthers' coach yelling at the refs and throwing his clipboard on the ground. By contrast, the Cougars' coach stood on the sidelines as cool as a tall glass of sweet tea. Only his intense gaze gave Coach Zach Zemaitis's turmoil away as he read the opposition's defensive line, signaled his boys, and adjusted plays. He loved ball. Had played it from as far back as he could remember, but there was no cause to get all uptight and bust something vital. Yeah, he'd been born and raised near Austin, and he knew that high-school football was as serious as a heart attack. He knew that some of these boys' futures depended on the outcome of the game, but he also knew it was supposed to be fun. Perhaps their last chance at ball in its purest form, before college scouts turned their heads around by attention, money, and the lure of NCAA scholarships.

The two teams continued to hammer at each other until the last few moments of the game, when the Cougars scored a touchdown that brought them within one point of a tie. With three seconds left on the clock, they lined up on the Panthers' two-yard line. The center snapped the ball and the quarterback handed off to his running back, who dove across the line for the two-point conversion. One side of the stadium went wild as the necessary two points flashed on the board. But unfortunately the same play that had saved the game for the Cougars sent their star running back to the West Central Baptist Hospital. There fluorescent light washed the emergency rooms in sterile white, and teal-and-maroon curtains separated the beds of patients suffering from assorted illnesses, accidents, and overdoses.

Zach Zemaitis stood with his weight on one foot and his hands on his hips as he gazed at the young man on the gurney before him. Pain etched Don Tate's thin black face.

Zach turned to the doctor beside him. 'How long?' he asked even though he'd played long enough that he pretty much knew the answer.

'After surgery, at least two months,' the doctor answered.

That's what he'd thought. 'Shit.' Still in his junior year, Don was the best damn running back in the history of Cedar Creek High School, maybe in the history of the whole damn state of Texas. So far, he'd rushed for more than fifteen hundred yards for an average of ten. Scouts from Nebraska, Ohio State, and Texas A & M had reviewed Don's tapes and were impressed with the seventeen-year-old boy. Football was Don's ticket out of West Texas, and now this. A knee injury that could sideline his career before it even began. Shit.

Don licked his dry lips, and fear pinched his brow. A real fear that Zach understood all too well. 'Coach, I can't be sidelined for two months.'

'You're going to be just fine,' Zach promised even though he wasn't at all certain. Don had torn two ligaments in his left knee, and some guys never recovered one hundred percent.

Zach dropped his hands to his side and made another promise he wasn't sure about, but one he'd try like hell to keep. 'No one's going to take your place on the team.'

'I gotta make All-State.'

'You will. Next year. Shoot, Gerry Palteer tore up his knee in a game against the Gophers in '89 and went on to make All-State the next year. He wasn't near as fast as you.' Zach raised his gaze from Don's eyes to the boy's mother, standing on the other side of the bed. A green-and-gold purse in the shape of a football with the word 'Cougars' sewn into the fake leather hung off one of Rose Tate's shoulders. The purses had been sold by the boosters that past summer to raise money for new helmets. 'How much is the surgery going to cost?' Rose stared at the clipboard in her hands as worry lines creased her dark forehead. 'Not that it matters, I suppose. If Don needs it, he needs it, but we lost our insurance when Gorman closed.'

A lot of families had lost good jobs when the software company had closed the year before.

'Don't worry about that, ma'am.' Zach held out one hand across the bed. 'I'll take care of the paperwork. The school has insurance that will pay for Don's care.' Rose handed him the clipboard, and he stuck it under one arm. 'You just see to your boy. I'll fill those out for you.' He returned his gaze to his player. In a few hours, Don would be transferred to the surgery center in Lubbock. 'I'll see you when you get home,' he said, and headed toward the foot of the bed. At the part in the curtains, he looked back over his shoulder. 'I know you want to get back into the game, but don't you push yourself faster than your body can heal,' he added and walked out into the hall. He moved to the nurses' station to fill out the rest of the paperwork.

'Good game tonight, Coach Z,' a nurse said to him as she walked behind the counter.

Zach glanced past a pair of pale blue eyes, flanked by a set of deep crow's-feet, up to a pile of wispy blond hair. 'Thanks, honey. I appreciate it.' The game hadn't been pretty, but they'd won.

'My grandson played for the Cougars back in '02. Defensive lineman.'

Zach hadn't lived in Cedar Creek in '02. He'd been playing ball in Denver and living a whole other life. Now, six years later, he was living a life that hadn't been in the game plan.

'I understand Don Tate is heading to the orthopedic center in Lubbock.'

'That's right.' Zach returned his gaze to the insurance forms. With a population somewhere around fifty thousand, Cedar Creek didn't have the resources of a bigger city.

'What's this mean for our rushing game?'

Zach smiled, but he wasn't surprised by the woman's question. 'It means Tyler Smith is going to get his chance at playing varsity ball,' he answered, referring to the junior varsity running back.

He signed his name and handed the clipboard to the doctor as he approached.

The doctor looked it over. 'I take it there is no school insurance.'

'None that'll cover everything, but Miz Tate doesn't need to know that.' He shook the doctor's hand. 'Thanks for takin' care of Don.'

The black soles of Zach's Pumas smudged the floor in a few places as he walked from the emergency room. The automatic doors opened and closed behind him, and he moved from the harsh light and out into the Texas night lit by millions of stars all crammed together in an endless black sky. He zipped up his green jacket with the words, Cedar Creek Cougars written in gold across the back. The lot had thinned since he'd arrived a few hours ago with a few circles of light illuminating patches of asphalt. He reached for the cell phone clipped to his belt and powered it up as he moved across the lot toward his silver Escalade. His choice in SUVs had nothing to do with Cadillac Pimpin' and everything to do with room. At six-four and 220 pounds, Zach liked most things a little roomy. He'd owned a Porsche once, but he'd returned it after three weeks. Driving it had felt like being stuffed inside a soup can.

The cell phone beeped, and he looked down at the lighted screen. Using his thumb, he scrolled the missed calls list and paused on the last number. He hit the call button, and, after a few rings, his thirteen-year-old daughter's voice filled his ear.

'Where are you?' she asked.

When he was late, Tiffany worried. 'Exactly where I told you I'd be.' It was understandable, but it'd been three years since the death of her mother, Devon, and she still freaked out if she couldn't get ahold of him. 'What do you need?'

'We're out of Coke cola. Can you pick some up?'

Zach glanced at the silver Rolex watch he'd been given the day he'd retired from the NFL. 'Tiff, it's after midnight.'

'We're thirsty.'

Tiffany had a girlfriend spending the night. Normally, he would have been home long before now, but after the game, he'd driven straight to the hospital. 'And we need some chips,' she added.

He shoved his hands in his front pocket and pulled

out his keys. 'I'll stop at the E-Z MART on my way.' He spoiled his daughter. He knew it, but guilt did that to a person. He hadn't been around a lot for the first ten years of Tiffany's life. Now, he was both mother and father, and he was fairly certain he was screwing it up. 'What kind of chips do y'all want?'

'Lay's barbecue.'

He glanced over the hood of his vehicle to the maroon Celica, with its front pointed toward his SUV, and his gaze stopped on the long legs and round behind of a woman standing at the open passenger's side door. One of her hands held the door open as she spoke to someone inside the car. She wore jeans and a white sweater, and she stood just inside the pool of light that shined in her long, curly hair.

'Daddy?'

Her thick blond hair reminded Zach of a girl he'd known once. A girl with big turquoise-colored eyes and soft pink lips. A girl whose soft gasps had driven him wild every time he'd kissed the sweet spot just below her ear.

'Daddy?'

One corner of Zach's mouth lifted into a smile. He hadn't thought about that girl in a while.

'Daddy, are you there?'

He tore his gaze from the woman and looked down at the keys in his hand. 'I'm here. What else do you need?' He unlocked the Escalade and slid inside.

'Nothin'. Just hurry.'

'I'm on my way, baby girl.' He started the SUV and glanced at the woman one last time. She bent forward to help someone out of the car, her sweater slid up her back, and her hair fell over the side of her face. Zach pulled out of the hospital parking lot and flipped on his headlights. As he drove toward the E-Z MART, his mind turned to the game against the Panthers, and he replayed it in his head. With Don out for the rest of the season, the team was going to have to rely more on its passing, which had some problems. The biggest was that the quarterback, Sean McGuire, needed to work on passing quickly against the rush. Sean was shorter than most quarterbacks and had a tendency to hold on to the ball a few seconds too long looking for a lane. Sean's height disadvantage could be overcome with drills, and there was no doubt in Zach's mind that the kid would work hard. What the young quarterback lacked in height he made up for in self-discipline, a tough competitive streak, and natural leadership. Those were things that could not be taught. Zach had known a lot of players who'd had talent but lacked discipline. Talent usually got those players into the NFL, but most of them didn't last long before fame and excess took their toll.

Zach stopped at a red light and hit the window switch. As the glass slid silently down into the door, the cold night breeze brought the smells of autumn into the SUV, of cooling earth, dying leaves, and the Concho River. Three years ago if someone had told him he'd be living in Cedar Creek, Texas, coaching high-school ball, he would have laughed his ass off. If they'd told him he'd be living in Cedar Creek coaching football and *liking* it, he would have laughed his ass off and said they were nuttier than a pan of his momma's peanut patties.

The light changed, and he drove through the inter-section and into the E-Z MART parking lot. Once inside the store, he grabbed a six pack of Coke, a bag of barbecue chips and a box of cornflakes because he knew they were out of cereal. When his wife, Devon, had been alive, she'd let Tiffany eat crap twenty-four/seven. Now, Zach didn't mind a little junk food; he had a fondness for Ding Dongs that would not be denied, but he tried to limit his and Tiffany's crap consumption to the weekends. Tiffany because she needed nutritious food to grow, and him because he didn't need to grow.

'Good game tonight, Coach Z,' the checker said as he placed the Coke and chips in a bag.

'Thanks.' Zach handed over a twenty to the young man, who wore the kind of eyeliner and Mohawk rarely seen in west Texas.

'My twin brother played for the Cougars back in '04. He's playin' for Ohio now.'

'Did you play?'

'Nah.' He gave Zach his change. 'I'm an art student at the University of Portland in Oregon.'

Zach chuckled. That explained the Mohawk.

'I'm heading back next semester.'

'Good luck in Oregon,' Zach said, and shoved his change in his front pocket. He grabbed the bag of groceries and headed outside. As he climbed into the Escalade, he thought back on what he'd been doing in '04.

Four years ago, he'd been living in Denver, while his wife and Tiffany lived in Cedar Creek. He'd visit or they'd visit, but for the most part, they'd lived separate lives. For the last seven years of their ten-year marriage, they'd lived in different states. He and Devon had liked it that way.

In his last year at UT, his touchdown passes led the

nation and he'd been picked up by Miami in the first round of the drafts. The summer after graduating from UT, he'd gone off to the Dolphins' training camp while Devon had stayed in Austin to have Tiffany. After Tiffany was born, the two packed up and moved to Florida.

For the next three years, they'd been happy living in Florida. Devon had loved Florida, and he'd thought she'd loved him, too. But after three years with the Dolphins, Zach was traded to the Broncos. He was thrilled to be out from under Dan Marino's long shadow, but Devon had hated living in Denver. After six months, she'd packed up Tiffany and moved back to the small Texas town where she'd been raised. Back to being a big fish in a small pond, and he'd discover that she loved being the wife of Zach Zemaitis more than she'd loved him.

For seven years they'd lived a life that suited them. She in Texas. He in Denver. He loved playing ball for the Broncos and figured he had a good five years until he retired, but that all changed one November 18 in a game against Kansas City. He didn't remember much about that day except waking up in the hospital and getting the news that his career was over.

During his ten years in the NFL, he'd sustained eight concussions. And those were only the ones serious enough to report. After a series of scans and tests, he was told that one more concussion would likely kill him. He'd been forced to retire at the height of his career. At the age of thirty-two.

He might have fallen into a deep depression if he hadn't been offered a sweet job with ESPN. While at UT, he'd managed to get his degree in communication and had been in negotiations with the sports network when his wife had been killed and his life took a complete one-eighty.

Zach slowed the Escalade and turned toward the river. It had been his intention to pack up Tiffany and move her with him, but the day of Devon's funeral, he'd realized he couldn't move her away from her friends and the only home she'd ever known. As he'd sat in the pew staring at his wife in her coffin, he'd felt his life change. With each tear his daughter had shed into the lapels of his suit, *he'd* changed. Like a compass showing the way north, his life spun in a completely different direction.

Before Devon died, he'd been able to tell himself Tiffany was better off living in Texas with her momma. God knew that if Devon wasn't happy, then no one was happy, and Devon seemed to be happy only living in Cedar Creek. But sitting in church that day, all the lies he told himself fell away, and for the first time in a long time, he put the wants, needs, and desires of his child first.

Zach turned into a gated community and hit three numbers on a keypad clipped to his visor. During the day, the gates were opened to allow workers and visitors easy access, but they closed at eight p.m. each night. The gate lifted and closed behind him, and he drove past the Cattail Creek clubhouse and driving range. On his left, a Mediterranean-style villa glowed an eerie white in the dark Texas night. He turned right at the clubhouse and moved past a French modern that looked like three houses piled on top of each other, a Victorian with turrets, and into the long drive of a ten-thousand-square-foot Tuscan-Plantation-style house.

The garage door opened as he drove past the portico, and he parked inside next to a twenty-four-foot Sea Ray.

Devon had built the house shortly after she'd moved back to Cedar Creek, and while the home was beautiful, it reflected little of Zach's personal style. He liked things roomy, but ten thousand square feet with a guesthouse, and maid's quarters across the yard from the pool, was excessive. Too big for three people, one of whom only lived there occasionally.

During its construction, he'd asked Devon why she wanted to build a huge Tuscan Plantation house in the middle of Texas. She'd looked at him and said as serious as a heart attack, 'For the same reason I drive a Mercedes and have a five-carat diamond ring. Because I can.' Which pretty much summed up his dead wife and was one of the many differences that had driven them apart. Just because people let you get away with being an ass didn't make it right. It was something he'd learned and Devon hadn't.

Zach grabbed the E-Z MART bag on the seat beside him and headed across part of the courtyard and into the house. As he walked past the laundry and storage rooms, the thud of shitty hip-hop music assaulted his ears from the sound system built into the house. He moved into a small room where every aspect of the house could be controlled, and he turned the system off. After living in the house full-time for three years now, he'd mastered most of the gadgets, buttons, and switches.

'Tiffany,' he called out as he moved into the kitchen and set the groceries on the honey-colored marble counter. He heard footsteps running down the terra-cotta stairs a few seconds before his daughter appeared.

Her long blond hair was pulled back in a ponytail, and she wore a blue T-shirt and flannel pants. Tiffany's arms and legs were long and thin, and she had yet to grow into her wide mouth and big green eyes. When she did, there was little doubt she'd be as beautiful as her mother.

A girl with dark brown hair and startling blue eyes followed in Tiffany's wake.

'Did you get the Coke cola?' his daughter asked as she tore into the bag.

Zach didn't feel the need to answer because his daughter pulled the six-pack from the sack and headed to the stainless-steel refrigerator. 'Sugar, you need to introduce your friend.'

'Oh, yeah.' Tiffany grabbed two cans of cola and shut the refrigerator. 'Kendra, this is my daddy.' She moved to the other girl and handed her a Coke. 'Daddy, this is Kendra. She's new to my school.'

'It's a pleasure to meet you, Kendra,' he said as he opened a cupboard and put away the box of Corn Flakes. 'Where are you from?'

'Fort Worth.'

'Are you a Cowboys fan?'

'No, sir. I don't watch football.' She popped the top on her Coke and took a drink. 'My daddy used to take me to see my grandmomma in South Carolina, and we'd go to Darlington sometimes.'

'Ah, you're a NASCAR fan.'

She shrugged and looked about the kitchen. 'It was kinda boring.'

'Can you believe she doesn't like football?' Tiffany asked as she grabbed the bag of chips. 'I've never known anyone who doesn't like ball.'

'I used to play on my school's soccer team.' Kendra returned her gaze to Zach. 'It's kinda the same.'

Tiffany gasped, and Zach laughed. 'Don't say that too loud around here,' he said, and changed the subject to save her from uttering any more unforgivable faux pas. 'What brings you to Cedar Creek?'

'My momma used to live here. She and my daddy are getting a divorce, so we moved here for a while.'

Kendra didn't offer more, and Zach didn't pry.

'Come on.' Tiffany opened the chips as she walked past her friend. 'Let's go watch a movie.'

'I'm going to bed, so keep it down. And try to get to sleep at a reasonable hour.' Zach spoke to the girls' backs as they headed down the stairs to what his wife had called the 'theater room,' which was more like a big family room with a seventy-two-inch high-definition TV.

Zach left the kitchen light on, but turned the others off as he moved through the house. In the living room, the leather sofas, chairs, and wooden end tables had been pushed to one side. Tiffany had obviously been practicing her dance routines, which also explained the loud music when he'd first arrived. Unlike her mother, Tiffany was not a cheerleader. Instead, she much preferred her school's dance team. She'd inherited coordination and timing from both parents, but her fierce competition came directly from him. People had accused Devon of being competitive, but she hadn't been so much competitive as she'd been territorial.

He moved past the entry and down a short hall to his bedroom. The house had been built with his and hers walk-in closets, but Zach had never cared about clothes. He had a few nice suits, but he preferred hundred-percent cotton, and as a result, his closet was fairly empty. Until a year ago, when he'd finally convinced Tiffany that it was time to donate her mother's clothes to the Junior League, Devon's clothing had filled her closet and half of his.

The soles of Zach's shoes sank into the thick beige carpeting as he moved across the room to a set of dresser drawers. The headboard of his king-size bed rested between two large windows covered in green-and-blue-striped drapery. Once he'd decided to move into the house, he'd had his bedroom furniture shipped from his condo in Denver, and he'd replaced the pastel colors Devon had favored with bolder, more masculine prints. The bedroom was the only room in the house that reflected Zach's tastes, and it was one of a very few rooms in the house he could walk into without seeing photographs of his dead wife.

Zach stripped down to his boxers, remembered that Tiffany had a guest, and pulled on a pair of gray sweatpants. His daughter wasn't ready to put away Devon's pictures, and while having Devon's green eyes watching him from one end of the house to the other was kind of weird, Tiffany found comfort in the images.

Zach set his watch on a maple chest of drawers. During the ten years he'd played pro ball, he'd thrown close to four thousand passes and rushed for over a thousand yards. He'd been in three pro bowls, won a Super Bowl, and been voted MVP. He'd be eligible for induction into the Pro Football Hall of Fame in two years, and it was expected that he'd be voted in on his first attempt. He had more money than he could spend in two lifetimes and made more every day from investments. He owned memorabilia businesses, and he was coaching high-school ball for twenty-five grand a year.

Zach moved to one of the windows that looked out the backyard and over the lighted grounds and pool covered by a thirty-six-foot-by-sixty-eight-foot retractable Plexiglas dome. He really didn't have any complaints. His life was surprisingly good . . . except for his sex life. Having a teenage daughter made it very difficult, if not downright impossible, to have any sort of sex life. Out of all the things he missed about his former life, and there was a lot to miss, he missed his sex life the most.

He pressed a hand to the cool glass window and thought about the woman he'd seen in the hospital parking lot. He thought about her nice behind and her long blond curls. He thought about the girl he'd known in his senior year in college and how she'd driven him insane with just a look from those big blue eyes of hers.

He hadn't thought of Adele Harris in a long time, but all these years later, the memory of her was still clear. After a lifetime of knocks to the head that made it hard to remember some things, he remembered her wild hair and amazing eyes, and he had no trouble remembering how she felt beneath his hands and how her hands had felt on him. He had no problem remembering the first time he'd kissed her in her dorm and the day he'd touched her through her clothes. They'd only dated for a short time, but he remembered her. He supposed it might have something to do with the fact that she'd been a virgin until the night she'd let him touch her without her clothes.

Zach looked down at the patio and across to the guesthouse. In a lot of ways, Adele had been different from the other girls he'd dated, and he'd really loved that about her. Hell, at the time he'd thought that maybe he'd loved *her*.

Now, he was older and supposed to be wiser, and he wasn't even sure he knew what that meant anymore.

3

The house was huge. Even by Texas standards. It
was made of stucco and stone and had a red tile
roof. Adele supposed it was supposed to look like a
Tuscan villa of some sort, but it had a slight *Romano's
Macaroni Grill* look to it, and she got an urge for shrimp
scampi. Or maybe she was just hungry from spending
all night in the hospital.

She parked her sister's car under the portico, then
moved beneath the vine-covered walk to a set of heavy
wood doors with wrought-iron handles. She rang the
doorbell and folded her arms against the morning chill.
She'd run out of the house in such a hurry the night
before, she'd forgotten a jacket.

The moment she'd driven into the gated community,
she'd felt a slight unease. It reeked of the kind of money
and exclusion that had always made her uncomfortable.
Like an interloper. It wasn't that she herself didn't feel
good enough. She was successful and made a very good
living off her writing, but being back in Cedar Creek
again reminded her of growing up in the small town. Of
growing up just inside the boundary between the haves
and have-nots.

As a kid, she'd been bused to schools in the

wealthier neighborhoods, and she'd never really fit in. Partly because her family had been middle class, and partly because she'd lived a lot in her own head. She'd made a few friends in middle and high school, but she'd lost track of them after she'd left for UT.

She fit in a lot better with the good friends she'd made in Idaho. She felt like she belonged there more than she ever had in the place where she'd been born and raised. But here she was back in Texas, standing on the porch of a mansion, out of place in her coffee-stained, thin white sweater that zipped up the front.

She'd been back in town a week. Seven exhausting days of helping her sister that had culminated in rushing Sherilyn to the hospital the night before. At least Adele had been able to wash her face and use a toothbrush she'd bought in the gift shop before she'd left to pick up Kendra.

One side of the heavy doors swung open, and a girl with long blond hair stood just inside. 'Are you Kendra's momma?' she asked, flattening her vowels like a true Texan.

'I'm her aunt.' The girl was very thin, and there was something vaguely familiar about her. Something Adele couldn't put her finger on. Then again, maybe there was nothing. She was exhausted, and her mind was fuzzy.

'I'm Tiffany.' She swung the door open and smiled, showing a mouthful of braces. 'Come on in. We're just finishing up breakfast.'

Adele stepped inside and onto terracotta tiles with a Marcala medallion in the center of the large entry. Her flip-flops slapped her heels as she followed Tiffany down a hall and into the kitchen, where everything was made of marble, granite and stainless steel. Morning sunlight spilled through a large leaded-glass window, throwing odd patterns on the floor and commercial-grade appliances.

Within a splash of white light, Kendra stood with one hip shoved into a counter. Except for the Harris eyes, she looked just like her father, William.

'Where's Mom?' Kendra asked, and took a bite of a Pop Tart with pink icing.

'I had to take her to the hospital last night.'

Kendra straightened and swallowed. 'What's wrong? Is she still there? Is she okay?'

'She has something called preeclampsia.'

'What's that?'

Adele herself wasn't quite sure. The doctors had talked a lot about high levels of protein and dangerously high blood pressure, but Adele had not really understood the how and why of it. Only that it was very serious. She explained the best she could. 'It's something that happens in the placenta that causes high blood pressure.' Maybe. 'She's okay, but the doctors say she has to stay in the hospital for a while.' There was a good chance Sherilyn would have to spend the four remaining months of her pregnancy in the hospital, which meant Adele was going to be stuck in Texas for longer than she'd planned. A lot longer.

'Is the baby okay?'

'He's fine.' For now. 'Go get your stuff, and I'll take you to see her.'

Kendra nodded, and her fine dark hair fell across her cheek. She walked from the kitchen, her Pop Tart forgotten in her hand. Adele wished she knew her niece better and knew what to say, but she didn't, and she felt a little guilty about that. Adele hadn't seen Kendra since her niece's seventh birthday, and she'd grown up a lot in six years. Her body was maturing, and she'd started to wear a little bit of makeup to school this year. Not a lot, but it wouldn't be long until she was smack-dab in the middle of her teenage years.

'Are you from Fort Worth?' Tiffany asked.

Adele turned her gaze to the young girl in front of her. 'No. I'm from Idaho.'

Tiffany nodded and pushed her hair behind her ears. 'I've been to Des Moines.'

That was Iowa, but Adele didn't bother to correct Tiffany. A lot of adults thought Idaho was in the Midwest, too. 'Did you girls have a good time last night?' she asked in an effort to hold up her side of the conversation. She hadn't been around teens since she'd been one herself and didn't really know what to say to someone twenty-two years younger. What did teenage girls do these days?

'Kendra's gonna try out for the dance team, and I'm helpin' her with the routines. Two girls got cut on account of gettin' caught at a beer party doin' keg stands.'

Apparently teens were doing keg stands. Adele hadn't begun her keg-standing career until college.

'Kendra danced at her old school, but you probably know that.'

Actually, she didn't. Adele listened as Tiffany rambled on about her dance team and their chances of making it to nationals this year. And the more she talked, the more Adele felt there was something familiar about the girl. But that something wasn't quite clear in Adele's tired brain.

'I can't find my dance shoes,' Kendra said as she

walked toward them, her sweatshirt in one hand and a backpack slung over one shoulder. Her eyes were red and her cheeks smeared with tears as if she'd just wiped a palm across her face.

Tiffany turned on her heels and walked from the kitchen. 'You probably left them in the living room.'

Adele put her arm around her niece's shoulders, and they followed Tiffany. 'Your mom and the baby are going to be just fine. When I left, she was eating breakfast, and the baby was kicking.' Not that she'd felt any kicking herself.

'Really?'

'Really. She's going to need lots of rest, but I'll be around to help out.' They moved into the dark living room, and Adele gave her niece's shoulder a squeeze before she dropped her arm to her side. 'Try not to worry.'

'I always wanted a little brother,' Tiffany said as she flipped a switch. Delicate wrought-iron chandeliers lit up a large room with the furnishings pushed back against the walls. The large rugs had been rolled up leaving the middle bare. 'But my momma and daddy only had me,' she added.

'I always thought it would be nice to have an older brother.' Adele moved farther into the room and glanced about for Kendra's shoes. At the far end, a fireplace made of gold-and-brown marble dominated one wall. Columns and leaves were carved into the smooth stone, and like the rest of the house, it bordered on over the top. 'A little brother would have been really ni—' She stopped in midsentence, her mouth fell open and the air whooshed from her lungs. Above the mantel, caressed by the warm glow of special lighting,

Devon Hamilton stared down at her from a life-sized portrait. Her green eyes cold and her lips pressed into that I'm-better-than-you smile Adele recognized.

Tiffany moved beside her and looked up. 'That's my momma.'

Adele moved her mouth to speak, but no words came out. Shock hit her stomach, while hot little pinpricks spread up her chest to her face. She took one step back, then another.

'She died a few years ago.'

Adele stopped. Shock number two. *Devon is dead?* 'I'm sorry,' she whispered past the clog in her throat.

'Wasn't she beautiful? Like an angel.'

'Mmm-hmm,' she managed.

'It's just me and Daddy now.'

Daddy. Tiffany and Kendra went to school together, which meant Tiffany was also thirteen. Which also meant . . . holy crap. In her shock over Devon, she'd forgotten all about *Daddy.* 'Kendra, we've got to go. Now!'

Both girls looked at her, and Kendra said, 'I need my shoes.'

'Get them another time.' Adele headed toward the door.

'Maybe I left them downstairs.'

'I'll wait in the car,' Adele said over her shoulder as she moved through the entry and out the door. 'This can't be happening,' she whispered to herself. Her fingers felt cold, and she shook her hands. She twisted an ankle on the uneven cobblestones in the walkway, but she didn't let a little thing like pain shooting up her shin slow her down. 'Oh my God. I can't believe this.' She hooked a right beneath the portico and moved toward Sherilyn's Celica. At one time or another, every woman alive fantasized about running into an ex and making him sorry he'd dumped her. Adele had had those fantasies. She'd had them a time or two about Zach Zemaitis, but she'd always pictured herself sizzling hot, not looking like crap with coffee down her sweater.

She pulled a set of keys from the pocket of her jeans. *God, just get me out of here.* She looked up, and the keys fell from her numb fingers at the sight of shock number three jogging up the driveway toward her. The sunlight caught in Zach Zemaitis's hair like a halo and a pair of Oakley Thump Pros rested on the bridge of his nose. Her heart pounded in her ears as the soles of his running shoes pounded the uneven cobblestones with ease.

Within the shadow of the portico, Adele stood frozen, afraid to breathe as he jogged up the drive. He gazed straight ahead, and with any luck, he'd run right on by without seeing her. But lately, Adele's luck had been fairly shitty, and just before he disappeared from sight, his head turned, and he looked right at her. His footsteps slowed and stopped. He retraced a few steps backward, and a crease furrowed his brow. For several long seconds, he simply stared at her, pinning Adele with a gaze she could feel rather than see. He was breathing a bit heavy as he pulled air into his lungs, and he slowly raised a hand to his temple and turned off the MP3 built into the slim frame of his glasses. He pulled the little speakers from his ears, then pushed the black sunglasses to the top of his head. Across the distance he looked at her through the dark brown eyes that used to make her heart squeeze and her stomach ache. His brows lowered over his steady gaze, and he walked from the sunlight into the shadow. With each step of his jogging shoes, her heart pounded a little faster in her chest, and she put a hand on the trunk of the car to keep from keeling over . . . or passing out . . . or jumping in the car and locking the doors.

After all these years, he still moved the same. Relaxed as if he was saving his energy for something important. Like throwing a long bomb, sprinting past a determined lineman, or exerting himself in bed. Sweat dampened the armpits of a blue X-TERRA T-shirt that fit loose about his wide chest. A pair of gray cotton jogging shorts rested low on his hips and fell midway to his powerful thighs. He was bigger than she remembered. His jaw was stronger, his cheekbones more defined. Age had not robbed him of one ounce of his good looks. If anything, he was even more gorgeous than she remembered. And as she forced herself to stand there and face Zach instead of jumping in the car and peeling out on his nice cobblestone driveway, she held on to a desperate hope that perhaps he didn't recognize her.

'Adele?' So much for her desperate hope.

'Hello,' she managed. 'How are you, Zach?'

'Surprised.' His voice was different. Deeper. More masculine than she remembered, but his accent was pure Texas. 'It's been a long time.'

Fourteen years.

His gaze moved across her face to her unruly hair. 'You look the same.'

He didn't. He looked better. More like a man. 'I'm here to pick up my niece, Kendra.'

'Oh.' His gaze returned to hers and after several

long heartbeats, he said, 'I'll get her.' He turned toward the door and took a few steps.

'She knows I'm here.'

He turned back toward her and the early-morning sun filtered through the vines above his head and cut slashes of light across his eyes and the full crease of his mouth.

'I had to take her mother to the hospital,' Adele explained. 'She's still there.'

A single bead of sweat ran down his right temple. He raised his arm and wiped the side of his face with the short sleeve of his T-shirt. 'You took her last night?'

'Yes.'

He dropped his arm to his side and lowered his gaze to the coffee stain on her sweater. 'Nothing serious, I hope.'

'Not really,' she lied, and clenched her hands to keep from covering the stain. 'I heard about Devon.'

He looked up. 'Yes. She was killed in a car accident three years ago.'

'I'm sorry for your loss.' Shock number four. She'd actually said that without choking.

'Thank you.' He took a few steps toward her, and she had to remind herself to breathe. 'The Junior League isn't quite the same without her.' He bent forward and picked up the keys at her feet. 'Or so they tell me.' He rose to stand, so close that the scent of his warm skin touched her nose. There had been a time when she would have breathed deep and sucked the scent of him deep into her lungs, but those days were long over. 'I didn't realize you live in Cedar Creek,' he said.

'I don't. I'm just here until my sister has her baby.'

'When's the baby due?' When? He was so close that

she took a step back and bumped into the trunk of her sister's car. 'Around Valentine's day,' she answered.

'Four months.' He reached forward and grasped her wrists. He slid his warm palm to the back of her hand and turned it up. 'That's a long visit,' he said, and dropped her keys into her hand.

'Yes.' Her gaze lowered to their hands and the words 'Carpe Diem' tattooed in bold script on the inside of his forearm from elbow to wrist. Unless he'd had it removed, he had a pair of interlocking tattooed Z's circling his left biceps, too.

The heavy door to the house opened and shut behind Kendra and Tiffany, and Adele closed her hand and pulled it from his grasp. 'Too long.' The girls moved from beneath the vine-covered walkway into the shade of the portico. 'Did you find your shoes?' she asked, and purposely turned her attention to her niece.

Kendra nodded. 'Thank you, Mr Zemaitis. I had a really good time.'

'I'm sorry about your momma.' He took a few steps back, and Adele quickly slid around the side of the car. 'Let us know if there is anything we can do for y'all.' His deep voice held a hint of a smile when he added, 'It was nice to see you again, Adele.'

Adele reached for the door handle and looked across at him. His lips were curved up at the corners, but she couldn't say that it was nice to see him. Beyond the shock of seeing him after so many years, she felt nothing. No lifting of her heart. No butterflies in her stomach or warm tingles at the backs of her knees. 'Good-bye, Zach.' She joined Kendra in the car and refused to look into the rearview mirror until she pulled away. Through the glass, she caught one last glimpse of the man who'd once crushed her heart. He put his arm around his daughter's shoulders and moved toward the house.

Adele returned her attention to the driveway and pulled out into the street. He'd been the first man with whom she'd had sex. She'd saved herself because she'd thought she had to be in love to make love. 'Right.' She made a scoffing sound and reached for her sunglasses. She'd never made that mistake again. As she'd discovered in the past fourteen years, sometimes some of the best sex had nothing to do with love. Sometimes it was just a hot release of pent-up lust. Although lately, she wouldn't know. Being cursed played hell with her sex life.

'Did anyone call Daddy?'

She slid the glasses on her face and glanced at Kendra. 'I'm not sure.' But she doubted it. 'Do you want to call him?'

Kendra shrugged. 'I don't know if he cares what happens to us.'

Adele turned her full attention to Kendra and issues more important than an old boyfriend, lack of sex, and curses. 'I'm sure he cares what happens to *you*.'

'No.' Kendra shook her head. 'I thought when he found out the baby was a boy, he'd want us all to live together again. But he only cares about Stormy.'

'*Stormy*.' Adele made a gagging sound and wrinkled her nose as if she'd smelled something rotten. 'What a stupid name.'

'She's a bitch.' Kendra glanced at Adele out of the corners of her eyes as if she expected to be reprimanded for swearing.

'Yeah. A bitch with a stupid name,' Adele added as

she drove through the gates and out into the real world where the air was a bit easier to breathe.

'Momma says I shouldn't hate anyone, but I hate Stormy.'

Adele reached for her water bottle between the two front seats and unscrewed the cap. Sherilyn had always tried to be so good. The perfect Southern lady and look where that had gotten her. Adele had never tried to be perfect like her sister, but she had always tried to be kind. To be thoughtful of other people, and look where that had gotten *her*. She took a long drink and replaced the cap. She might not be alone and pregnant, but she was alone and cursed with one bad date after another. 'I hate a lot of things.' Being surprised by an old boyfriend was currently at the top of the list.

'I hate peas.' Kendra fiddled with the zipper pull of her backpack. 'I hate Cedar Creek. It's just so small.'

'True, but you've already made friends. Tiffany seems like a nice girl.' Which was true and also a surprise, given her mother. Although, Zach had always been polite. Sometimes sarcastically so. He'd once told her that the fear of three-hundred-pound linebackers was nothing compared to slipping with a curse word or being disrespectful in front of his mother.

It was nice to see you again, Adele, he'd said, but he was probably just being polite. Not that she cared.

Adele had lost her accent. A smile curved Zach's lips. Well, she might have lost that Southern, melt-you-like-butter voice spilling from her full red mouth, but she was still as hot as all hell. Still had those long curls and turquoise eyes that looked slightly drowsy even when she was wide-awake. Still looked good in other places, too.

Zach dried his hair with a towel, then hung it on the heated towel rack in the bathroom. He grabbed his electric razor and walked into his bedroom. He had half an hour to get to his office at Cedar Creek High to review last night's game tapes with the other coaches. He shaved as he dressed in blue boxers, a pair of Levi's, and a Cougars Coaching Staff sweatshirt.

She hadn't seemed very happy to see him, though. In fact, she'd been all fired up to leave. Which was probably for the best. He wasn't the kind of guy who lived in the past or thought much about what might or could have been. He didn't relive his glory days in the NFL, nor did he rehash his mistakes. God knows there'd been enough of those.

Zach pointed his chin to the ceiling and shaved just below his jaw. When he did look back on his life, he saw it in three distinct parts. Before the NFL, during, and his life now. He'd known Adele a few lifetimes ago, and he had little interest in a trip down memory lane. Especially with a woman who clearly wanted nothing to do with him.

He shut off his razor and tossed it on the dresser. She did look good, though. As beautiful as ever, and the front of her sweater had been real interesting. His smile tilted up a bit more. She'd obviously been cold.

'Daddy,' Tiffany called out a second before she knocked. Typical of her, she didn't wait for an answer before she stuck her head inside. 'When ya gonna be back?'

'Probably around two.' He sat on the edge of his bed and pulled on a pair of clean socks. The team needed to work more on their passing game now that Don was out for the rest of the season. Zach had a lot of tricks in his playbook and running the Pistol offense was one of them. He'd talk to the other coaches, but it was a lot easier to run play action out of the Pistol.

'Can I have a few friends over while you're gone?'

'You need to put the living room back together while I'm gone.'

Tiffany's shoulder slumped. 'Daddy.'

He shoved his feet into his black Pumas and bent over to tie the laces. 'And the television room is a mess. There are dirty cups and bowls all over the place.'

'We need a maid,' she said through a long, drawn-out sigh and folded her skinny arms over her skinny chest.

When Devon had been alive, they'd had a full-time maid. Now they had a maid service once a week. 'No.' He stood. 'We need you to pick up after yourself.'

'If I clean up, can I have a get-together?'

He moved to his dresser and slid his watch onto his wrist. 'When and what kind?'

'Next weekend. The girls from my dance team.'

Twelve thirteen-year-olds. Twelve *emotional* thirteen-year-olds prone to high-pitched screaming and drama. Last summer, one of Tiffany's friends had locked herself in the bathroom with a cell phone and had cried to her boyfriend all day. What was a thirteen-year-old girl doing with a *boyfriend* anyway? Zach would rather get kicked in the nuts than go through that again. 'Next game is on Saturday in Midland. Kick off's at one, so I'll be leaving Friday sometime.'

'Is Leanna coming over?' she asked, referring to the neighbor girl Zach hired to stay with Tiffany when he had to go out of town overnight.

'Yep.'

'Cool. Can I have my party Sunday? You'll be home.'

'Honey,' he said through a sigh, 'I'm goin' to be tired, and you have school the next day.'

'You can sleep in, and I'll do all the work.' She dropped her hands to her sides. The girl was relentless as her mother had been. 'And I'll make sure everyone is out of here early. Please, Daddy?'

He frowned, and she took it for a yes and bounced up and down on her heels with excitement. 'If it's nice, can we barbecue outside?' she asked.

'I doubt it will be that nice.' He moved across the room. 'If it is, I don't see why not.'

She put her palms together like she was praying and clapped her fingers. 'Yay. Can I invite boys?'

He stopped and looked down into her face. She'd never shown any interest in boys before. 'No. No boys.' He pointed a finger at her nose. 'Ever.'

'Why?'

He continued out the room and down the hall. Because he knew thirteen-year-old boys. He'd been one himself. 'Stay away from boys.'

'You're a boy.'

He walked into the kitchen and grabbed a bottle of water from the refrigerator. He didn't want to talk about boys. Talking about boys would lead to talking about sex, and that was one conversation he didn't want to have with his little girl. Not yet. She was too young. A few months ago they'd had the first bra conversation, and that had about killed him. 'Your new friend Kendra seems nice,' he said, changing the subject.

'Yeah. I think she's good enough to make the dance team.'

'Why's her momma in the hospital?' He unscrewed the lid and took a drink.

'She has high blood pressure.'

Zach licked a drop of water from his lip. High blood pressure? It was obviously more serious than it sounded. 'Did you talk to her aunt?'

'She was kinda weird.'

He looked down at the bottle. 'Weird how?'

Tiffany shrugged. 'Kind of in a hurry.'

He'd noticed that. He raised his gaze to his daughter. 'Is she from Fort Worth, like Kendra and her mom?'

Tiffany shook her head. 'She said she's from Ohio. Des Moines, I think.'

'Honey, that's Iowa.'

'Oh.'

He slowly screwed and unscrewed the cap. 'Did she, a . . . mention if she's married?' He hadn't noticed a ring when he'd placed her keys in her palm, but that didn't mean anything. For whatever reason, a lot of married people didn't wear rings.

'She didn't say.'

'Kids?'

'I don't know.' A suspicious frown appeared between Tiffany's eyes, and she looked just like Devon. 'Why?'

Yeah. Why? Zach shrugged one shoulder and took a drink of water.

'You don't think she's cute, do you?'

Cute? Puppies were cute. Kittens were cute. Adele Harris was sexier than a row of pole dancers, and since it had been a long time since Zach had seen dancing of any kind, mattress, pole, or otherwise, that sounded pretty damn sexy to him. He lowered the bottle. 'Sugar, I just like to know who Kendra's people are,' he lied because some thoughts were better left in his own head.

Tiffany smiled. 'Momma liked to know the same thing.'

Yeah, he knew that. Devon had been real big on people's people.

Tiffany wrapped her arms around his waist and rested her head on his chest above his heart. 'I miss Momma, but I've got you, and we don't need anyone else. Do we?'

He wrapped his arms around her skinny shoulders and pressed a kiss into the part of her light blond hair. 'No,' he answered because he knew that's what she needed to hear. No women with curly hair, turquoise-colored eyes and interesting points on her sweater.

'William finally called,' Sherilyn announced, as Adele walked into her hospital room Monday afternoon.

Adele set a vase of white daisies and blue carnations and a bag of Gummi Bears on the stand next to her bed. 'It took him long enough,' she said as she fussed with the flowers. The hair at the back of her neck was still wet from her shower, and she'd thrown on a black-ribbed Van Dutch sweater and Lucky jeans after her five-mile jog.

She turned to look at her sister, propped up and wearing a white nightgown with lace trim at the throat and cuffs. She looked like Nicole Kidman, with her shiny blond hair pulled back into a smooth knot at the back of her neck, all slick and proper. She looked delicate and beautiful ... except for the tired lines at the corners of her eyes and the puffiness in her face and hands. Both were symptoms of her toxemia and the irritability due to her headache caused by high blood pressure.

'What did he say?' Adele prompted.

'He wanted to know if there was anything he could do for me. I told him there was just one thing.' Sherilyn rested her hands on her rounded belly, and Adele hoped her sister hadn't done something pathetic like grovel and beg. Adele would have called him an a-hole and hung up. Sherilyn probably hadn't ever said 'a-hole' in her life. She'd always been too busy trying to be a lady.

'What's the one thing?' She picked up a gold plastic cup with one hand and a matching pitcher of ice water with the other.

'Well . . . I told him to go fuck himself.'

Adele gasped, and her hands stilled. The spout of the pitcher was inches from the cup. The woman in front of her looked like Sherilyn, but an alien must have taken over her sister's body. Sherilyn would never drop the f-bomb.

'I know it's really vulgar and ill-bred, but I've wanted to say it for a while now.' She slid her hands in circles over her belly as if she were caressing her baby. 'Go fuck yourself, William.'

A woman in a fuzzy pink robe pushed an IV stand past the open door, and Adele composed herself enough to pour the water. She set the cup and pitcher on the tray, then placed her hand on Sherilyn's forehead. Adele didn't recall if the doctors had mentioned fever as a symptom of preeclampsia, but there was definitely something weird going on.

'I'm fine.' Sherilyn looked up into Adele's face and pushed her arm away. 'Well, except for the dangerously high blood pressure, headache, and puffiness.'

'I found your Handycam in a box with your computer,' Adele said, in an effort to take her sister's mind off her troubles for a little while. She sat on the bed next to her sister's hip and hooked the toe of her black leather pump behind her knee. 'The batteries are all charged up and ready to record Kendra at dance-team tryouts.'

'I wish I could be there.'

'As soon as the tryouts are over, we'll come here and watch them together.'

'Kendra's had such a hard time. First her daddy leaves, and now this.' Sherilyn held her hands up and dropped them to her sides. So much for taking her mind off her troubles. 'I made her leave her home and all her friends, and now she . . .'

She has to live with an aunt she doesn't even know, Adele thought. 'She's making friends at school. Tiffany seems like a nice girl.'

'I hope so. Kendra needs a nice friend. You met Tiffany's daddy Saturday, right?'

She'd met Tiffany's daddy before Saturday. 'Yeah.'

'What did you think of him?'

For the past few days, she'd been trying *not* to think of him. Not to think of the way he looked all hot and sweaty, strolling toward her, each step slow and easy. 'He seemed okay.' She shrugged. 'Why?'

'Kendra said that he's the football coach over at Cedar Creek High and that he used to play professional ball. She couldn't remember the team, but she said Tiffany showed her posters and bobble heads and football jerseys in glass cases.' Sherilyn leaned her head back against her pillow and sighed. 'I guess he seems okay, but I always like to meet the parents of Kendra's friends just to make sure she isn't hanging out with children whose parents are too permissive.' A little frown appeared between her tired blue eyes. 'A year ago we got crosswise when she befriended a little girl who didn't have a curfew, dressed like Britney Spears, and was trying to grow up way too fast. Suddenly Kendra wanted to wear a short skirt and thong underwear.'

'I'll keep my eyes and ears open, but I don't think you have to worry about Tiffany.'

'Kendra says there's no mother in the home, and it sounds like her father is really busy.'

Busy with work or women? she wondered. She thought of that horrid life-sized portrait of Devon, and figured any self-respecting woman would likely run away if she had to look at their boyfriend's dead wife glaring down at her all the time. 'Her mother died a few years ago.'

'Oh poor thing.'

'You remember Devon Hamilton.'

Sherilyn closed her eyes and thought a moment. 'Isn't she the one who used to torture you about your hair?'

Among other things. 'Yes. That was Tiffany's mother.'

Sherilyn's eyes flew open, and her gaze met Adele's. 'You're kidding?'

'Nope.'

Sherilyn reached for the Gummi Bears and opened the bag. 'Small world.'

She had no idea.

'I feel so helpless. I can't keep an eye on my daughter.' She popped a red bear into her mouth. 'And with everything going on with William, I haven't bought a thing for the baby.' She rubbed her stomach. 'Poor thing.'

For a type-A control freak like Sherilyn, being confined to bed had to be hell. 'Kendra and I will get everything ready for the baby. It'll be fun.' And as soon as Sherilyn had the baby, and everything was okay, Adele was out of there. Back to her own home and her friends and her life.

'Great.' Sherilyn tossed the bag of Gummi Bears on the tray. 'The baby's moving.' Counting kicks and paying attention to movement was important in a preeclampsia pregnancy. 'Give me your hand.' She grabbed Adele around the wrist and placed her palm on the left side of her belly.

'I don't feel anything.'

'Shhh . . . there. Did you feel that?'

Adele shook her head. Yesterday, she hadn't felt anything either. Or the day before that.

After a few moments, Sherilyn let go. 'I guess he went back to sleep.' She pointed to the nightstand. 'Get a piece of paper and pencil and write down everything I tell you.'

An hour later, Adele had a three-page list of what the baby needed as well as a list of appropriate behavior, activities, and television programs for Kendra. Basically, anything that had cursing in it was forbidden. Which meant Adele would have to catch up with some of her favorite shows after Kendra went to bed.

Adele shoved the list into her purse, hopped in Sherilyn's car, and headed to Sterling Park Middle School. The second she entered the old gym, she was struck by two things. One, it looked smaller than she recalled. And two, it smelled the same. Like hardwood floors and rubber balls. A red-and-black-painted stallion took up the center of the floor, and at the far end, Kendra and a few dozen or so girls stretched and tied their dance shoes. Kendra had pulled her hair back and tied a white-and-red ribbon around her ponytail. Adele gave her niece a big wave, but Kendra must not have seen because she turned her back. Adele shrugged and moved up the bleachers to take a seat three rows up. On the floor below her, four teachers and three students sat at a judging table. One of the students was Tiffany Zemaitis with her hair pulled back in a claw and a pencil in one hand.

Just a few short weeks ago, Adele never would have imagined that she'd find herself sitting in her old middle-school gymnasium. She wrote about the bizarre and unlikely, but she never would have imagined that someday she'd watch her niece try out for a dance team on which Devon and Zach's daughter was the captain. Not in a million light-years.

She set the Handycam next to her and put her elbows on the bench behind her to stretch out and wait. Neither would she have ever pictured herself the interim de facto parent of a thirteen-year-old. She knew nothing about children. She hadn't been responsible to another living thing since her veiled chameleon, Steve, died of old age five years ago. And a teen required much more than some misting water, a clean basking area, and a few crickets.

Whatever it was that Kendra required, Adele hadn't figured it out yet. Kendra hated chicken because it was 'veiny.' She hated salad because lettuce tasted like 'dirt,' and she hated bananas because they were 'mushy' even when they weren't.

Since the age of eighteen, Adele had lived alone and really didn't cook much. She usually just threw steak or chicken on her George Foreman and made a salad. Something quick and easy, but Kendra wanted stuff that had to be planned out and cooked, like spaghetti or enchiladas. Or better yet, she wanted fast food. When Adele had explained that she couldn't have McDonald's or Taco Bell every day because it was very unhealthy and filled with trans fats, Kendra had looked at her, and said, 'That's gay.' As Adele had quickly discovered, anything that Kendra didn't like or didn't like to hear, was 'gay.' Adele might have pointed out that saying everything was 'gay' wasn't very p.c., but she figured Kendra would just look at her as if she were old and stupid and 'gay.'

A girl in black spandex moved to the center of the gym, put her head down, and waited. Within a few seconds 'Get Ready 4 This' blasted from a CD player in front of the judges' table. The girl began to dance, and it wasn't so much that she was bad, as she just wasn't very good. The second girl was a bit better, but unfortunately, the loud squeaky doors to the gym opened and slammed shut three times during her performance, prompting one of the judges to make a sign and hang it on the outside. After that people filed in through the locker rooms.

Half a dozen girls danced before Kendra took the floor. She put her CD in the player, then waited for the first few beats of Kelly Clarkson's 'Since U Been Gone.' Adele stood, and through the Handycam's screen, she watched her niece. Kendra had mentioned that she'd been in dance classes since the age of four. Adele had taken dance classes throughout her life, too, and she recognized someone with natural talent. When Kendra finished, Adele gave a few whoop whoops, then stuck two fingers in her mouth and whistled. She'd probably just acted really 'gay' in Kendra eyes, but she was too excited and proud not to make some noise.

Several more girls danced after Kendra, and by the time everyone finished trying out, it was past six. Adele stuck the Handycam in her shoulder bag and moved down the bleachers. She moved a few feet from the judge's table, where the girls had gathered.

'You were awesome,' Adele told Kendra, as her niece separated herself a bit from the other girls.

Kendra shook her head. 'I messed up twice.'

'I didn't notice.' She lowered her voice, and added, 'You were a lot better than everyone else.'

Kendra tried and failed to hide her smile. The first really genuine smile Adele had seen on her niece's face. 'I hope so. A few of the girls were good.'

'Grab your stuff, and we'll run to the hospital to show your mom what a great job you did.'

Kendra pointed past Adele's left shoulder. 'We have to wait until they announce the winners.'

Adele turned to the judges' table near her. Their heads were all together, and they spoke in hushed tones. 'They're going to announce the winners now?'

'Yeah.'

The doors to the gym banged open, prompting everyone to turn as Zach Zemaitis walked in, trailing the last remnants of the setting sun. Apparently he hadn't bothered reading the note stuck to the door. The door banged shut behind him, and he stopped just inside and looked around. He wore a black Nike hooded sweatshirt and a pair of faded-out Levi's. A whistle circled his neck, and the curved brim of his cap shadowed his face and hid his eyes. He folded his arms across his chest and looked intimidating and massive standing there framed by the door and glancing about.

His arms fell to his sides, and although she couldn't see his gaze, she knew it had stopped on her. She could feel it move up and down her body, touching here, stopping there.

'Hey, Daddy,' Tiffany called out to him.

He took off his hat and walked across the gym to the judges' table. He ran his fingers through his hair as his unhurried stride carried him closer. He didn't so much as glance at Adele, and she wondered if she'd imagined that whole feeling-his-gaze-on-her thing. She wondered if he'd even seen her at all.

Zach stopped next to Tiffany and tossed his hat on the table. 'Are you just about done here, sugar bug?'

'Yep.'

One of the female teachers looked up. 'Hello, Coach Z. How're you doin'?'

'Can't complain, Mary Jo.' The corners of his mouth turned up into a smile that oozed Southern boy charm. 'You look awfully pretty,' he told the woman old enough to be his mother. 'Did you do something with your hair?'

'Got it done at the Clip and Snip,' she said through a little giggle.

Adele rolled her eyes and turned her attention to her niece. 'I think we need to celebrate. Let's go to McDonald's on the way home from the hospital.'

A frown wrinkled Kendra's flawless forehead. 'We don't know if I made it or not.'

'Doesn't matter. You did a good job and tried your best. That's all that counts,' she said, as a small crowd filtered down from the bleachers and waited for the judges. A lot of them called out 'heys' to 'Coach Z.' Most of them were women.

'I'm going to go stand with the other girls,' Kendra said as she abandoned Adele and moved a few feet away.

'Adele Harris. I thought that was you.'

Adele turned and looked into a pair of blue eyes that would have been on the same level as hers if she hadn't been wearing three-inch heels. 'Cletus Sawyer?'

'Yeah. How are you?'

'Good.' She gave him a quick hug, then stepped back to look at him. In school, Cletus had been a geeky nerd and they'd belonged to the same drama club. In *The Tempest*, she'd been Ariel, and he'd played Prospero. He'd been skinny and buck toothed, but he'd filled out some and gotten his teeth fixed. He was still fair-skinned with red hair, but he'd matured into a handsome guy. Not as handsome as the man standing directly behind him, sucking up the attention of every female in the gym. But there really weren't many men who were better-looking than Zach Zemaitis.

'It's good to see you,' she said through a smile. 'What have you been up to?'

'Just livin'. I teach math here at Sterlin' Park.'

A *math teacher*. Zach looked over the math teacher's head at Adele. Surely she didn't see anything remotely attractive in a guy with a pocket protector.

'What have you been up to?' the math teacher asked.

Zach would like to know that himself.

'I write science-fiction and fantasy novels.'

'Wow. Are you published?'

'Yes. I have ten books published, just turned in my eleventh and am about ready to start my twelfth.' She glanced up past the teacher's red hair, and her gaze met Zach's. He wasn't all that surprised that she wrote fantasy novels. She'd been interested in fairies and druids and other weird shit when he'd known her. He was also not all that surprised that she was a published author. She'd been one of the smartest girls he'd known.

'Do you publish under your own name?'

Her beautiful blue eyes looked into his for several more seconds before she returned her gaze to the teacher. 'Yes.'

'Hey, Zach,' LaDonna Simms called out as she walked toward him. LaDonna had been a good friend of Devon's and was a member of the Junior League.

'Hey, LaDonna.' She stopped in front of him, and he looked past her big blond hair and returned his attention to Adele. He'd noticed her the second he'd stepped into the gym. Noticed her butt inside her tight jeans. Not only had she been smart, she'd always had a nice butt. Still did.

'Did you get your invitation to the Night of a Million Stars benefit?' LaDonna asked.

'Yeah I did, but I don't have anyone involved in the Junior League these days.' Just like last year and the year before.

'Oh well.' LaDonna leaned closer and put her hand on his arm. 'We all loved Devon so much, we consider you part of the League family. Unofficially of course.'

'Of course.' As LaDonna rambled on, Zach tuned her out and listened to the conversation a few feet away. It was much more interesting than pretending interest in the Junior League. Eavesdropping was rude. His momma had always told him so, but he didn't particularly give a damn.

'You sure look good,' the math teacher said, and Zach could practically hear him drool.

'Thank you, Cletus. I jog five miles a day.'

'I work out sometimes,' the nerd said, which Zach figured was pretty much bullshit. 'We should get together and catch up.'

Adele hesitated, and Zach thought she was going to turn him down. Instead, she pushed her heavy hair behind one shoulder and smiled. 'I'd like that, Cletus.' She gave him her phone number and the little guy programed it into his cell.

'Can I have everyone's attention,' Tiffany called out as she stepped up onto her chair. 'We'd like to thank y'all for coming out this afternoon and trying out for the Stallionettes. But there are only two available spots.' She looked down at her notes. 'It was a really hard decision, but we'd like to welcome Lisa Ray Durke and Kendra Morgan to join the team.'

Applause and a few shouts of joy accompanied the announcement. Several other girls burst into tears and fell on each other crying. Zach watched Adele's smile reach her eyes as she turned her gaze from the math teacher and toward her niece.

'Oh shoot.' LaDonna dropped her hand. 'Roseanna didn't make it,' she said referring to her daughter. 'She's just devastated and crying her little eyes out. Excuse me.'

Evidently, Roseanna was one of the girls carrying on. Zach didn't understand why girls had to get so emotional about everything and why they had to get all emotional in public. Not making a dance team wasn't like losing state or a bowl game, for God's sake. Now that was damn traumatic.

'Hey, Daddy.'

Zach dragged his attention from Adele and her niece to his daughter. 'Are you ready to go?'

'Just a sec. I have to talk to Kendra and Lisa Ray first.'

'Don't take all night,' he said, and shoved his hat back on his head. He sat on the edge of the judging table as the gym began to clear out. He figured he'd waited about five minutes before Tiffany, Kendra, and Adele moved toward him.

'Congratulations, Kendra,' he said, and rose to his full height. 'I guess this means we'll be seeing you at the house practicing some more.'

'Oh yeah,' Tiffany answered for the other girl. As the four of them headed across the gym, she added, 'Kendra has to learn the dances really quickly. Our next competition is in a few weeks.'

'I'll be ready,' Kendra assured her.

The heels of Adele's shoes tapped across the hardwood floor, the sound of a pair of sexy shoes filling his head with ideas.

'I'm having a barbecue this Sunday for all the girls,' Tiffany announced. 'You have to come, Kendra. It'll be fun.'

Kendra looked across her shoulder at Adele. 'Can I?'

'We'll talk to your mom, but I don't know why not.'

Zach opened the door for the two girls, and as Adele passed, he heard himself say, 'You should come, too.' He hadn't meant to invite her. Wasn't even sure it was a good idea. No, strike that. He was sure. It wasn't a good idea.

She paused, the curls resting on her shoulder a few inches from his chest. Her eyes looked into his. 'I don't think so.'

He should be relieved. For some reason he wasn't. 'Are you afraid?'

'Of?'

She looked good and smelled better, and he answered, 'Of about a dozen thirteen-year-old girls runnin' around screamin' and gigglin' and blastin' shitty music.'

She almost smiled as she shook her head and stepped outside. 'I'm busy.'

'With the redhead?' He followed, and the door shut behind him. If he didn't know himself better, he'd think he sounded jealous. Which was ridiculous. Even if he had an interest in pursuing something with Adele, which he didn't, he wasn't jealous of a redheaded math teacher.

'Maybe.' She dug around in her purse and pulled out a set of keys. 'Catching up with Cletus will be nice. After the week I've had, I'm ready for a good time.'

'Good time?' He reached for the brim of his hat, slid it back, then settled it in the same place. 'Impossible.'

She stopped and looked up at him. 'Not that I really care, but why?'

'He'll bruise like a peach.'

'I'm going to talk to him.' She frowned and shook her head. 'Not punch him.'

Clearly they were talking about two different kinds of 'good times.'

'Hey, Z,' the middle-school football coach called out as he approached. 'That was some game last weekend. Shame about Don.'

Adele looked up at Zach and into the shadow his hat created. Z. That's what everyone had called him at UT. Hearing it brought back a flood of memories. Memories of his smile and laughter. Of the touch of his hand in the small of her back.

'How's the boy doing?' the middle-school coach asked.

'I just talked to his doctors up in Lubbock this morning. He's doing good.'

Adele took a step back. 'Excuse me,' she said as she walked around Zach and headed toward the parking lot. She thought of the double-z tattoo circling his upper arm. The last time she'd seen it, they'd been naked, and she'd been running her hands and mouth all over his hard body.

'Adele,' he called to her.

A cool breeze blew a few strands of hair across her face as she looked back over her shoulder.

'See ya around.'

She didn't answer, just kept on moving. Obviously, she was going to run into Zach now that Kendra would be spending so much time with Tiffany. She would be polite, but that was it. She didn't feel anything for him anymore. She didn't love him, but she wasn't interested in reliving memories. She didn't hate him, but she wasn't interested in being friends.

She and Kendra made the short drive to the hospital in just about ten minutes and showed Sherilyn the tryout video. Afterward, they drove through McDonald's, and Adele had a salad while Kendra pigged out on a Quarter Pounder with cheese, fries, and a Coke. When they got back to the condo, Kendra did her homework while Adele did laundry.

Over the next few days, Adele's life settled a bit and fell into a pattern. She woke every morning, took Kendra to school, then jogged her five miles. She visited her sister in the hospital and listened to the latest updates on Sherilyn's and the baby's progress. Sherilyn would add to the to-do list, and Adele would run around town whittling it down the best she could. At around noon, she'd return home to work on the opening of her next book, a futuristic set in an alternate universe. During her breaks in writing, she caught up with her friends in Boise via e-mail. She'd met the three other writers years ago when they'd all attended the same librarian conference. The things they'd had in common – deadlines, writers' block, and bad relationships – had made them fast friends. And even though Adele was the only one suffering from bad relationships these days, they were still great friends. Once Sherilyn had her baby, and everything was fine, Adele could not wait to go home and catch up in person.

By the time Saturday rolled around, Adele was ready for a break. Cletus Sawyer had called during the week to say he'd pick her up for dinner at seven. Kendra had been asked to babysit the five-year-old in the condo next door, and in case of an emergency, Adele programed her phone number into Kendra's cell.

An hour before Cletus picked Adele up, she threw on a long-sleeved red dress and shiny red pumps she pulled from Sherilyn's closet. She didn't bother with nice underwear, not that she'd packed her nice stuff anyway. Even if the date went really well, and she discovered an overwhelming attraction to Cletus, she had to be home when Kendra got home at eleven.

Over appetizers, Cletus told Adele about his divorce and his two-year-old daughter. He asked questions about her life and seemed genuinely interested. They laughed about things that had happened to them in school, but by the time Cletus paid the check, Adele knew nothing was going to happen with him. Ever. He was really nice, but she had absolutely no desire to get naked and freaky with him, which was kind of sad because the date was going surprisingly well. So well that she was beginning to wonder if the curse was broken.

At around ten he drove her back to the condo and walked her to the door.

'When can I see you again?' he asked.

She wouldn't mind having Cletus for a friend. 'I don't know.' She dug her keys out of her clutch purse. 'I'm really busy with my sister, and I don't have a lot of free time. Call me though, and maybe we can get together for coffee.'

'Oh. You're one of those.'

One of those?

'You think you're too good for me. You think because I teach math that I'm not any fun. You think I'll be pacified with a little coffee date.'

'Cletus, my sister's in the hospital, and I have to take care of my niece,' she said through a sigh. 'I just don't have a lot of time for real dates.'

'Sure you don't. I bet if I had a lot of money, you'd find the time. If I'd been one of the popular guys in school, you'd be dying to date me.'

Adele looked at him, and she couldn't get angry. It wasn't his fault he'd turned into a jerk. It was hers. She was still cursed.

One hundred fifty miles west of Cedar Creek, Zach was beginning to wonder if he was cursed, too. Cursed with a defense that hesitated on the snap and couldn't get past a determined offensive line to rush the quarterback.

Within the guest locker room of the Grande Communications Stadium in Midland, he and his assistant coaches stood surrounded by the rattle of Tylenol bottles, the rip of athletic tape, the smell of grass, sweat, and frustration. In the first half of the game against Midland, the Cougars were behind by fourteen points.

Zach folded his arms across his dark green Cougars football jacket while the defensive coach, Joe Brunner, drew a diagram of the zone blitz on a marker board. 'We spent all goddamn week reviewing the Bulldogs' tapes,' Joe said as he drew x's and o's on the board. 'We knew goin' into this game that they play their zone better than any team we've been up against this year. Their goddamn quarterback is just sittin' back in the pocket lobbing balls to the soft spot, and you guys aren't goddamn rushin' him.' Joe drew dashes and arrows from the linebackers through the o's as he continued.

Zach liked Joe. He respected his knowledge and devotion and his gut instinct. Joe had played corner-back for Cedar Creek and later for Virginia Tech in the nineties. No one loved football more than Joe Brunner, but he had a problem that held him back from ever being a head coach. He cracked under pressure. Right in half like someone split him with an ax, and out came a spitting, whirling devil. It was every coach's job to get their boys to pull their heads out of their asses and turn games around, but that was hard to do if the fifty-three players in front of you were trying not to laugh.

Zach stood with the offensive coach to one side and watched to make sure Joe didn't crack. They interjected when necessary and were relieved that only two veins popped out on Joe's forehead. For most of Zach's life, he'd been a quarterback, not a coach, but he'd played ball for some of the best coaches and some of the worst. He'd led teams to championships, and he knew the difference between being stern and going off on a tirade. He knew that players would leave their blood on the field for someone they respected and who respected them. A good coach inspired that kind of respect.

When Joe was finished, Zach stepped in front of the marker board. 'Y'all know what you gotta do,' he said. 'You go out there and make those Midland boys sorry that they showed up today.' He pointed to the defensive ends. 'If you get blocked, I better hear it from where I'm standin', and I don't want to see you getting stopped by any more of those pussy finesse blocks. You get around those boys and run upfield like someone lit your ass on fire. You go after that quarterback and *force* him to get rid of that ball before he's ready.' He pushed his ball cap to the back of his head and gathered the team around him. 'The first half of this game is history, gentlemen. There isn't anything we can do about it now. Let's put it behind us.

'Last week when we lost Don, everyone started saying we were done. But I don't believe that. One player does not make a team great. It's what's in each player's heart and gut that makes a team great. It's your job to go out there and show you have the guts and heart to turn this game around. I know you can do it. Tonight's battle is not over. We're not finished. We're only down by two touchdowns, let's go show 'em y'all are winners.'

He looked them all in the face. 'So let's hear it together: hearts, guts, glory.'

'Hearts, guts, glory!' the team shouted as they butted helmets.

'Now get out there and kick some Bulldog ass!'

Zach and the other coaches followed behind the team, the sound of cleats on concrete bouncing off the tunnel walls. The Cougars broke onto the field running as the Cedar Creek band played the school fight song. The players butted chests and helmets and fists, and in the second half, the defense finally broke through the Midland offensive line and rushed their quarterback. The Cougars closed the gap in the score and in the last few seconds of the game kicked a thirty-seven-yard field goal to win by three points.

As Zach filed off the field with his boys, he thought about the mistakes made in the first half. Next Friday night's game was against Amarillo in Lubbock, and the Sandies had one of the toughest defenses of any team they'd played so far. If the Cougars played like they had against Midland, they'd get their asses handed to them and their run for the state championship would be over.

After the game, more than a dozen buses waited outside the stadium to be filled with players, cheerleaders, band and drill-team members, sponsors, and Cedar Creek students. Zach had driven his Escalade to Midland, preferring the comfort and speed of his Cadillac to that of a bus.

Usually, he brought Tiffany with him to the games. She liked watching Cedar Creek play but not if it meant traveling over three hours each way.

He made it home in two and a half hours and fell into bed at 1:00 a.m. There was never practice on Sundays, and he planned to take advantage of it and sleep. Tiffany had other plans.

'Daddy,' she said, shaking his shoulder.

He cracked his eyes open. 'What time is it?'

'Nine.'

'This had better be an emergency.'

'It is. We need to get stuff for my party.'

'What party?'

'My dance-team party. It's today. Did you forget?'

For a few blissful hours he had forgotten that his house would be invaded by a dozen screaming thirteen-year-olds. 'Christ on a crutch,' he groaned.

'Don't swear,' his thirteen-year-old said, sounding a lot like his mother.

'Sorry.'

'Get up. We gotta get some burgers and stuff 'cause I wanna barbecue outside. You *said* we could, remember?'

'Don't you girls just want to sit around and quietly watch the tube?'

'Daddy, you're so funny.' Tiffany laughed. 'I turned the heat up in the pool and told the girls to bring their swimsuits, if they wanted. I figured we could drag those big heater things out of the guesthouse and set them up on the lower terrace. Or maybe we can push everything out of the entertainment room and set up some tables so we can eat in there after we swim. What do you think, Daddy?'

Zach turned on his stomach and pulled a pillow over his head. 'Just shoot me now.'

Midafternoon sunshine poured through the windshield as Adele pulled the car over to the side of the road and covered her face with her hands. She'd held it together in the hospital. She'd had to be strong for Sherilyn, but she'd never been so frightened in her life. For the last two hours, she'd stood in her sister's hospital room, holding Sherilyn's hand and watching her blood pressure rise. The intense beeps of the fetal heart monitor still echoed in her ears.

The doctors had come within minutes of wheeling Sherilyn to the delivery room and taking the baby before her blood pressure had slowly lowered out of critical range. At twenty-one weeks, the baby had a chance of surviving outside the womb, but not without the risk of serious health complications.

'It's okay. It's okay,' she'd told her sister over and over when everything was clearly *not* okay. But she hadn't known what else to say. What to do besides stand there and watch and wait and hold it all together.

Tears slid from behind her lids, and she opened her mouth to gasp for air. She sobbed past the clog in her throat, and all the fear and sorrow and anger that she'd kept inside for her sister's sake tore at her lungs, and she cried into her hands. The last two hours had been the worst hours of her life, and as she'd stood there helpless, trying to be strong for Sherilyn, she couldn't help but hate William Morgan more than she already did. It should have been him there. Holding his wife's hand and fighting for his baby. Instead, he was off acting like an idiot and boning his young assistant.

Adele took a deep breath and let it out slowly. Her tears slowed, and she rubbed her hands across her wet cheeks. As she dug around in the console between the seats in search of a Kleenex, she reached in her purse for her cell phone. Sherilyn being Sherilyn, had a little pack of tissues in the console, and Adele pulled one out of the package as she flipped open her phone.

It was half past three, and she was a little late picking up Kendra from her dance party. She dried her eyes and blew her nose, and instead of calling Kendra, Adele dialed her sister's old home phone number in Fort Worth, where William still lived. The answering machine picked up after the fifth ring.

'This is Dr William Morgan,' he began, and in the background a female giggled, 'and Stormy Winter.' Bitch. 'I am indisposed at present,' William continued. 'Please leave a brief message and a telephone number where you may be reached.'

It was so like William to leave a pompous message while his girlfriend giggled in the background. A-hole.

Beep.

'William, this is Adele. I'm calling to tell you that . . .' She paused. The last thing Sherilyn needed was for the a-hole to call and upset her. Besides, he didn't deserve to know. 'I just called to tell you to go fuck yourself,' she said, and closed her phone. Okay, so that wasn't very mature. But Sherilyn was right. It felt good.

She glanced into the rearview mirror and groaned out loud. Her eyes were red and the skin beneath splotchy. There was no way that she wanted to knock on Zach's door looking like crap. Yet again. She flipped open her phone and tried Kendra's cell. If she could get Kendra to wait for her outside . . . perhaps at the end of that long driveway . . . but Kendra didn't answer.

Sherilyn had a little baggy for garbage stuck on the gearshift, and Adele tossed the Kleenex inside as she eased off the brake. She pulled back onto the road and dug around in her purse for her sunglasses. She tried Kendra's cell three more times before pulling into the gated community.

'Damn.' She sighed and shoved her black sunglasses onto her face. She tossed the cell phone onto the passenger's seat and drove around some fancy-schmancy clubhouse before turning into Zach's cobblestone driveway. She'd thought about calling Kendra from the hospital to tell her she'd be late, but she hadn't wanted to worry her niece since there wasn't anything anyone could do. In hindsight, she should have so that a parent could have dropped Kendra off at home.

Two Mercedes and a Ford truck were parked beneath the portico, and Adele parked her sister's car beside the truck. She tried Kendra's cell one more time as she grabbed the blue Hard Tail hoodie that matched her sweatpants and shoved her arms inside. No one answered, and she was forced to get out of the car and move through the walkway to the front door. The hooded sweatshirt had a red star and black wings across her breasts, and she zipped it halfway up her chest. Her sweats were nice, but nothing fancy. Nothing to make a man regret he'd dumped her, but her eyes looked like crap, so a killer outfit would have been a total waste.

She stepped onto the porch, settled her glasses, and knocked. But really, who cared if she looked horrible – yet again – she told herself. She didn't care what Zach Zemaitis or anyone else thought about her. Zach was a jerk. In fact, people were jerks. Her brows lowered, and she was somewhat taken aback by her cynical attitude. Somewhere in the past few weeks, she'd lost her usual optimism.

The door swung open and Zach stood in front of her, tall and ridiculously good-looking, but with Zach it had always been more about his confidence that hit women like a testosterone fireball than his looks. It had always been more about the cockiness that he backed up with enormous talent that drew women to him. Or at least it had been for her.

'I'm so sorry I'm late,' she said as she gazed at him through the dark lenses of her glasses. 'I was at the hospital and there was a problem and . . .' And why would he care? 'I should have called to let someone know I'd be late. Sorry.'

He wore a white long-sleeved T-shirt advertising Moose Drool beer on the front and down one arm, Levi's, and black flip-flops. And if she'd been a weak woman, she would have been tempted to breathe into her hand and check her breath.

'Kendra's in the pool,' he said, dragging out the vowels to the end of next week.

'It's what . . . fifty-five degrees?' Although in some states that was considered balmy for November.

'Fifty-seven, and the pool's covered in winter.'

Of course. 'Could you tell Kendra I'm here.'

His gaze lowered to the wings on her hoodie, then rose slowly to her eyes. 'Come in.'

'I'll wait in the car.' She turned and pointed to the Toyota. 'Just tell Kendra that I'm—'

'What are you afraid's gonna happen?' he interrupted her.

She turned and looked at him. 'Nothing.'

He took a step back into the house, and she could barely see him through her sunglasses. His voice came out of the shadows, low and almost rough, 'Then come in, Adele.'

'Are you always this bossy?'

He shrugged. 'Are you always this difficult?'

'Fine.' She folded her arms beneath her breasts and walked into Zach's house. He shut the door behind her, and she followed him through the entry and into the living room.

'Have you gone on your date with the red-haired guy?' he asked over his shoulder.

'Cletus? Yes.' Unlike the last time she'd been in the house, the expensive furniture and rich rugs were in place. She kept her gaze pinned on Zach's wide shoulders and the back of his blond hair touching his neck so she wouldn't make full eye contact with the big portrait of Devon staring down at her. Wherever Devon was buried, Adele was sure she was spinning in her grave. After everything Devon had done to keep Zach and Adele apart, here she was, in Devon's house with Devon's husband. Adele might have taken a moment to enjoy that delicious slice of irony if not for the fact that she didn't want to be there any more than Devon would want her there.

'Wow. The guy works fast.'

'The date was nice.' Right up until he'd turned into a jerk.

'It would never work out you know.'

Yeah, she knew that. She was cursed. 'Why? Because he'll bruise like a peach?' She followed him into the kitchen. 'And I figured out that you weren't talking about me slugging Cletus, by the way.'

He opened a refrigerator and pulled out a plate of sliced tomatoes, pickles, and lettuce. Several high-pitched screeches from somewhere outside penetrated the house, and Zach winced. 'You used to be quicker.'

'I used to be a lot of things.'

'I remember.' He shoved the plate at her, and one corner of his mouth turned up into a smile. 'I remember a lot of things about you.' With her hands full, she was unable to stop him as he reached for her sunglasses and pushed them to the top of her head. 'I remember your eyes, turquoise except when they turn a deeper blue.'

He'd been the first man to tell her that her eyes got darker when she got turned on. She remembered they'd been in his truck the first time he'd said it. He'd been kissing her mouth and touching her through her clothes and she'd wanted to eat him up.

'So tell me, honey,' he said just above a whisper, 'what's got your beautiful eyes so sad?'

A plate of veggies separated his stomach from hers, and she didn't think to ask why he'd shoved the plate at her. For a few brief moments, she forgot he was a jerk. She was a woman who hadn't had a decent date in years, and he was a man. An incredibly hot man with a soothing Southern accent that touched the places deep in her soul. The hot, itchy places that wanted to be soothed.

Adele's lips parted, and she took a breath. It would have been easy to unload her problems on his big shoulders.

'Life's not so bad,' he said.

Showed how much he knew. 'My life sucks.'

'Why?'

So many reasons. 'My sister is in the hospital fighting for the life of her baby, and it should be her husband holding her hand. Not me.'

Zach lowered his gaze to Adele's mouth. 'Where's her husband?'

She was so disconcerted by his attention to her mouth that her brain got a little fuzzy, and she blurted, 'Off boning Stormy Winter somewhere.'

Confusion wrinkled his brow but he didn't look up. 'Stormy Winter?'

'His girlfriend.'

'Ah.' He slid his brown gaze back up to hers. 'Stripper?'

Adele smiled. 'His "dental assistant".'

A door opened, and Zach looked up past Adele. 'Shit,' he said through a groan.

'I thought you might need some help,' a female voice said, followed by the click of heels on the stone floor.

Zach returned his gaze to Adele's and replaced her sunglasses on the bridge of her nose. 'Thanks, Genevieve, but I found a helper. You shouldn't have troubled yourself.'

Behind the lenses of her glasses, Adele closed her eyes. *Please God, not Genevieve Brooks.*

'It's no trouble,' Genevieve Brooks assured him as she stepped into the kitchen.

'Why am I holding this plate?' Adele finally thought to ask.

'In just a minute, I'll need you to carry that outside.' Zach turned and walked back to the refrigerator, and Adele lowered her gaze to the back of his Levi's. His wallet made a bulge in one pocket, and he bent forward slightly to pull out a big tray of hamburger patties and hot dogs. 'You can grab the buns over there on the counter, Genevieve,' he added as he shut the door.

The heels of Genevieve's pumps tapped across the tiles as she moved to the counter. She was as tall and lean as Adele remembered, and she wore a white blouse, beige pants, and cardigan. Probably St Johns. Several ropes of pearls circled her slim neck, and she wore a diamond the size of a marble on her ring finger. 'Those girls are going to be starving,' Genevieve said. She grabbed the buns, then turned to Adele. 'Hello. I'm Genevieve Brooks-Marshall. Lauren Marshall is my stepdaughter.' Genevieve's makeup was understated and perfect, and her black hair was cut into a straight bob.

Adele assumed Lauren was on the dance team. 'Kendra Morgan is my niece,' she said.

'One of the new girls?'

Adele nodded as Zach walked past her through the kitchen, and she followed him into the dining room. 'I'm obviously interrupting your dinner plans,' she said to his back. 'So, if you'll just show me where to set this, I'll grab Kendra, and we'll leave you to your guests.'

He opened one of the French doors, and Adele stepped out onto a terrace. 'What was your name?' Genevieve asked as she joined them.

'Adele Harris.' Adele waited for any sort of recognition from the woman with whom she'd gone through twelve years of school, but there was none. Adele wasn't all that surprised.

Zach closed the door, and the two women followed him down a set of stone steps to the lower terrace and cobblestone courtyard. It was a clear November day, and Adele felt like she'd stepped into a fall issue of *Better Homes and Gardens*. Beyond the courtyard, sunlight fell on an expanse of pruned gardens, sculpted shrubbery, and a lawn that separated the main house from two smaller dwellings.

To her left, girls from Kendra's dance team swam and jumped into a full-sized pool enclosed in steamy glass. Adele obviously wasn't the only late parent.

She followed Zach toward a turbo-sized barbecue set into a stone island and past several tables set with yellow tablecloths. Between the tables were five commercial-grade patio heaters, each warming up the twenty feet around them. Adele set her plate next to bags of chips and pasta salad on a long table. A man wearing a ball cap stood next to the monster-sized grill. The second woman standing beside him laughed at something he said. As Zach approached with the tray of meat, the guy in the cap opened the big chrome lid and scraped the grill with a wire brush.

Adele didn't belong there and planned to make a quick getaway. She turned toward the pool, and the closer she walked to the enclosure, the more she was able to see that she'd either been mistaken about the time, or there were a lot of late parents. She opened the glass door and the smell of chlorine and the sound of high-pitched laughter hit her like a brick to the head.

She spotted Kendra hanging on to the side of the pool and knelt on one knee beside her. 'Am I late?' she asked above the noise, and pushed her sunglasses to the top of her head.

Kendra wiped water from her eyes. 'What time is it?'

'About a quarter to four.'

'The party ends at six.'

'I thought you said three.'

'No.' Kendra shook her head. 'Six. We practiced new dances until three. Maybe you got confused.'

'Obviously.' And Zach hadn't bothered correcting her. 'I'll come back in a few hours.'

'Okay.' Kendra smiled. 'How's Momma?'

The last thing Adele wanted was to wipe the smile from her niece's face. 'She's fine. The baby's fine.' She stood. 'Have fun, and I'll see you later.'

Kendra sank into the water, then pushed off and swam toward a group of girls on the other side of the pool.

The door opened, and Zach stepped inside, carrying a glass of red wine. 'It's time for y'all to get out of the pool,' he said in a loud, clear voice, and the noise in the pool house suddenly quieted. Then he started issuing orders like he was calling plays on the football field. 'Get dressed. Dry your hair. You've got fifteen minutes. Go.'

Adele half expected him to yell a few hut huts, then drop back for a pass. Instead, he moved toward her, grabbed her hand, and pressed the glass into her palm.

'What's this?' she asked, and glanced up from the wine and into his face.

'Wine,' he answered. 'I thought you could use it.'

'I don't suppose telling you I don't want wine will make a difference.'

'Sure it will.' He shrugged one big shoulder. 'Are you an alcoholic?'

'No.'

'Allergic?'

'No,' she answered, as the girls began to drag themselves out of the water and move toward the far end of the pool, where Tiffany handed out thick white towels.

'Cheap drunk?'

'No.'

'Mormon?'

'No.'

'One of those girls who gets drunk and wants to get naked?'

'No.'

'You sure?'

'Yes.'

'That's a shame.'

She smiled despite herself.

'Let's get the hell out of here before these girls start with those ear-piercin' screeches that they mistake for talkin'.' He placed his palm in the small of her back and steered her toward the door.

Through her sweatshirt, his touch pressed into her spine, light and heavy at the same time, spreading a warm, aware rush across her skin and bringing back visceral memories of his hand sliding to her waist and pulling her against his side. She took a drink of a very fine Merlot and was extremely grateful when he dropped his hand and opened the door. She stepped outside onto the walkway and felt she could breathe again. All that steam in the pool house had made her feel a little light-headed.

'If any of those girls get the sniffles, their mommas

are goin' to come after me,' he said, as they moved toward the courtyard.

Adele glanced at Genevieve and the other women standing around the barbecue and wondered if they, too, had gotten the time wrong. 'I thought I was late picking up Kendra. So, why didn't you tell me I'm actually early?'

'My momma told me I shouldn't ever correct a lady.'

Adele lifted a brow and looked up at him. 'Uh-huh. Try again.'

'I knew you'd hop into your car and peel out on my driveway.'

He was right.

'And I don't think it's right that I have to suffer through this party by myself.'

'Isn't that part of your job as a parent?'

'To suffer?' He nodded as they walked past the heaters in the courtyard. 'Yeah, but what no one told me was that cleanin' stinky drawers was goin' to be the easy part.'

'You cleaned stinky drawers?'

'When I was home.' They stopped beside the grill, and Zach introduced her to Cindy Ann Baker. Next she met the guy in the cap, Joe Brunner, defensive coach for the Cedars Creek Cougars. 'And you've already met Genevieve,' Zach said as he grabbed the tray of burgers and dogs and lifted the huge barbecue lid.

Genevieve hardly acknowledged Adele with a breezy 'Yes' before she turned her attention to Zach, and asked, 'What can I do to help you?'

'Nothin',' he answered as he picked up a spatula and placed patties on the grill. 'You just relax.'

'Oh, you know I have to feel like I'm doing

something useful.' Genevieve picked up a glass of Merlot and took a drink. She moved closer to Zach and spoke low so no one else could hear her.

'Which daughter is yours?' Cindy Ann asked Adele.

'It's my niece, and she's one of the new girls, Kendra.'

Cindy Ann looked like one of those stocky women who'd been a gymnast in a former life. Short, compact, perky. Hair cut into a blond wedge. 'Do you have children?'

Through the white smoke rising up around Zach's head, Adele caught his gaze and looked away. 'No.'

'Married?' Cindy Ann asked.

'I came close once,' she fudged, and she figured if Dwayne hadn't gone insane because of the curse, she might have married him.

'Boyfriend?'

She shook her head. 'My pregnant sister is in the hospital with preeclampsia. I'm taking care of her and Kendra, so at the moment I only have time for my family.'

'Did you go to Cedar Creek High?' Joe asked as he looked straight at Adele.

'Yes.'

'We were in the same art class. I graduated a year after you.'

That finally got Genevieve's attention. 'You went to Cedar Creek?'

'Yep,' Adele answered, and told her the year she'd graduated.

Genevieve studied her face. 'Oh. I remember you now.' She turned to Zach. 'Did you get an invitation to the Night of a Million Stars benefit?'

'Yes.'

'You're going, aren't you? I know it will be painful

without Devon. We still miss her horribly, of course.'

Zach placed hot dogs next to the patties, then set the tray down.

'We were best friends since our very first Little Miss Sparkle Pageant. We were close as sisters. Devon was just one of those special people, and the Junior League just isn't the same without her.'

'So I've been told.'

'I know how much you loved her, we all did.' Genevieve shook her head, and her perfect bob brushed her chin. 'Life just isn't the same without Devon.'

'True.' Zach rearranged the hot dogs. 'But somehow we manage to live on.'

Adele looked down in her glass of wine and almost felt sorry for Zach. He must have loved Devon a lot. For years she'd told herself that they were miserable together. That he'd only married Devon out of responsibilty. That they weren't in love. Not really. Not the kind that lasted a lifetime. It made her feel better to believe it, but it wasn't true. It had never been true.

She thought of the life-sized portrait in the living room. That scary freaky picture of a dead woman. Zach must have loved Devon. He must still love her a lot.

Z ach had wanted out of his marriage. An hour before Devon t-boned that garbage truck, he'd handed her divorce papers. After ten years, there'd been no love left. Just a civil, if not always peaceful, coexistence that had no longer been enough. At least not for him.

The difference between them had been that Devon had wanted to go on living that way forever. She'd loved living the life of an NFL quarterback's wife, even a retired quarterback, far more than she'd loved him. She'd loved the cachet that it gave her, especially in the small Texas town. For a long time, he hadn't minded living in a shame marriage. If he was honest, he'd admit to himself that it had worked for him. He'd lived in Denver. Devon in Texas. He'd lived his life. She'd lived hers. She hadn't really cared what he did as long as it didn't hit the news and embarrass her in front of her Junior League friends. He hadn't cared what she did as long as it didn't affect Tiffany.

By the time he'd filed for divorce, he hadn't loved his wife. He hadn't even liked her much, and he'd wanted out before that growing dislike turned to something stronger. She'd been the mother of his only child, and the last thing he'd ever wanted was a court battle, but that's exactly what she'd promised that morning he'd handed her the papers.

'You can't do this to me, Zach. I won't let you,' she'd vowed, just before she'd slammed the door and sped away to one of her meetings. As he'd watched her go, he hadn't been surprised by her response. He'd known the day he'd contacted his lawyer that he was in for a shitstorm.

Zach closed the lid on the barbecue and looked up. Through the smoke he watched Adele swirl the wine in her glass. He couldn't say that he knew her, but he was pretty sure that she wasn't the type of woman who wouldn't care what the hell her man did as long as it didn't hit the news.

Adele glanced up and again he felt like he was back at UT, staring at her from across a classroom. Like there was something about her that he wanted to know better. Something that drew his gaze and attention. Something more than the heavy pull of desire. Back then he'd wondered what her hair would feel like tangled up in his fingers. Tonight he wondered how long it would take him to make those eyes of hers turn a deeper blue. A smile curved his lips as he remembered a night when he'd kissed a little fairy she had tattooed on the right side of her belly just above her panties.

As if she read his thoughts, her cheeks turned pink, and she turned and moved toward the table a few feet away.

'I'm sure you'll be interested to know that the governor will be attending the benefit,' Genevieve said, interrupting Zach's thoughts, which he figured needed to be interrupted before he got too carried away and embarrassed himself.

'Really? Huh.' Zach had met a lot of governors and a few presidents, too. He'd been to the Playboy mansion and partied with a lot of famous people. Some he'd liked. Others had been pompous tools. If Genevieve knew him at all, she'd know he wasn't easily impressed. Especially by stuck-up society women who married old men for their money, then cheated behind the suckers' backs.

Genevieve had invited herself to the party, and he wasn't fooled by offers of help. Not that she was trying to fool him. He'd been around women like Genevieve all of his career and most of his life. Women who offered up their bodies, and while he'd sometimes taken what they'd wanted to give, he'd never screwed around with married women nor women he didn't even like. He wasn't desperate enough to start now.

'I'll go check on the girls,' Cindy Ann volunteered, and took off toward the pool house.

'Thanks,' Zach said, and watched her go. Cindy Ann Baker was a perpetual volunteer mother, a former gymnast, and a woman who had it bad for Joe Brunner. Once Cindy Ann had seen Joe's truck parked out front and noticed Genevieve, she'd quickly volunteered to 'stay and help out, too.' Only Joe was so oblivious during football season, that he wouldn't recognize an attractive woman if she tackled him. And while Cindy Ann wasn't Zach's sort of woman, she was cute and perky and athletic.

The barbecue sizzled and sent smoke into Zach's face as he flipped a few more burgers. He waved the smoke away with one hand and glanced over at his defensive coach standing at the end of the table, chatting it up with Adele. The spatula paused in midflip, and a burger fell on its side on the grill. Maybe he'd been wrong about Joe. He watched Adele smile at his friend, then Joe leaned in and said something that turned her smile into soft, sexy laughter. Adele shook her head and patted Joe on the upper arm. Zach wondered if she'd be so friendly if she knew Joe had been married and divorced twice. If she'd be so touchy-feely?

Zach had invited the defensive coach over to help him out with the barbecue, not hit on women.

A frown pulled Zach's brows together, and he righted the burger on the grill. Joe was a good guy and a great buddy who had a bad habit of dating and marrying the wrong kind of women. He needed someone who was as much into sports as Joe was. Someone like Cindy Ann. Not a woman like Adele, who could not care less. At least she hadn't cared fourteen years ago.

Adele was beautiful, with a wonderland of a body, and Zach really couldn't blame Joe for chatting her up. And really, why should he care who talked to Adele? He shouldn't, and he didn't.

Across the lawns, the door to the guesthouse opened, and twelve hungry thirteen-year-olds headed his way. Their hair was dried, and they all seemed subdued, whether from exhaustion or hunger, Zach wasn't sure but was very grateful. They each grabbed a plate and loaded up on pasta salad, chips, hamburgers, and hot dogs.

'Did you burn mine black?' Tiffany asked as she moved next to the grill.

'You know it.' Zach speared the darkest hot dog on the grill and shoved it in a bun. Once the girls were all seated at tables beneath the heaters, he loaded Joe up with a double burger, Cindy Ann with a hot dog, and Genevieve just took pasta salad. 'What's your pleasure, Adele?' he asked. 'Hot dog or hamburger?'

She looked up from the seat she'd taken a few feet away. 'Neither thanks. I ate a huge lunch.' She stood and pointed to the side of the house. 'Can I get to the driveway through that gate?'

'If I unlock it. Why?'

'I left my cell phone in the car and I have to call my sister and tell her we won't be able to visit her until after six.'

Zach shoved a black hot dog in a bun and closed the lid to the grill. 'Use the phone in my office. It's closer.' He took a big bite and chewed. 'It's through the room with the big TV,' he continued, and pointed to a set of big glass doors. 'Down the hall. Last door on the left.' As he watched her walk toward the house, his gaze moved from the top of her head, down her curly hair, to the angel wings and heart on the nicely rounded ass of her sweatpants.

Just before she disappeared inside, he lifted his gaze to the small of her back. He'd touched a lot of women there. It meant nothing. Just being a polite gentleman like his momma had taught him. But earlier, when he'd touched Adele, his thoughts had been anything but polite.

He took another bite of his hot dog and washed it down with Lone Star. Like Tiffany, he liked his dogs crispy on the outside, but unlike his daughter, he didn't like ketchup. With his beer in one hand and hot dog in the other, he took a seat next to Joe and the two bullshitted about their Super Bowl picks. Joe was a die-hard Cowboys fan, but Zach liked the look of New England's offensive line.

'I don't care if they have Owens,' Zach argued. 'You can't build a team around one player.' He polished off his hot dog. 'Especially a pain-in-the-butt whiner.' Most wide receivers complained about not enough ball time, but Owens took it to the media.

'You're going to have a lot of free time on your hands once football season is over,' Genevieve said as she sat across from Zach and raised her wine to her lips. She looked at him over the brim of the glass, and her lids lowered a fraction. 'What will you do?'

Zach recognized the invitation. He'd seen it a thousand times in the eyes of a thousand different women. If it had been anyone but Genevieve Brooks-Marshall staring back at him, he might have given it some thought.

'I'll figure something out.' He stood and moved to a garbage can behind the grill. He tossed his empty beer bottle and walked into the house. He moved past the leather couches, chairs, and seventy-two-inch high-definition television and into the bathroom. Most of the house was exactly the way Devon had left it, except for the HDTV. Zach wasn't the kind of guy who had to have the biggest rig or fastest car, but he did like a big TV. With over two million pixels, sometimes bigger really was better, he thought as he zipped up his pants.

As he opened the bathroom door and shut off the light, he heard soft laughter from down the hall. He followed it past the weight and sauna room and stopped in the doorway of his office. He shoved one shoulder into the frame and crossed his arms over his chest. Adele sat on one edge of his big desk, talking on the phone. 'I didn't leave him a prank call on his answering machine,' she said, as she looked down at the cord she twisted around one finger. 'What a total loser. I called to tell him about what happened today with you and the baby, but at the last minute I decided he didn't deserve to know. Maybe I should have just hung up, but I didn't. I told him he should go fuck himself, and you're right. It felt great.'

Adele had a potty mouth on her. Zach lowered his gaze to her lips. Not that he held that against a beautiful woman.

'Let him.' She made a scoffing sound and shook her head. 'What judge is going to care? Compared to a man leaving his pregnant wife for his twentysomething dental assistant, a few messages are nothing.' She glanced up, and her gaze met Zach's. Her hand stilled, and she stood. 'Listen, Sheri, I've gotta go, but we'll come by on the way home. I know Kendra wants to tell you about her day.' She pulled her finger from the twisted cord. 'I'll see ya in a while,' she said, then hung up the phone.

'I thought you might've gotten lost.' He pushed away from the door and walked into the room.

'No.' She shook her head and brushed her hair from her face.

'How's your sister?'

'Better.' She sucked in a tired breath and let it out slowly. 'After Sheri has her baby, and everything is okay with them, I'm going home to my real life and sleep for about a year.'

'Where's home?'

She dropped her hands to her sides and looked up at him. 'Idaho.'

'Idaho?' He thought Tiffany had said Iowa. 'Is that where you disappeared to when you left UT?'

Adele stared up into Zach's handsome face, past his strong chin and firm mouth and into his eyes the color of warm coffee. She was tired and didn't want to talk about the past. Especially with the man responsible for so much pain. 'I didn't disappear.' She pulled her gaze from his and moved to a built-in bookcase. 'I went to stay with my grandmother in Boise. I liked it and never left.' She picked out an oversized *Sports Illustrated NFL Football's All-Time Greatest Quarterbacks* and pulled it from the shelf. 'Are you in here?' she asked, and looked over her shoulder.

'Somewhere.'

She cracked the cover and turned her attention to the glossy pages. 'You don't know where?'

'Page thirty-two.'

She chuckled and flipped through the book. The slick paper was cool to the touch, and she thumbed through until she came to a page filled with the image of Zach in a blue-and-orange jersey with the number twelve on the front and on the big padded shoulders. A pair of tight white pants fit him like a second skin, and a white towel was tucked into his waistband and hung over his laces like a loincloth. Zach's intense brown eyes stared out from within the face mask of his blue helmet, and his lips were flattened against his teeth. His left hip turned downfield, his right arm extended behind him, the photographer snapped the picture just before he snapped the ball forward.

'You ranked number eleven,' she said, then read out

loud, ' "Zemaitis played the game in his head. He had the ability to see each play before it happened. He played strong and smart ball and could kill with perfect spirals and long bombs." ' She turned the page to another photograph of him, standing behind the center, knees bent, head turned to one side as he called the play and waited for the snap. She read the caption to the side of the photo. ' "Girls always wanted to know what it was like to have Zach's hands all over my butt" – Dave Gorlinski.' She looked up at him. 'Who's Dave Gorlinski?'

'Center at UT.' He grabbed the book and tried to take it from her.

She didn't let go and read another caption. ' "Zach Zamaitis had the most skilled hands of anyone who's ever lined up underneath me" – Chuck Quincy.' Adele bit her top lip to keep from laughing. 'Who's Chuck?'

'Center for the Dolphins my first three seasons.' This time he succeeded in taking the book from her. 'Try not to laugh too hard,' he said, and tossed it on his desk.

'Well, it does sound kinky.'

'Honey, that's nothin'.' He tilted his head to one side and smiled. 'I could tell you stories if you're interested in kinky.'

'No. That's okay.' She turned her attention to the big glass case filled with everything from trophies to signed footballs and a pair of cleats. On just about every inch of the walls hung his old football jerseys encased in Plexiglas as well as plaques and photographs of Zach at various stages in his career, starting as a kid wearing shoulder pads that looked too big for his body and ending with his retirement.

'Impressive.'

He shrugged. 'Devon decorated this room a year or two before she died, and I've just left it. It's too crowded, but what else am I going to do with all this stuff?'

'I think you should leave it.' Adele turned to face him. 'It looks good, and you should be proud of yourself. And . . . I'm sure since Devon . . . you know.' She dropped her gaze to the Moose Drool beer on his wide chest. *Think of something nice to say about Devon.* 'I'm sure you miss her, and it must be a comfort to come in here and see something she decorated herself. Even if it is a bit crowded.' Well, that wasn't exactly nice, but it wasn't exactly rude.

He chuckled without humor, and she looked up into his face. 'I didn't mean to imply that she decorated it herself. She had someone do it. Devon never did anything herself.' He lifted a hand and brushed a few strands of hair from her cheek. 'I don't want to talk about Devon.' The tips of his fingers touched her cheek as his eyes searched her face. 'I want to talk about you.'

A hot little tingle spread down the side of Adele's neck and across her chest. It tightened her breasts and messed with her breathing. 'There's nothing to say.' She tried to laugh, but it sounded nervous even to her own ears.

'I doubt that.'

'Really.' She moved past him and headed for the door before the hot little tingle burned its way through her entire body. 'I'm very boring.'

A few feet from the entrance, his hand on her arm stopped her. 'Don't pretend you're not the least bit curious.'

'About?'

'What it would be like if I kissed you again. We're older. Have more experience.' She refused to turn around, and he slid his hand up her arm to her shoulder. 'Would it be as good as it was fourteen years ago?'

If it had been so good, why had he left her for Devon? She closed her eyes. They both knew the answer to that, but the fact that Devon had been pregnant hadn't made it any less painful. Not for her. It didn't hurt any longer, but there was absolutely no way she would ever get involved with him again. 'No. I'm not curious. I never look back.'

As if she hadn't spoken, he pushed her hair to one side. 'Would you drive me insane like you used to?' He lowered his face, and his breath warmed the side of her neck. 'And honey, you drove me out of my mind.' He slid one big hand around her side to her flat stomach and pulled her back against his hard chest. 'I was the first man to make love to you. I haven't forgotten that.'

'It was a long time ago.'

'You haven't forgotten, either.' His lips brushed her heated skin, and those hot little tingles she'd worried about spread warmth all over her body. It had been a long time since she'd felt the secure arms of a man. A long time since she'd felt the hot rush from a man's touch flow through her and the delicious pull of lust tugging at all the right places. 'I might not have thought about it in a while,' he continued, 'but I haven't forgotten that night we drove to the La Quinta off I-35. Not the best place, but not exactly a dump. I didn't have much money back then.'

She hadn't minded.

'We had sex at least five times.'

Seven if a person counted the next morning. She took short uneven breaths in the top of her lungs as he kissed the side of her throat. The scent of his skin filled her head, and it would have been so easy just to sink back into him. To close her eyes and just feel his big chest and arms around her. 'I don't remember,' she lied, because telling the truth would make things so much harder.

He slid his palm up the front of her hooded jacket, and her uneven breath got caught in her throat. His hand lightly skimmed across the top of her chest to her shoulder. Slowly he turned her and looked into her eyes. He smiled as his hands slipped to the side of her head, and he plowed his fingers into her hair. He tilted her face up, and her lips parted. 'Liar,' he said just above a whisper, then he lowered his face and kissed her. A light teasing brush of his firm lips. A wet smear across her mouth, and she stood perfectly still.

'This is much more fun if you participate,' he whispered.

She stood still while every nerve ending in her body screamed at her to grab him by the ears and participate the hell out of him. To let him make her feel good, to mold herself against him and use him to satisfy her hunger and need like a succubus, but she knew better. Nothing good would ever come out of kissing Zach. Sometimes the price of satisfaction was too high.

She wrapped her hands around his wrists and took a step back. 'I can't do this,' she said. 'This can't happen again.'

His hands dropped to his sides, and he took a deep breath. He looked down at her through narrowed lids. 'It's going to happen, Adele. If not now, another time.'

He looked so sure, her mouth got suddenly dry and she shook her head. 'No, Zach. Not with you. Not ever.' She couldn't breathe around him and walked out of the office like demons were nipping at her heels.

The next few minutes were a blur of restless nerves and raw emotion. Adele pleaded a splitting headache, which wasn't a huge stretch from the truth, and Cindy Ann volunteered to drop Kendra off at home after the party. As she drove from the gated community, she called Sherilyn and told her sister that she and Kendra would be in later that evening.

Once she was home, shut safely inside Sherilyn's condo, she took a deep breath and slowly let it out. Zach was wrong. Nothing was going to happen between them. Ever.

She moved through the entry to the kitchen and set her purse on the granite counter. Before Sherilyn had gotten ill, she'd been in the process of painting the mostly beige kitchen a cheery yellow. As a result, the kitchen walls were painted halfway down.

Adele took the extra house key out of a bowl in the cupboard and tied it to the string of her sweatpants. Like everything else about the sisters, Adele's tastes were the total opposite. She preferred white walls and colorful furnishings while Sherilyn preferred color on the walls and subdued furnishings.

She grabbed a scrunchie off the counter and pulled her thick hair into a ponytail as she walked back out of the house and locked the door behind her. She'd jogged earlier, but she didn't know what else to do with the restless energy humming through her veins. Her head really was starting to ache, and she didn't want to think about Zach.

She stepped from the porch and took off at a familiar, even pace. The steady beat of her heart and the routine rhythm of her feet were usually a comfort, but today it was as if her past was riding her heels. She couldn't outrun it, and it caught up to her at the corner of Crockett and Third. Her feet slowed at the bus stop near the corner and she took a seat on the hard bench advertising Tina's Taco-rama. An old truck with a red bone hound in the back drove past, stirring up the leaves on the road and rattling the cool air with its busted tailpipe.

Would you drive me insane like you used to? he'd said as he'd lowered his face to the side of her neck. *And honey, you drove me out of my mind.*

She'd driven them both insane. Him because she hadn't jumped in bed with him, like every other girl on the UT campus, the first time he kissed her. Her because she'd wanted to wait until she'd been sure she loved him, and he loved her, too. She'd waited a *whole* month. A short time that had felt like forever. Looking back, she couldn't say that he'd pressured her to have sex. Not unless she counted the way he'd kissed her. So hot and intense he'd left her breathless. And not unless she counted the way he'd touched her. Slow and unhurried, a light teasing stroke to her stomach and breasts, he'd driven her crazy until all she could think about was feeling his hands on her. She'd wanted to feel her hands on him, too.

She'd had boyfriends in the past. Some with whom she'd thought she might be falling in love. Things had gotten fairly hot with some of them, but she'd never been sure they were *it* for her. *The* one. Her *soul* mate.

Looking back, the thought of saving herself for a

soul mate seemed like an immature romantic fantasy. An embarrassing ideal that she blamed on too many fairy tales as a child, but back then she'd thought Zach was all those things and more. The man meant for her, and she recalled perfectly the moment she'd slammed headfirst in love with him. Up until that moment, she'd tried to take it slow. Tried to put the brakes on her runaway feelings, but the day he'd shown up at her dorm room with an illustrated book of flower fairies in his big hands, there was no slowing the beat of her heart or stopping her headlong fall.

The book hadn't been expensive, but it had been perfect. Six months before she'd met Zach, she'd had the fairy queen, Titania, sitting on a rose petal, tattooed low on her abdomen, her wild blond hair strategically covering parts of her nude body.

Adele hadn't believed in fairies for a long time, but she'd still loved the art and Scottish folklore of the Seelie Court. She had wonderful memories of her grandfather sending her out to the garden with a net to hunt the fairies he'd assured her lived amongst the roses and buttercups.

'I saw this, and it reminded me of the story you told me about your grandfather,' he'd said as he handed her the book.

She'd only mentioned it in passing, and he'd laughed at her and told her he thought she was cute. Looking at the gift in her hands had shocked her so much she'd blurted, 'You went into a bookstore?' Silence fell between them, and she glanced up.

Some of the pleasure drained from his face, and he crossed his arms over his chest. 'Yeah. Go figure. I can read *and* play ball.'

'I didn't mean it like that!' But she sort of had meant it. As long as she could tell herself that Zach was a stereotypical jock, the more she felt they were on equal ground. She was the brains to his brawn, but Zach wasn't dumb. Far from it. 'What I really meant was, did you make a trip to a bookstore just to buy this for me?'

He looked down at her for several moments, judging whether to believe her or not before his hands fell to his sides, and he shrugged. 'I thought you'd like a book more than anything else.'

'But you didn't have to get me anything.' She felt her heart swell a little in her chest. He'd bought her a book on fairies, not because he liked them but because she did.

'Look at this one,' he said, and pulled the book from her hands. He turned to a picture of a fairy sitting on a crescent moon, her blond curly hair blowing about her head and nude body. 'This one reminded me of you.'

Adele glanced down at the page, then back up into Zach's brown eyes. Her swelling heart ached, and she felt as if she were being slammed up against something bigger than she. Bigger than her ability to stop it. She wrapped her arms around his neck and fell into that something bigger. 'I love it. Thank you.' She closed her eyes and breathed in the smell of his skin. *I love you.*

He tossed the book on the small desk in her dorm and turned his face into her hair. 'You're welcome.' He ran his hands up and down her spine and she lifted her mouth to his. She poured everything she felt into the hot, hungry kiss. Her heart. Her soul. The love pounding through her veins.

He groaned against her lips as he slid his hands down her back to her behind and pressed his erection into her. 'You make me so hard,' he said, just above her mouth. 'I want you.'

She knew the feeling and pulled her T-shirt over her head and tossed it on her twin bed. She reached for him, but his hand on her bare stomach stopped her. His gaze lowered from hers, down her chin and throat to her breasts cupped in a sheer white nylon bra. Her nipples made hard points in the center of each cup. He stared for so long she raised her palms to cover herself, but he grabbed ahold of her wrist. He looked at her as if he'd never seen a naked girl before, but she was certain he'd seen more than his fair share of breasts.

'Zach. You're making me self-conscious.'

'Why?' He glanced up into her face then back down again.

'I don't know what you're thinking.'

He chuckled, low in his throat. 'I'm thinking that you're a beautiful girl, and I'm a lucky guy. I'm thinking that after all this time, I'm really looking at you.' A sexy smile curved the corner of his mouth. 'At least that's the cleaned-up version of what I'm thinking.' Then he kissed her, working his way down her throat until his hot, wet mouth covered her nipple through the sheer nylon. His hands moved to the hooks at her back, and the bra fell to the floor. He whispered something unintelligible as he sucked her naked flesh.

They'd never gone that far before, and this time he'd been the one to stop it. He hadn't wanted her first time to be in a dorm room with thin walls or in a house filled with football players. The next day, he rented a room at the La Quinta and made it so good, she'd fallen even harder. He'd been the one with all the experience, and he'd taught her what to do and where to touch him.

He'd taught her what good sex felt like. Later, she would learn that sometimes there was a difference between hot sex and making love. Zach had given her both. She would learn that hot sex without strings could be very satisfying, but that the best heart-pumping, mind-numbing, rock-you-like-a-hurricane sex, involved both.

She would also learn that if something burned too hot, it burned out too fast. But even if it hadn't been for Devon, Adele doubted her relationship with Zach would have lasted past graduation. It had all been too much. *He'd* been too much. Sooner or later he would have broken her heart.

With Zach, it had been sooner rather than later. Her one true love, the guy who she'd thought was *it* for her, left her after two months. The night he'd told her that Devon was ten weeks pregnant, Adele had been devastated beyond words. He'd ripped her heart from her chest and made a mess of her life. She'd loved him with every aching cell of her body, and getting over him had taken her years.

It's going to happen, Adele, he'd said earlier. *If not now, another time.*

Adele stood and turned back toward Sherilyn's condo. She was only in Texas for a few months, but even if she lost her mind and moved back for good, the last thing she was ever going to do was get involved with Zach Zemaitis.

Monday morning Adele worked on the outline for her latest futuristic series. She'd worked out the plot lines for the first three books, but the fourth and fifth weren't so clear. She wasn't too worried about it though. By the time she sat down to write those books, she'd know the direction each was meant to take. Hopefully.

After lunch she e-mailed her friends in Boise. Writing in a room by yourself was solitary and often lonely, and she needed contact with the outside world. Within an hour they returned her e-mails, and she learned that Lucy was diligently writing and that she and her husband Quinn were busily working on having a baby. Clare was leaving to travel with her freelance journalist husband, Sebastian, to Russia. Maddie had just inked a deal with Hollywood to have her latest book made into a film, and she was planning her wedding.

Adele looked around the small bedroom where she worked in Sherilyn's home and sighed. While her friends were happily living their lives, making a baby, traveling, and planning a wedding, she was stuck in Cedar Creek. She was cursed with bad dates, vexed with a former boyfriend who gave her hot little tingles despite her desire to feel nothing, and annoyed with playing her sister's gofer.

On the small desk next to her laptop lay a notebook filled with Sherilyn's notes and to-do list. Adele looked forward to the day when Sherilyn was home and able to take care of herself and her children, but each time she thought about that day and looked forward to it, she felt guilty. It wasn't her sister's fault that she was in the hospital. If anything, Sherilyn hated *not* working her to-do list and playing gofer more than Adele hated working it. Still, each time Sherilyn added yet one more thing to the list, Adele fought an urge to grab the pencil and snap it like a dry twig. And that made her feel guilty *and* selfish.

Adele closed her laptop for the day and glanced about at the boxes of baby furniture and bags of baby clothes and diapers and baby . . . *stuff* littering the room. Number five on Sherilyn's growing to-do list was: Paint and set up the baby's room. Adele figured she had a few more months to get it done and was busy concentrating on the everyday wants and needs of a thirteen-year-old. Although really, she wasn't sure what those wants and needs were because they seemed to change day by day. Sometimes minute by minute.

Just yesterday morning Adele had made Eggos for breakfast. Kendra had looked up from her plate as if she'd been served freshly toasted crap and had insisted that she hated Eggos and only wanted Cinnamon Toast Crunch. Then just this morning she'd thrown a fit because she got up too late to have an Eggo.

'I thought you hated Eggos?' Adele had reminded her.

Kendra frowned and shook her head. 'No. I love Eggos.'

A pain had stabbed Adele's forehead as she'd stared across at the niece who looked like a regular girl but was obviously an alien pod person who'd been sent from another world to drive Adele crazy.

You think you're cursed, she reminded herself. Okay, cra*zier*! She scrubbed her face with her hands and let out a deep breath. She was out of her element. She and Kendra weren't all that much closer now than they had been the day Sherilyn had picked her up at the airport, and Adele didn't have a real clear idea of how to rectify the situation. She supposed she could ask her sister, but she didn't want Sherilyn to stress out about her and Kendra. Besides, it wasn't as if they didn't get along. They did; it was more like they were two people living in the same house who didn't talk about anything important. Adele would like to know Kendra better before she left, and she could think of only one way to make that happen.

A month ago when she'd packed her suitcase, she'd anticipated a trip of no more than two weeks. As a result, she hadn't packed all that many clothes and was getting really sick of the things she had packed. She needed to do some serious shopping, and she'd thought that maybe she and Kendra could do a little retail girl time. All teenage girls liked to shop, didn't they? Maybe she and Kendra could bond at Dillard's in the new mall downtown.

Adele stood and walked into Sherilyn's bedroom, where she had moved her things. With Sherilyn in the hospital until she had her baby, Adele didn't see any reason to sleep on the hide-a-bed sofa. The queen-size bed was covered in a simple red duvet made of cotton. On her bed at home, Adele had a puffy silver silk quilt with real silver threads woven into it. Adele didn't consider herself materialistic, but she did love good bedding.

She gathered up the laundry and was again amazed at how much wash a teenager generated in one week. At three, she left to pick her niece up from school. As she pulled the Toyota to a stop in her usual place, Kendra and Tiffany walked toward the car.

'Can you give Tiffany a ride home?' Kendra asked as she opened the door and stuck her head inside. 'Her daddy can't get away from his football practice over at the high school.'

'Sure,' Adele answered, and both girls climbed into the car. As she pulled away from the curb, Tiffany buckled herself in and asked from the backseat, 'Would you mind taking me home the rest of the week? My daddy is really busy, and I don't want to get stuck waiting around for him.'

Adele looked in the rearview mirror. With Zach at football practice, it wasn't likely that she would run into him. 'I don't mind.'

'And maybe next week too? It just depends on if the Cougars win their game Friday night.' Tiffany zipped up her hooded sweater and rearranged her backpack. 'I don't want to ask any of those stupid moms to take me.'

Adele suspected there was more to the story, and after they dropped Tiffany at home, Kendra filled her in. 'She doesn't like some of the girls' mommas.'

'I got that. Why?'

''Cause she thinks they only act nice to her 'cause of her daddy. I guess after the party last night, some of the mothers hung around, and Tiffany said they were flirting and acting dumb.'

Adele pulled out of the gated community and imagined it was something Tiffany was going to have to get used to. Zach was very good-looking and rich and . . . well, he was Zach Zemaitis, and this was Texas. 'She doesn't like woman flirting with her father?'

'Oh no.' Adele looked across at her niece who shook her head. 'She doesn't like women around her daddy. *At all*. She says they want to marry him, and she doesn't want a stepmomma.'

Adele thought of Genevieve and didn't think the woman's interest was in marriage. 'Not all women are interested in a husband. Some just like to go out and have fun. He's single and . . . attractive.' Which was such a ridiculous understatement. Saying Zach was attractive was like saying a hurricane was a slight breeze.

'Yeah, Mr Z's cute. For an old guy.'

Adele chuckled. *For an old guy*. As she drove across town to the hospital, she thought about the brush of his mouth against hers and the seductive pull of his touch. Fourteen years ago, Zach had had moves well beyond his years. He'd known his way around a girl's body, and she had a feeling he'd only gotten better.

When they walked into Sherilyn's hospital room, she sat in a chair by the window waiting for them.

'The baby is really active today,' she said, a smile warming the tired lines at the corners of her eyes.

Kendra dropped her backpack on the bed and moved to her mother's side. She placed her hands on Sherilyn's belly and waited.

'Did you feel that?' Sherilyn asked.

Kendra nodded and her dark hair fell over one shoulder. 'That was a good one.'

Sherilyn lifted a hand from her belly and motioned to Adele. 'Come feel.'

'He always stops when I touch your stomach.' She moved to her sister's other side and Sherilyn grasped her hand. She placed it on her belly and waited. Just as Adele was about to pull away, she felt movement beneath her palm. She paused and was rewarded with a strong kick.

'Oh my God!' She looked up into her sister's face and grinned. 'Was that him?'

Sherilyn nodded.

'What's he doing? Tae kwon do?'

'Maybe he's trying to kick his way out,' Kendra suggested, as they all three stared at Sherilyn's belly. Through the thin cotton of Sherilyn's nightgown, her taut skin warmed Adele's palm. A new life grew beneath her touch, and for the first time it seemed real to her. He seemed real to her. Sure she'd seen his sonogram images, but they'd looked more alien than human. She'd heard his heart beat dozens of times, but that sounded weird and squishy, not like the beating of a human heart.

'Have you decided on a name?' she asked. They'd talked about names, but now that he was suddenly real, it seemed right that he have a name.

'I think Harris. He'll have his father's last name, but I'd like him to have my maiden name.'

'Harris Morgan.' Adele's smile grew. 'I like it.'

Kendra shook her head. 'I like Nick.'

'That's because you like Nick Jonas,' Sherilyn said.

Adele hadn't known that Kendra liked a boy. 'Does he go to your new school?'

Kendra glanced across her mother's stomach at Adele and rolled her eyes. 'Nick is part of the Jonas Brothers. They sing "Hold On".' She didn't say *duh*, but she might as well have.

Beneath Adele's hand, the baby kicked again, and it felt as if he'd kicked something loose that lodged in the middle of her chest. Something she hadn't really given much thought to lately because there hadn't been a man in her life for several years.

Yeah, Mr Z's cute. For an old guy. Zach was the same age as Adele. She dropped her hand and walked to the side of the bed. She watched Kendra and Sherilyn talk and laugh as they tried to get the baby to move.

'There it was again,' Kendra said through a great big smile.

Being here with Sherilyn, feeling the baby move and watching Kendra touch her mother's stomach, it struck Adele that she was watching a family. Yeah, William was an AWOL a-hole, but that didn't make Sherilyn, Kendra, and the baby any less a family.

Adele wanted that. She'd always wanted a family. When she'd had single girlfriends, she could tell herself that there was still time. But one by one her friends were all married or getting married and starting families of their own. Adele wanted her own family, too. A man to love her and her children. Children who would grow up and demand Eggos one day only to look at her like she was a moron the next and declare they hated Eggos.

'That was huge!' Sherilyn laughed.

It wasn't as if Adele was standing there, watching her

sister, and suddenly hearing the ticking of some biological clock. It was more like a glimpse into her future.

There's always time, a little voice in her head reminded her. But was there? That's what she liked to think, but she was thirty-five and hadn't had a good date in three years. She was either cursed or crazy and what were the chances of finding a man who would marry a cursed or crazy woman?

Good. Crazy people have a way of finding each other. Look at Bonnie and Clyde. Ozzy and Sharon. Whitney and Bobby. Okay, so what were the chances of finding a nice *normal* man who would marry a cursed or crazy woman?

Not so good. And she didn't want to purposely raise a child by herself. Some women did and were good at it. She just didn't think it was for her. Maybe she'd change her mind in a few years, but for now, she wanted the whole package.

'This Thursday night there's a rally at the high-school gym, and the Stallionettes are gonna dance,' Kendra announced, and pulled Adele's thoughts from her troubles.

'Why is the junior high having a rally at the high school?' Adele wanted to know.

'It's the high-school football rally.' Kendra looked across at Adele. 'You'll film it again, right?'

'Of course.'

Kendra removed her hands from her mother's stomach and bounced up and down on the balls of her feet with excitement. 'The high school's dance team is out of town at a competition, so they asked us. How awesome is it that we get to perform at Cedar Creek the night before a playoff game?'

Watching Kendra dance again – very awesome. Seeing Zach again – *not* very awesome.

Inside the Cedar Creek gymnasium, gold and green streamers wafted from the rafters. Since the last time Adele had been in the gym, the packed bleachers had been painted green and gold. The wooden floor had a new snarling cougar logo that was very fierce, and a few new championships had been painted on one wall.

Adele stood just inside the door, Sherilyn's Handycam in her shoulder bag. The Cedar Creek marching band stood in the center of the gym as cheerleaders jumped about to the blasting horns and thumping drumbeat of the school song. Adele didn't consider herself a particularly sentimental person, but hearing the old familiar tune hit her with a touch of nostalgia, like thumbing through an old photo album and seeing a picture of her first dog, Hanna.

The band finished on a booming note, then filed out two opposite doors. With the floor cleared, Adele looked for Kendra and found her across the gym, sitting on a bottom row in front of the football team. She wore her black footless unitard, purple sparkly vest, and soft leather dance shoes. Her dark hair was pulled to the back of her neck, and she'd painted her lips a deep red.

Since Kendra had found out that her team would dance at the high school, she'd been extremely nervous. What if she didn't get her sparkly vest in time? What if she tour jeté when she was supposed to do a stag leap? What if she didn't give the crowd 'energy'? Evidently, 'energy' was big in the dance-team world because Kendra worried about it a lot.

Her gaze moved across the row of football players,

all suited up in their team jerseys, to the coach sitting on the far side. Zach wore a black long-sleeved polo and a dark green ball cap that shaded his eyes. He rested his forearms on his Levi's-covered thighs, and his attention was directed at the center of the gym, where a man with a white cowboy hat and boots took the microphone.

'Hello, Cougars! For those of you who don't know, I'm Principal Tommy Jackson.' Applause broke out that mostly drowned out a few stray boos. 'We're all here tonight to show our support for our football team and to cheer them to victory tomorrow night.' Adele moved farther into the gym as the principal thanked the boosters and the students and teachers who'd hung the streamers and made posters. Adele found a seat near the middle, three rows up, and sat.

'The boosters have graciously provided ice cream to be served in the cafeteria directly after the rally. So y'all be sure to wander in that direction.' He paused to take his hat off and revealed a dark wreath of hair. 'A year and a half ago, when Coach Wilder passed away unexpectedly, we didn't know what would become of our football program. We had some mighty fine assistant coaches, but none were fully prepared to take over the job of head coach. Then someone' – he looked over toward the bench of players – 'I believe it was you, Joe, suggested that we ask a man who certainly knows his way around a football if he could step in and help us out.' The crowd whooped and hollered and stomped their feet. The bleachers shook, and Zach looked down at the floor between his boots. The bill of his hat hid the top half of his face and the shadow rested just above the bow of his top lip. 'Now, let's hear it for the man who's gonna take us all the way to State! Coach Zzzz!'

The crowd grew even louder, chanting his name, buzzing the air with excitement. Zach stood, pulled his hat from his head, and tossed it on the bench. As his long legs carried him to the center of the gym, he combed his fingers through his blond hair.

'Okay, y'all. Settle down a minute,' he began, the epitome of cool under pressure. He grabbed the microphone and adjusted it to reflect his height. 'First off, I'd like to thank y'all for coming out tonight and showing your support. I know it means a lot to the boys.' He placed his hands on his hips and rested his weight on one booted foot. 'We're all mighty happy to have Don suited up in his jersey tonight.' The gym broke out in wild applause, and he leaned forward, closer to the microphone.

'I just talked to his doctors this afternoon, and he'll be ready to play next year. When we lost Don, people said we were done for the season, but I never believed that. Don is one hell of a player with a big future, but we have a lot of boys on this team who can play ball. Who come ready to play at every practice and give me 110 percent. Who come to the games and leave their blood on the field. I am proud of every one of those boys, and I want to thank all the mommas and daddies who raised them up right.' He straightened as the crowd filled the air with whoop whoops.

'I'm not gonna lie. Amarillo is a tough team, and they're going to show up to win. Our boys are tough, too, and it's goin' to come down to who wants it more. I'm bettin' we do. I'm bettin' we have the heart, guts, and the glory to show those Amarillo boys how we play ball down here in Cedar Creek.' The crowd exploded, whooping and hollering and pounding the air with raised fists as if they were at a rock concert.

Zach turned his head and looked in Adele's direction. Across the distance, his gaze skimmed past her only to return abruptly as if he was a magnet and she was a shiny piece of metal. He waited a few seconds for the noise to die down before he continued. 'I know the boys will appreciate it if y'all can drive up to Lubbock tomorrow night and show your support.' He looked at the crowd in the seats above her, then raised a hand. 'Thanks again for coming out tonight.'

His easy confident stride carried him back to the bench, and he reached for his hat. As he sat, he slid it back on his head, then leaned to one side to listen to one of his assistant coaches. The Stallionettes rushed onto the floor, and Adele broke out the camera. She recorded Kendra as she danced her heart out to N'Sync's 'Bye Bye Bye,' and cheered the loudest when the show was over.

Next, the Cougar cheerleaders took the floor and jumped about, calling out cheers. They did lots of backflips, and an impressive human pyramid. Through the stack of arms and legs, Adele's attention was drawn to Zach. She could not see his eyes, but she knew that he was looking at her. His jaw was set. His chin squared. If she knew him better, she might think he was angry, but she didn't know him. Not at all.

After fifteen more minutes of cheering, the pom-pom squad ran out of the gym, and the football players followed, high-fiving each other on the way. The crowd in the bleachers began to file out, and Adele made her way to Kendra, who stood in a knot of dancers and their mothers. She recognized Cindy Ann Baker from the barbecue at Zach's.

'Are you ready?' Adele asked her niece.

'Can't we stay for ice cream?'

She glanced behind her and spotted the top of Zach's hat. He was surrounded as if he was a superstar, and she guessed he was. 'I've got to work tonight,' she said, which wasn't even a lie. She hadn't worked very much that morning and had to make up for it tonight.

'Please,' Kendra begged. 'All the girls are staying.'

'We'll take her home,' Cindy Ann volunteered. 'You go on to work before you're late.'

'Thanks.'

'She works at home.' Kendra picked up her bag. 'She can't be late.'

A little wrinkle appeared between Cindy Ann's light blue eyes. 'What do you do?'

'I'm a writer.'

Cindy Ann froze, and her brows rose up her forehead. 'Oh my God! You're Adele Harris. Aren't you?'

It wasn't like Adele was recognized every day. Or even often, but she did have a fairly large readership. 'Yes.'

'The other day at the party I thought you looked familiar. But when you said you went to Cedar Creek, I thought I must be wrong 'cause I just moved here from Alabama a few years ago.' She placed a hand on her chest. 'I've read every book you've ever written. My favorites are your books with the Brannigan fairies. Although I just love your Star Ship Avalon series, too.'

'Thank you. I'm glad you enjoy them.' Normally she liked to fly under the radar. At home, no one at her grocery store knew who she was, and she liked it that way. She liked running into the grocery store for a pound of chocolate and a box of tampons, looking like complete crap.

'What are you working on now?' Cindy Ann wanted to know.

Before Adele could answer, Joe Brunner approached. 'Hey, ladies.'

'Hey there, Joe.' Cindy Ann smiled at the assistant coach. 'Did you know Adele here is a published writer?'

'Why no. What do you write?'

Zach excused himself from the parents surrounding him and moved to Don's side.

'Be careful now,' he cautioned. 'I want you back to a hundred percent next season.'

Don stuck crutches under his arms and hopped along on one leg. His mouth pulled into sullen lines. 'I hate sittin' out, not playin' ball,' he grumbled.

'It's only one season.' But in football that meant a lot, and they both knew it. 'Just a few games, if you think about it.'

They passed Joe, chatting it up with Cindy Ann and Adele. From beneath the brim of his hat, Zach glanced at Adele, standing there in a pair of jeans and the same white sweater that zipped up her front she'd worn the day he'd seen her standing beneath his portico. Tonight, her hair hung down her back in sexy, wild curls, and she was doing a stellar job of ignoring him.

That was fine by him. He didn't need some uptight woman from his past getting him all hot, then telling him nothing was going to happen between them. *Not ever.*

'Careful now,' he said, as Don teetered. Hell, it wasn't as if he had even been meaning to start things between him and Adele the other day. At least not there. Not in his office with twelve thirteen-year-olds outside. One of whom was his daughter. When he'd walked into his office that day, he hadn't even thought about kissing her. Then he'd touched her cheek, her goddamn cheek was all, and he'd wanted more. In seconds, he'd turned hard as a rock, and the memory of the night he'd taken her to the La Quinta flooded his head. The memory of her naked body pressed to his had lowered from his head to his dick, and damned if he hadn't wanted to relive that night. All five times and twice in the morning.

Slowly, he and Don moved through the gym as people called out to them. Zach nodded and smiled and waved and wondered how his life had come to this. Lusting after a woman who clearly wanted nothing to do with him. That had never happened to him before, and he didn't know why it was happening now. Maybe his system had gone all peculiar because he was a full-time dad. Although, what that had to do with it he didn't know.

Someone he didn't recognize called out to him and he smiled and waved. 'Hey there. How you doin'?' More than likely, though, the peculiarity to his system had something to do with his lack of a sex life. It was making him screwy. So to speak.

'Hey, Coach Z.'

'Hey there, Miz Owens,' he called out to Alvin Owens's mother.

Maybe during the Christmas break, he'd drop Tiffany off at his mom's in Austin and take a little trip to Denver and hang out with some of his buddies. He'd drink a few beers and get laid. A lot. That ought to take care of it. At least enough so he'd quit fantasizing about an old girlfriend who'd made it really clear she wasn't interested in the likes of him.

Don stopped at the door to talk to a girl, and Zach continued through the halls of the school to the cafeteria, which had been decorated with paper cutouts of each boy's jersey. The boosters had set up a table and were selling pennants and foam fingers. Zach grabbed a strawberry ice-cream cone and took a big bite out of the top. Baskin-Robbins might have thirty-one flavors, but he was a strawberry man. Always had been.

'Did you catch the game last Monday?' one of the boosters asked him, as he wiped the corners of his mouth with a napkin.

He didn't have to ask which game. Not in the heart of Cowboy country. 'Sure did. Romo looks good in the pocket this year.' He shoved a hip into a vending machine and talked ball for several more minutes before Joe entered the cafeteria, followed by Tiffany, Kendra, and one of the other dancers. Cindy Ann's girl maybe. Adele wasn't with them. Not that he cared one way or the other. Just a mild observation.

He took a big bite out of his ice cream. If he wasn't careful, he was going to give himself a brain freeze. 'Denver is playin' Pittsburgh Saturday night,' he said, as Joe walked toward him. Tiffany had some sort of dance-team sleepover that night, and pizza, beer, and a ball game with the guys sounded good to Zach.

Joe smiled and rocked back on the heels of his Tony Lamas. 'I have a date Saturday night.'

'Good for you.' If anyone needed to get laid, it was Joe. Hell, maybe even more than he did. Zach took a big bite of his cone. 'With Cindy Ann?'

'No, that writer.' Joe shook his head and crossed his arms over his chest. 'The one with the curly hair and great behind. She was at your barbecue last weekend.'

'Adele?' Zach swallowed, and his brain froze, but he wasn't sure it was from the ice cream. Adele couldn't go out with Joe. She belonged to Zach. He straightened away from the vending machine as if he'd been jerked by invisible strings and threw the rest of his cone in a lined garbage can.

'Yeah. I think I'll take her somewhere nice. Try and impress her.' Joe grinned, and joked, 'Maybe get her good and drunk so she'll come home with me.'

Normally Zach would have laughed, but he suddenly wasn't in a laughing mood. No, he was in the mood to kick Joe's ass, which was a strange feeling for Zach, who'd never been a particularly possessive guy. Adele wasn't his, and he didn't know where the feeling that he wanted to kick anyone's ass was coming from. She could do whatever the hell she pleased. Joe could do whatever he pleased, too. They could do what they pleased together, and it wasn't any of Zach's business.

He clapped Joe on the shoulder as he walked around him. 'Have fun.'

Zach's lengthy strides carried him back through the empty gym toward the coach's office. To get there he had to pass through a long hall lined with glass cases, which were filled with trophies and team photos dating back to 1953, the year Cedar Creek High opened its doors.

A stack of game footage waited for him on his desk, and he wanted to study the Amarillo offense a few more times before tomorrow night's game. If the Sandies had a weakness, it was their running game.

As Zach stepped into the hall, his gaze landed on Adele and Cindy Ann, the only other people around. He paused for several seconds before continuing toward them.

'That was the one and only year I was in flag corps,' Adele said, pointing to an old photo and plaque behind the glass. 'My dad told me I looked like one of the soldiers from *The Wizard of Oz*.'

'I was in gymnastics most of my life,' Cindy Ann said, and glanced up at the sound of Zach's bootheels on the linoleum. 'Hey, Zach.'

'Cindy Ann.' Zach looked into Adele's eyes. Those captivating eyes that sometimes turned a deeper blue. 'Hello, Adele.'

'Zach.'

'Weren't the Stallionettes great tonight?' Cindy Ann asked.

At the moment, he couldn't recall. 'They danced their little hearts out.'

Cindy Ann turned to Adele. 'Well, I'll let you go so you can get to work.' She adjusted an armadillo bag hanging off one shoulder. 'And remember, if you ever decide to write more books about the Brannigan fairies, I'd love to read them.'

'I'll think about it. Thanks for taking Kendra home.'

'You're welcome.' She walked toward the door, and said over her shoulder, 'Bye, Zach.'

'See ya.' He lowered his gaze from Adele's face, down her throat and the round swells of her breasts beneath her thin sweater to the lower right side of her belly. 'Are you still into fairies?'

'Not so much these days.' She moved to step around him, but his hand on her arm stopped her.

'That's too bad,' he said, and looked back up into her face. With no more than the touch of her arm beneath his hand, a hot ball of lust hit him behind the button fly of his jeans. 'I have a few fond memories of kissing that fairy you have tattooed just above your panties.'

Her lips parted and color rose up her cheeks. 'That was a long time ago.'

'You keep saying that.'

'It's true.'

'True but memorable. Right up there with winning the Super Bowl. Or throwing that fifty-yarder to DaShaun Wilson in the last three seconds of the game against Chicago. And, honey, that was the perfect spiral. ESPN still shows that clip.' If they'd been somewhere more private, he would have given serious thought to falling to his knees and getting reacquainted with her fairy, but she was right. It had been a long time ago. Several lifetimes, and he looked into her face, seeing the resemblance to the girl he'd once known and the differences, too. Her mouth was a little wider and her lips softer than he remembered. Her pale skin was still smooth and her hair wild, even when she tried to tame it. Her eyes were the same. The same blue that did things to his insides when she looked at him.

'Joe tells me you have a date.' Zach couldn't recall ever feeling so possessive before. Not over a woman. Any woman.

'That's right.'

'First the redhead, and now Joe.' He moved his hand up her arm and shoulder to the side of her neck. Beneath his thumb, he felt the quickening beat of her pulse. 'Why?'

'They must think I'm nice and want to spend time with me.'

They didn't think she was nice. They thought she was hot, and the time they wanted to spend with her was in bed. Maybe he was projecting his own wants, but he didn't think he was alone. 'I know why they ask you out. I'm not so clear on why you say yes.'

Her brows lowered as if he was crazy. He felt crazy. 'Why wouldn't I say yes?'

'Because you don't really want to be with them, Adele.' There were a million reasons, all of them good, why he shouldn't want Adele Harris again. At the moment, none of them mattered. He didn't give a rat's ass as his hands cupped her face. 'You want to be with me.'

The corners of her full mouth turned downward. 'You're still as arrogant and full of yourself as you ever were.'

He smiled. 'Probably.'

'That wasn't a compliment!'

'Doesn't matter. I'm right.'

She wrapped her hands around his wrists. 'No, Zach. You're mistaken. I don't want to be with you.'

If she'd wanted him to stop, she'd said the exact wrong thing. He looked into her eyes, a subtle shade darker than they'd been a moment ago, and felt her pulse kick up a notch. 'You're not any better a liar now than you used to be.' He turned his face to the side to keep the bill of his hat from hitting her forehead and kissed her. A nice soft kiss that belied the savage lust beating his chest, pounding his groin, and urging him to push her up against the trophy case. Instead, he lightly pressed his mouth into hers, and his thumb brushed her cheek. Her lips parted with a little gasp, and she pulled his breath into her lungs. She put her hand on his chest, and the warmth of her palm spread fire across his skin and twisted his belly with pleasure and pain. She exhaled against his mouth, a slight puff of warm air that turned the pleasure and pain into an almost mindless need.

Adele pulled away, and Zach's hand fell to his side. Within her chest, she felt her heart pounding, and she could hardly breathe. She looked into Zach's sexy, sleepy eyes and she remembered his sneaky ways from fourteen years ago. How his light, teasing touch had ruthlessly made her want him even more. 'You're slick.'

He actually smiled as he reached for her. 'Thank you.'

She took a step backward, out of his reach. 'Again – not a compliment, Zach!' Every cell in her body was on fire. All he had to do was touch her, and every nerve ending twisted into a ball of yearning.

His hand fell to his side. 'Honey, come here.'

She shook her head and took another step backward. 'I don't trust you.'

'Baby, you don't trust yourself.'

That was true. She didn't trust herself not to give in to his sneaky, slick ways, and that just made her mad. 'What's the matter, Zach? Can't you find a willing woman to harass?'

Instead of getting angry like she'd intended, he laughed. 'Finding willing women has never been a problem for me.'

'God, you can't help yourself. You're a pathological bragger.' She held her hand up and took another step back. 'Not a compliment.'

'Arrogant. Slick. Pathological bragger. Anything else wrong with me?'

'You don't have all night.'

'I've got ten minutes.'

'Not enough time.' She took another step back and stopped by the sign to the girls' bathroom.

'That's where you're wrong, sweetheart.' He hooked his thumbs inside the front pockets of his jeans and drew her attention to the huge bulge beneath his button fly. 'The right man could have you in the zone and screaming Hail Marys in ten minutes.'

He turned her insults into foreplay. Worse, it was working. She licked her lips and her brain went kind of fuzzy. 'I'm not Catholic.'

'Doesn't matter.' He shook his head and moved

toward her. 'Everyone has a come to Jesus moment on fourth and goal.'

'That's something only a dumb jock would say.' Then, like the mature woman she was, she spun to her left and practically dove into the bathroom. She moved to the sink and placed a cool hand on the porcelain and one on her hot cheek. That was real adult. Call him a dumb jock and run away.

The door swung open and banged against the wall. 'Stop running, Adele.'

She spun around and gasped. 'You can't come in here.' He closed the door and leaned back against it. She pointed to the tampon dispenser and stated the obvious, 'This is the girls' bathroom.'

He glanced about at the six stalls and two sinks before his gaze returned to her. 'So it is.'

'You'll get caught in here.'

He pushed away from the door. 'It won't be the first time.'

'You're crazy.'

'I wasn't until you came back into my life.' He moved across the floor toward her and took off his hat. 'I see you, and I remember kissing you and touching you and making love to you. I want you more than I think I've ever wanted any woman.' He tossed the hat on the counter between the sinks. 'I can't help but wonder why you're back in my life.'

'I'm here because my sister needs me.' She placed her hands on his chest and, for every step he took, she took a step back.

'I need you.'

'No. You want me.'

'Same thing.'

'No. Oxygen is something you need.' Her back hit the wall next to the last bathroom stall.

'Just be still,' he said, and placed his hands on her shoulders. 'And stop running from me.'

'Stop coming after me.'

He shook his head as his brown gaze stared into hers. 'I'm beginning to think I need you like I need oxygen.'

She knew the feeling. From beneath his cotton shirt, his hard, defined muscles warmed her palms, and instead of dropping them to her sides like a smart girl, she slid her hands up his chest and wrapped her arms around his neck. *What the hell. The curse will kick in.* She lifted her face as he lowered his mouth to hers. His hands on her shoulders tightened, and for several long heartbeats, he remained perfectly still. Then he groaned deep in his throat and slid one hand to her waist. He brought her against his chest and kissed her. Like always, soft and sweet, creating a yummy suction as he drew her tongue into his mouth.

Adele dropped her purse to the floor, then plowed her fingers through the sides of his fine hair. Heat radiated from his chest and warmed her breasts. Her stomach felt light, her breathing heavy, as her nipples puckered into excruciatingly hard points. While his mouth made love to hers, she tried to remain still. She tried to keep her hands on the sides of his head and not roaming the hard contours of his chest and back, but then he slid his fingers beneath the bottom edge of her sweater and pressed his thumbs into her stomach, and she let her fingers do some walking all over him.

She pressed her legs together against the hot need pooling between her thighs. She reminded herself that they were standing in the girls' bathroom at Cedar Creek High, and she could not pull his shirt from his Levi's and feel his bare skin. She definitely couldn't run her mouth all over him and eat him up like a hot fudge sundae, but until the curse kicked in and put an end to this madness, she was going to feel sexual desire pour all over her.

His thumbs fanned her skin and the tingling sensation spread up her chest. She turned her head to one side and turned up the heat. She gave him long, feeding kisses, and he pressed his erection into her pelvis.

'Mmm,' she moaned into his starving mouth, and wanted more before it all had to stop. He shoved a knee between hers as one hand moved from beneath her sweater to the top of her zipper. While his tongue plunged into her mouth, his fingers pulled the zipper down until it came free at the bottom. Then his hands were on her breasts, cupping her through her white satin bra.

He slid his mouth to the side of her throat, and her head fell to one side. 'You don't know how much I want you,' he groaned, as his hands slid to the back of her bra.

'Hooks in the front,' she whispered. Actually, she did know how much. He felt enormous and so hard that the pressure against her pelvis was almost painful. She lifted her knee up his thigh and wrapped her leg around his waist. He unhooked her bra and she rocked against him, feeling the hard pressure through her jeans and his.

His harsh breathing lifted his chest, and he pushed her sweater and the straps of her bra from her shoulders and down her arms. He pulled back to look at her, down at his big hands filled with the weight of her breasts.

'You're the same as you were in college,' he said, his voice a harsh whisper.

'I'm older.' She gasped as his thumbs lightly stroked her puckered nipples, and she recalled the book about quarterbacks in his office and the quote about his 'skilled hands.'

'Better.' He turned one hand and slowly brushed the backs of his knuckles across the aching tip of her breast. 'Perfect.'

Adele looked up into his face, at his parted lips and brown eyes drugged with desire. Somehow she'd lost control of him and her and the situation. She'd waited for the curse to kick in. It hadn't, and she'd lost the will and good sense to stop. She tore at the sweater and the straps of her bra, holding her wrists at her side, until they fell to the tiled floor. Then she slid her palms over his hard chest and shoulder and leaned forward to kiss him. He tasted good in her mouth, like hot, turned-on man. It had been three years since she'd felt anything so wonderful as Zach's hands, his hot mouth, and his hard penis shoved against her.

Like the flash point of an escalating fire, the kiss ignited and turned all carnal and feeding, with hungry mouths and tongues. He rocked against her, rubbing the wet, aching places and stoking the fire. Her skin tingled, her breasts felt heavy, and her nipples painfully tight. It had been so long since she'd felt such delicious pleasure.

'Stop,' he groaned, as his hands moved to her behind and he shoved into her, pinning her hips to the wall. The wall felt cool against her back, and beneath her hands, his muscles turned hard as stone, and he froze. His lungs expanded as he inhaled a deep breath, and he whispered into her hair, 'Tell me no.'

'No?'

'Sound more convincing.' His warm palm slid up from her waist, and left a hot trail up her bare stomach. 'Slap my face.' His thumb brushed the underside of her breast. 'Tell me we can't do this here.'

She might have laughed or cried or kissed his neck if the sound of voices hadn't penetrated her sexual haze and instantly doused the hot lust burning deep in her stomach. Zach reached for her sweater and pulled her into a stall as the door to the bathroom swung open.

'He's in my math class,' a teenage voice spoke. 'He's kind of cute.'

'He's hot.'

'He asked me out. Do you think I should go?'

Zach handed her the sweater and held it while she shoved her arms inside.

'I don't know. His girlfriend's Sara Lynn Miller.'

'She's ugly.'

'Yeah, you're cuter.'

The sound of running water drowned out the girls' voices as Adele put the ends of her sweater together and zipped it up.

'Someone left their hat in here,' one of the girls said as the water turned off.

Adele glanced up into Zach's face. He stared straight ahead as if he could see through the door. His expression was stony.

'It's a Cougars football hat. Only the players wear

these.' There was a pause and then, 'Who's number twelve?'

Zach closed his eyes as if someone should just go ahead and shoot him.

'I don't know.'

'How did it get in here?'

Good question. Adele opened the stall door and closed it behind her. Out of the corner of her eye, she spied her white purse and bra where they'd fallen on the white tile floor. She moved to the sink toward two girls dressed in cheerleader outfits and hoped they didn't have to use the bathroom and notice her bra.

'Thanks,' she said, and plucked the black-and-green hat from one of the girls' hands.

'That's yours?' the girl asked.

'Yep.' Adele shoved it on her head and turned on the water. As she washed her hands, she looked through the mirror at one of the girls, who wore way too much eyeliner.

'Only the football players have those hats.'

And the coaches. 'This isn't one of the players' hats.' She turned off the water and tore off a paper towel.

'It sure looks like it.'

'It's similar.'

The girl with the eyeliner chewed her gum thoughtfully. 'Where'd you get it?'

From the guy hiding in the last stall. She shrugged. 'Internet.'

'Oh.'

They stared like they wanted to argue more, but in the end they gave her Kendra's favorite 'you're so gay' look and walked out of the bathroom.

'Coast is clear,' she said as she tossed the paper

towel into the garbage. The soles of her sneakers squeaked on the tiles.

'Zach?'

He didn't answer, and she pushed the stall door. He sat on the back of the tank with his booted feet on the seat. His forearms rested on his thighs, and his hands dangled in front of his knees. 'That was fucking close.' He looked up at her through his turbulent brown eyes. 'You still think nothing is going to happen between us? *Ever?*'

No, she wasn't sure. Not at all. 'We stopped.' Which she could admit to herself was a pathetic answer.

He pointed to his right. 'I was seconds away from getting you out of your pants and nailing you against that wall.'

She shook her head. 'I doubt things would have gone that far.'

'Who was gonna stop me?' He dropped his hand. 'You?'

She liked to think so, but she wouldn't swear on it. 'Clearly there are unresolved issues between us,' she said, striving to sound rational and make sense out of something that made absolutely no sense at all.

He raised one brow. 'Unresolved Issues?' He stood, and she took a step backward. 'I'd call what's between us good old-fashioned lust.' He hung a wrist over the top of the stall. ' 'Course, I'm just a dumb jock.'

'Zach, I didn't mean that. I'm sorry I called you a dumb jock.'

'I'm sorry I called you a cock tease.'

A frown wrinkled her brow. 'You didn't call me a cock tease.'

He smiled. 'No?'

'I'm not a tease!'

He leveled his brown gaze on her. 'Then run along out of here before I make you prove it.'

She didn't have to be told twice and grabbed her purse from the floor. She moved toward the door and walked out into the empty hall without looking back.

Adele opened the door to the condo then stuck her key back in her purse. She couldn't believe she'd left her bra in the girls' bathroom. She'd forgotten all about it until she'd been halfway home and glanced down at herself in the thin white sweater. For about half a second she'd thought about returning for it, but the idea of running into anyone with her nipples clearly visible had made her reconsider. She figured the bra would be discovered by the janitor and thrown away. Which was a shame since she'd liked that bra.

She smiled at the thought of the janitor finding it and trying to figure out how it got there.

She tossed her purse on the table in the small entry and moved to the kitchen. She'd lost her bra while kissing Zach in the girls' bathroom. How had it even happened? One second she'd been in control, and in the next she'd lost it. One second she'd told him that she didn't want to be with him, and in the next she'd told him her bra hooked in the front.

She opened the refrigerator and pulled out a Diet Pepsi. She'd waited for the curse to kick in and turn him into a freak who repulsed her. But for the first time in three years, the curse hadn't zapped anyone.

The one time she'd actually counted on the curse, it had let her down. With Zach. The last guy on the planet she should be kissing and touching. Especially in the girls' bathroom at Cedar Creek High. She should feel appalled and embarrassed, and she did feel those things. But probably not nearly as much as she should.

Not nearly as much as she felt the urge to smile.

For three long years, she'd believed she lived under a curse. Tonight, the curse hadn't shown up and turned Zach into a jerk. Maybe that meant it was broken. Perhaps there was a finite number of bad dates, and the curse had run its course. Or there never really was a curse at all. Either way, for the first time in a long time, she dared to feel free. Dared to hope that maybe the nightmare she'd been living was over.

Adele moved into the baby's room and pulled Zach's hat from her head, setting it on the desk next to her laptop. She dared to hope that Joe wouldn't turn into a jerk Saturday night when she went out with him.

She liked Joe okay, the little that she knew of him. He was kinda cute in a cowboy-redneck sort of way. The kind of cute you'd see in a John Deere ad. Along with his Southern accent, he seemed to have nice Southern manners, too.

That next Saturday night, over beef fajitas and a pitcher of margaritas at El Rancho Restaurant and Cantina, Adele discovered that Joe Brunner did have nice manners. He held the door for her and helped her on and off with her jacket. Mostly though, she learned that Joe loved three things. High-school ball. College ball. And pro ball.

'That game made history,' he said, referring to a game he'd played at Virginia Tech. He'd picked her up at eight, dressed like a lot of other guys from west Texas, in a beige Western shirt with mother-of-pearl buttons, new Wranglers, and a pair of Justin's. A straw cowboy hat covered his brown hair. 'You live in Boise, right? They have a good program up there in the WAC.'

Despite his obsession with football, she also learned that he really was a nice guy, and she felt like a horrible woman because she kept comparing him to Zach. He wasn't as tall or handsome, and when she looked at him, she didn't go all weak like she seemed to do when Zach was around. Which should have been a point in Joe's favor.

Several times during the course of dinner, Adele attempted to change the subject from football.

Not only because she wasn't a fan, but because the subject brought her thoughts back around to a certain retired quarterback. And when she thought of Zach, she thought of her shameful behavior in the girls' bathroom. And when she thought of her shameful behavior, her stomach got tight, and her skin got all hot.

'Tell me what you do when you're not coaching,' she'd asked Joe as she rolled up her first fajita.

'I own the Whistle Stop Mart.' His light green eyes looked into hers across the table, and he smiled. 'It's not very exciting, but I make good money selling gas and potato chips.'

When he smiled like that, she could almost forgive him for being such a ball fanatic. 'Do you like it?'

'I do. It has its challenges. Not like coaching though. I love coaching.'

Clearly. 'Who won the game last night?' she asked, giving in for the moment.

He paused in the act of eating and looked at her as if she had a single digit IQ. 'Cougars. Didn't you go?'

'I had to work.'

The topic changed to her writing for a few minutes, then Joe mentioned that he read books about sports, mostly football. Of course.

By the time Joe handed the waiter his credit card, Adele had caught a tequila buzz. Which helped dull the pain of so much football. 'Didn't you have a girlfriend you dated for quite a while in high school?' she asked, still making an effort.

'Yep. Randa Lynn Hardesty. She was a cheerleader.'

Figured. All ballplayers dated cheerleaders, didn't they?

The waiter returned with the check, and Joe calculated the tip and signed the receipt. 'And my first wife.'

'First wife?' Adele reached for her coat and slid from the booth. 'How many have there been?'

'Just two.'

Just two?

He stood and helped her as she slipped her arms into the sleeves. 'And you've never been married, right?'

She shook her head and looked up at him. 'Clearly, I'm a slacker.'

After dinner, Joe drove her home and held her hand as he walked her to the front door.

She wished she felt something. Even a little of what she'd felt when Zach put his hands on her would have been nice, but it just wasn't there. 'I had a great time tonight,' she said, and shoved her free hand into her coat pocket. 'Thank you.'

'I had fun too. Maybe we can go out again.'

'Maybe, but with my sister being in the hospital, I'm

really busy.' She remembered her date with Cletus, and she held her breath, waiting.

Joe smiled and squeezed her hand. 'I understand. With coaching and everything, I'm really busy, too. I don't have a lot of time to date. So, the next time I have a free night, I'll give you a call. If you're free, too, we can grab a bite again. No pressure.'

She felt such relief that she fought the urge to wrap her arms around him and give him a big hug. He hadn't turned into a jerk like Cletus. Maybe the curse really was over. 'I'd like that, Joe.'

'Good.' He dropped her hand and turned to go. At the bottom of the steps he stopped and looked up at her. A smile still curved his lips as he said, 'I imagine that you have some good-lookin' girlfriends.'

She thought of her friend in Boise. 'Yes.'

'It's not even ten. Why don't you call 'em up, and we can all party at my house. I'm in the mood for a skin sandwich.' He rocked back on his heels, and said, 'I'll provide the meat.'

Sunday afternoon football played out across Zach's huge TV, but he paid zero attention as Denver hammered the 49ers.

'She's pretty and interesting and I really liked her. I wanted to see her again,' Joe said from his side of Zach's big leather sofa. 'We kind of said that if we both weren't busy we'd go out again, and then . . . And then I kinda told her to get some friends so we could have a threesome. I said, "I'll provide the meat," and I don't even know where that came from, Z. One second I was looking up at her, thinkin' about how good she looked, and the next I was talkin' about a skin sandwich.'

Joe looked so miserable, Zach figured it was best not to laugh at his friend. 'Did you say "skin sandwich"?'

The defensive coach nodded and took a drink of his Lone Star. 'I'm pretty sure.'

But there was only so much a man could hear before he burst out laughing. It bubbled up from his chest and shook his shoulders. He had to set down his Pearl to keep from spilling beer in his lap.

'It's not funny.'

From where Zach sat, it was funny as all hell. And a load off, too. Joe hadn't so much as kissed Adele, and he was fairly sure there wouldn't be a second date between the two of them.

'I hadn't even been thinking about a threesome, and then I just opened my mouth and started going on about it. It was like something took over, and I had no control.'

Unfortunately, Zach knew the feeling, and his laughter died. Where Adele was concerned, he obviously had no control either. Just thinking about his loss of control scared him. Anybody could have walked into that bathroom while he'd had Adele up against the wall, his hands on her bare breasts, his hard-on pressed into the hot crotch of her jeans.

Not only did his lack of control scare him, it shocked him to the core. In his life, he'd enjoyed some fairly wild stuff, but he'd never put himself or his reputation at risk. He'd always kept control. Always called the shots. Been very careful not to create a scandal, and he didn't even like to think about what would have happened if the football coach had been discovered going at it in the bathroom by a couple of high-school girls.

'I've never had a threesome,' Joe grumbled as he took another drink of his beer. 'You probably have.'

Zach shrugged. 'They kind of lose their shine after a while.'

'I don't think I can ever face her again.'

There was no way Zach could avoid Adele. It just wasn't possible. Tiffany and Kendra were friends and on the same dance team. They were bound to run into each other again.

Unresolved issues. He reached for his beer as Denver scored a touchdown on a fifteen-yard drive.

That was one way of putting it, he guessed. He thought about her standing in that bathroom, her pink nipples pressed into his palms, and figured there was only one way to resolve those 'issues.' And it didn't involve avoiding Adele and walking around with a constant hard-on.

After the game was over, he showed Joe the door and made dinner for himself and Tiffany. He grilled chicken, tossed a Caesar salad, and warmed up a loaf of artichoke bread he'd picked up at the local deli. His daughter was unusually quiet, and he asked her if there was anything wrong.

'No.' She shook her head and played with her salad. He really didn't believe her, and it wasn't until the following Thursday morning that she finally let him know what had been on her mind.

'I have my first dance competition this Saturday,' Tiffany reminded him from across the table in the breakfast nook. 'I'm leaving for San Antonio tomorrow after school.'

Of course he knew. They'd talked about it all week. 'I wish I could be there, sugar bug, but you know I've got the Amarillo game in Lubbock that day.'

She stirred her cereal and sighed. 'I know. Not everyone's parents can go.'

Zach took a bite of a toasted bagel with cream cheese and wondered if she was purposely trying to make him feel guilty. Or rather, guiltier.

'Kendra's family can't go. 'Course that's because her momma's in the hospital, and her aunt has to stick around in case of an emergency.'

'Tiff, you know I'd go if I could.'

She nodded, and they ate in silence for a few more moments before she said, 'I'm thirteen.'

'Yeah. I know.'

'Old enough to go to dance competitions without you.'

'That's right.' His guilt eased a bit as he slathered strawberry jelly on his bagel.

'Old enough to pack enough money and make sure I don't miss the bus home.'

He took a bite and chewed. 'Yep. You're old enough to do a lot of grown-up things.'

'And old enough to wear makeup?'

He swallowed. 'What?'

She looked up at him. 'Daddy, everyone at school wears makeup.'

'No.' The thought of his baby all tarted-up with rouge horrified him. 'You don't need makeup.'

'Just a little bit?' she wheedled.

'No.'

'If Momma were alive, she'd let me.'

That was probably true, but it wasn't an argument that swayed him. 'Honey, you're pretty without it.'

'You never let me do anything the other girls do!'

'Now, that's not true.'

'It is! Last summer you didn't let me go to the fair with Lyndsy Shiffer, and everyone but me got to go.'

'That's because Lyndsy's momma does most of her parenting from a barstool over at the country club.'

'She wasn't going to be drinkin' that night.'

'Uh-huh.'

Tiffany stood. 'I hate my life! I want my mother. She'd understand!' She turned and ran up the stairs to her bedroom.

Zach stared at the empty stairway, then lowered his gaze to the bread in his hand. What the hell had just happened? Was Tiffany really that upset over a little mascara and lip gloss? It wasn't as if those things were really important. Nothing to get all worked up about.

He finished eating, then loaded the dishwasher. He didn't even pretend to understand teenage girls. They were so . . . emotional. He shoved his car keys into his pocket and headed upstairs. He'd given Tiffany a good fifteen minutes to cry whatever was bugging her out of her system. It was time he took her to school.

He rapped his knuckles on the door as he opened it. Tiffany lay on her stomach in the middle of a big pink confection of a bed surrounded by pillows and stuffed animals. Cinderella's castle was painted on one wall, complete with horse-drawn pumpkin carriage. The room had been designed for a little girl, not for the teenager sniffling under the gauzy pink canopy. The teenage girl who thought she was old enough to wear makeup.

Tiffany raised her head as Zach walked across the room. 'I miss Momma,' she whispered.

Zach glanced about at the many photographs of Devon in the room and sat down beside his daughter. 'I know you do.' He reached for Tiffany's hand and played with her silver ring. 'But she isn't here, and I'm trying to do what I think is best.'

Tiffany rolled onto her back and pulled her hand from his. 'If Momma were here, I could talk to her about girl stuff.'

'What stuff?'

She shook her head. 'Just stuff I can't talk to you about.'

'You can talk to me.'

She looked at him out of the corners of her eyes. 'I don't think so.'

'I know lots of girl stuff.' Which he figured was true, although his experience was more with big-girl stuff.

She shook her head and stared up at the ceiling. 'There's just stuff you won't understand.'

'Like makeup?'

'Yeah. And . . .'

'And what?'

'Why all the other girls at school got their period, and I don't.'

'Whoa.' Zach shot to his feet, and he heard ringing in his ears.

'See.'

He sat back down and felt heat creep up his neck. 'You can talk to me about that stuff.'

'Um-hum.'

'No, really.' He scrubbed his face with his hands. There wasn't a damn thing he knew about girls and their periods. Except maybe that they got bitchy around that time. God, he'd never thought about when girls should get theirs. He didn't want to think about it now. Not about Tiffany. 'So, all the other girls, huh?'

She looked over at him, his little girl who was trying so hard to grow up yet wasn't ready to give up her Cinderella bedroom. 'Dad. You don't have to talk about it.'

'No. No, this is good.' He scratched the back of his neck. 'Are you worried that there's something wrong with you?'

'Maybe.'

'Well, we can take you to see a doctor.'

152

'No!' She shook her head, and her cheeks turned pink.

'Okay. You can always call one of your grandmothers and ask them about it.'

Her nose wrinkled. 'Maybe.'

And because he felt so totally inept, so totally guilty for being out of his league, he said, 'And maybe you can wear a little lip gloss. Light pink.'

'And some mascara.'

'A little.'

'And eye shadow. Blue.'

'Good God, no.' The thought of his little girl tarted-up in blue eye shadow horrified him almost as much as the thought of her cheeks caked in rouge. 'The next thing you'll want is your nose pierced like that bull we saw at the fair last summer.'

She shook her head. 'Oh, Daddy.'

Wednesday afternoon, Adele pulled her hair back and made a mad dash to Kendra's school. She'd gotten wrapped up in her writing and was late picking up Kendra and Tiffany.

'Sorry,' she said, as they piled into Sherilyn's Toyota. 'I was working and lost track of the time.'

'No problem.' Kendra shut the front passenger's door and shoved her backpack onto the floor between her feet. 'Can you take us to the Estée Lauder counter at Dillard's?'

'Sure. What do you need?'

'I need some makeup.' Tiffany climbed into the backseat, and as soon as she buckled herself in, Adele pulled out into traffic.

Adele could use a few things herself. 'Is it okay with your dad?'

'Yes. Daddy gave me his credit card and said not to come home looking like a hooker.'

'Like Jenny Callaway,' Kendra said through a snort, and the two girls started to laugh.

The last time Adele had seen *Daddy*, he'd just come out of a bathroom stall. At first she'd been too blinded by the hope of no more curse to feel much of anything other than relief and pure joy over what had happened in that bathroom. A week later, she just wanted to curl up and groan. If those girls hadn't walked in, she wasn't so sure she'd wouldn't have ended up having sex with Zach against the wall. She didn't want to think about what might have happened if Zach hadn't pulled her into the stall before those girls opened the door.

'Aunt Adele?'

She looked over at her niece. 'Yes.'

'No, Kendra,' Tiffany whispered loudly from the back.

Kendra turned and looked between the seats at Tiffany. 'She might know.'

Adele looked in the rearview mirror at Tiffany shaking her head. Her eyes huge. She looked so much like her mother, it brought back memories of Devon making fun of the brand of pants Adele wore. 'What's up?' Adele asked.

Kendra sat back in her seat. 'When did you get your period?'

The car swerved a little as Adele glanced over at her niece. 'Why?'

' 'Cause Lilly Ann Potts got hers last week. That makes everyone in the eighth grade but Tiffany.'

Adele stopped at a red light and once again glanced in the rearview mirror. Tiffany leaned forward with her face buried in her backpack. She seriously doubted every girl in the eighth grade had her period but Tiffany. 'Are you worried about it?' Adele asked.

Tiffany shrugged.

'She thinks something might be wrong with her,' Kendra provided. 'And she doesn't have a momma to talk to her about it.'

The light turned green, and Adele drove through the intersection. At the age of thirteen, she hadn't had a mother either, and she knew what it was like to have that important piece missing in your life. To always feel the loss and sorrow and longing in your heart, but at least she'd had Sherilyn. Perfect, pain in the butt, Sherilyn to explain things to her. 'My mother died when I was ten. Just like you. Only I had an older sister to talk to about embarrassing stuff I couldn't talk to my daddy about.'

Tiffany lifted her head. 'I tried to talk to my daddy about it. He said I could go to a doctor, but I don't want to, and I don't want to talk to my grandmas either. And there might not be anything wrong anyway, but I saw a story on TV about girls who have too many boy hormones or something and they don't get their periods and they grow a mustache. I don't wanna grow a mustache.'

Adele had never heard of such a thing, but she supposed it could happen. 'I think I was thirteen when I got my period, but my friend Gail was fourteen. She was littler than I was and a late bloomer.'

'See. I told you not to worry.' Kendra picked at a blue patch of polish on her stubby thumbnail.

'I think my mom was a late bloomer,' Tiffany said.

'Yes. I think she was.'

Tiffany sat straight up. 'You knew my mom?'

'We graduated from Cedar Creek High the same year,' she said as she turned into Dillard's parking lot. 'We didn't hang around with the same group of friends, but I knew her.'

Adele parked the car, and the three of them got out and moved toward the front of the store.

'Did my momma have lots of boyfriends?' Tiffany asked, and folded her arms across the chest of her red sweater.

Devon had always dated a football player. 'I believe she did.'

'Were they cute?'

'Sure.' Adele hung her purse on her shoulder. 'Your daddy knew her better than anyone, I imagine.' They walked into the store and paused at the perfume counter. 'You should ask him about her.'

Tiffany shrugged and sprayed herself down with Juicy. 'I do ask him, but he didn't know her before UT. And he just says stuff like, "there was no one like your momma" and that she loved me.'

Zach was right. Adele had never met anyone else like Devon, which was a good thing. 'You should ask Genevieve Brooks.' Adele picked up a bottle of Burberry, pulled back her sleeves, and spritzed her wrists. 'She knew your mother better than I.'

Tiffany shook her head, and her golden blond hair brushed the shoulders of her sweater. 'She only talks to me so that she can be around my dad. The others, too.'

'Smell this.' Kendra held her wrist up to Tiffany's nose. 'It smells like grapefruit.'

They set down the bottle of perfume, and Tiffany asked as they moved to the Estée Lauder counter, 'What was Momma like in school?'

A heinous bitch. 'Well, she was perky and cute.' Adele dug around in memory for something nice to say. 'She was a cheerleader and popular.' Then she flat out lied. 'She was just plain wonderful.' She swallowed past her constricting throat. 'Really great.'

Tiffany grinned, showing a mouthful of metal. Her whole face lit up from the inside out. 'Everyone loved her.'

'Yes. Everyone loved her.' Adele smiled and was glad that she'd lied.

'Grandma Cecilia says that people loved her 'cause she was so sweet to everyone.'

Adele opened her mouth, but her throat closed completely. Apparently one lie about Devon a day was her quota. 'Mmm-hmm,' she managed and was saved further comment by an Estée Lauder salesclerk with a pile of blond hair and perfect makeup. The clerk set the three of them in chairs in front of mirrors and let them play with makeup as she gave them tips.

Adele felt bad for Tiffany. Going through your teen years without a mother was rough, and although she was positive Zach loved his daughter, he could never be her mother. She could never go to him with those excruciatingly embarrassing questions that every girl had when her body changed from a little girl's into a woman's. She wondered if she should tell Zach that Tiffany had talked to Adele about her worries.

While the girls applied a little pink rouge, Adele picked out liquid eyeliner and drew a narrow, plum-colored line across the base of her lashes. She pumped up the volume of her lashes with some Illusionist mascara, then turned to her niece. 'What do you think?'

'I like the eyeliner, but . . .'

'But what?'

'No offense, Aunt Adele, but the scrunchie has to go.'

'Go where?'

'In the garbage.'

She lifted a hand to the ponytail at the back of her head. 'What's wrong with my scrunchie?'

Tiffany leaned forward, and answered, 'It's so nineteen-nineties. Noooo one wears *scrunchies* anymore.'

'Jordon Kent's mom does,' Kendra said as she gazed at herself in the mirror. 'I saw it when she picked him up from school.'

'Yeah, and she wears mom pants and big bangs, too.'

Adele suddenly felt really old and lowered her hand. 'Really? My scrunchie is a fashion no?' How had she not known that? And how had she suddenly become so incredibly *un*cool?

'Your scrunchie is a fashion *heck* no.' Tiffany gave her a consoling smile. 'But you've got pretty eyes.'

Pretty eyes? Wasn't that what people always said to unattractive people when they couldn't think of something nice to say?

'And you're really cute when your hair isn't in a scrunchie,' Tiffany added, throwing Adele a bone.

Cute? 'Thank you.' She looked up at the saleswoman. 'I'll take the Illusionist mascara. The plum eyeliner and lipstick in maraschino.' She glanced at her watch, then she turned to her niece, 'What are you going to get?'

'Me? I don't have Mamma's credit card.'

'Don't worry about it. I have tons of credit cards.'

'Really.' Kendra smiled. 'You'd buy me some makeup?'

'Sure. I don't think your mother will mind, and I haven't given my cards a workout since I've been here. I'm feeling a little deprived.'

'Do you mind if I get concealer?' Kendra pointed to a pimple on her chin. 'This is so embarrassing.'

Adele looked at the choices of concealer the saleslady had placed before them and pointed to a small tube with a wand. 'Do you like this one? It looks like your color.'

Kendra nodded and the saleswoman turned and opened a drawer of concealer.

'Do you want to go see your mamma before or after dinner?' Adele asked her niece.

'After. Tiffany's coming over to your house, and her daddy's picking her up around six.'

'Oh.' The memory of Zach with his big 'skilled' hands on her breasts inconveniently popped into her head.

'I hope it's all right, but Daddy's practice is going to run a little late tonight.'

Adele didn't know if she was ready to see 'Daddy' so soon. She'd hoped to maybe avoid him until the memory of the bathroom incident faded a bit. 'Of course it's all right. Sheri won't mind if we come a little later than usual.'

The saleswoman piled the concealer and pink lip gloss with Adele's makeup and Tiffany pointed out the cosmetics she wanted. 'You're so lucky, Kendra,' Tiffany said, and sat back in her chair. 'I wish I was going to have a baby brother.'

'We get to feel him kick all the time.'

'You have to let me babysit with you.'

'Okay. I'll let you change his poopie pants.'

Tiffany wrinkled up her nose. 'Yuck.'

The saleswoman set curling mascara, two tubes of pink and rose lip gloss, and a clear cube with a pot of bright blue color in the center.

'Is your daddy going to be okay with that blue eye shadow?' Adele asked the thirteen-year-old.

Tiffany nodded and whipped out Zach's Platinum American Express card. 'He won't mind.'

At six fifteen, Zach stood on the porch of Sherilyn's condo wearing a bulky hooded sweatshirt. Gray November sky bathed him in a slight shadow and, like always, the sight of him did funny things to her insides.

'Hello, Adele.'

'Tiffany,' she called over her shoulder, 'your daddy's here.' She stepped out onto the porch and closed the door behind her. 'I need to talk to you.'

He looked down at her, his expression carefully blank. 'If it's about what happened in the bathroom, I think it's pretty safe to say that we both got carried away and . . .'

'It's not about that.' She took his arm and pulled him down the steps. He'd once told her that he was a human furnace, and he was right. Warmth radiated from him and heated up her hand and forearm. 'There's something more important for us to talk about than what happened in the bathroom.' After they'd returned home from Dillard's she'd thought about Tiffany's concerns about her body, and the more she thought about it, the more she'd figured she should talk to Zach. 'Tiffany told me that she's afraid that she'll never get her period and she'll grow a mustache.'

They stopped at the bottom of the stairs and he turned to face her. 'She told you all that?'

Adele nodded and let go of his arm. 'I thought you should know she talked to me about it.'

'She mentioned something about it the other day.' He looked down into her eyes. 'But she didn't mention the mustache.'

'Evidently she saw something on TV that's freaked her out.' Adele shrugged with one shoulder. 'I'm sure she's just a late bloomer. Devon was small.'

'Her momma was tiny, so maybe.'

Tiny and petite and beautiful. Adele looked away and folded her arms against the chill. She wore a long-sleeved shirt, but it wasn't enough protection against the cool night air. 'She asked me questions about Devon.'

They walked side by side down the walk toward his silver Escalade. 'What questions?'

'What she was like in high school. Stuff like that.'

'What did you tell her?'

Adele glanced up at him and said flatly, 'I lied.'

'About?'

'I told Tiffany that Devon was wonderful and everyone loved her.'

She wasn't sure, but she thought he smiled with one corner of his mouth. 'I take it not everyone thought she was wonderful.'

Adele stopped at the curb. 'No. Not everyone did.'

He shoved his hands into the pocket of his sweatshirt and looked over her head as if he was distracted by something going on across the street. 'Thank you. I know that Devon wasn't your favorite person.'

'No.' She glanced behind her, but no one was out and about but her and Zach. 'She made my life hell.'

'You weren't the only one.'

She wondered if Devon had made Zach's life hell, too. 'No matter what I think of Devon, or of you, Tiffany seems like a nice girl. She's been really sweet to Kendra at a very difficult time in my niece's life.'

'Tiffany *is* a nice girl.' His eyes narrow as he continued to stare over her head. 'I didn't know she was worried about growing a mustache, and I thought she could talk to me about whatever's on her mind. I guess there are some things she feels uncomfortable talking over with her dad.' He finally looked at her. 'If she says anything else, I'd appreciate it if you'd let me know.'

Adele nodded. 'I lost my mother when I was ten, so I know how she feels.'

'That's right. You told me that at UT.' His gaze slid to her mouth and down the front of her shirt. His voice got really low, his drawl more pronounced when he said, 'I've got something for you.'

She didn't think she wanted to know what he had for her. It might be something she hadn't had in a long time. Something she really wanted but really shouldn't want. She frowned to cover up her confusion. 'Grow up, Zach.'

He looked at her for several moments, then said, 'Sweetheart, you have a dirty mind.'

She placed a hand on her chest. 'Me?' Before she could respond further, the front door opened, and Tiffany moved from the porch and down the steps.

'You ready?' Zach asked, the hot lazy drawl gone from his voice.

'Yep.' Tiffany hung her backpack over one shoulder

and opened the Cadillac's passenger's door. 'Thanks for taking me to Dillard's.'

'You're welcome.' She placed her hand on Tiffany's shoulder. 'And just remember something. Being a late bloomer might suck right now, but when you're thirty, you'll look twenty-five, and all your friends will be jealous.'

For the first time in years, Zach dreamed of Devon. In the dream, he was back at UT, walking alone from the tunnel at Texas Memorial Stadium. The sound of his cleats echoed off the concrete and the helmet in his hand bumped his thigh. His footsteps slowed then stopped as he noticed Devon standing at the big gaping entrance wearing the Chanel suit he'd buried her in.

'Hello, Zach.'

A heavy, suffocating weight settled in his chest.

'Aren't you going to say hello?'

'Why are you here?'

She flipped her blond hair and leveled her green gaze on him. 'I'm pregnant.' She smiled and placed a hand on her flat stomach. 'You're going to be a daddy.'

The heavy, suffocating weight squeezed his lungs and closed his throat. He woke up gasping for air; his heartbeat pounding in his head. The quilt felt like lead, holding him down, and he pushed it off. He sat on the edge of the bed, never so glad to be awake in his life.

'What a fucking nightmare.' He stood and walked through the dark room toward the bathroom. The carpet beneath his feet changed to heated tiles, and he moved past the dais with the big spa tub. Moonlight shone down on him from the domed skylight windows as he pulled himself out of his boxer briefs and used the toilet. The last time he'd dreamed of Devon, she'd come back from the dead to yell at him for trying to divorce her. He preferred those dreams to this latest.

He tucked himself back into his underwear and flushed the toilet. He didn't know why Devon had popped up in his dream to tell him she was pregnant, he was just damn glad he'd woken up, and it hadn't been real.

The overhead moonlight ran down his spine and behind as he moved beneath the skylights to the bedroom. He thought back fourteen years when Devon had tracked him down at the house he'd lived at with a couple of football buddies. She'd told him she was pregnant. She'd conceived the last time they'd been together. Just a few days before he'd broken up with her.

'I'm not one of those girls who has children out of wedlock, Zach. I won't do it.' She crossed her arms over her chest, the implication clear.

As he'd looked at her standing there, a girl he'd once loved, he'd felt as if his life was slipping through his fingers like sand. There was only one thing he could do.

He'd done the right thing.

Goose bumps broke out across his chest as he moved through the house to the kitchen and opened the refrigerator. He reached inside and pulled out a gallon of milk. Within the glow of bright light, he drank straight from the container.

He'd been raised to do the right thing. There'd never really been a choice, but it hadn't been easy. Marrying Devon because she was having his baby caused problems from the beginning.

He lowered the carton and sucked milk from his top

lip. One of the biggest problems had been that he'd always wondered if the pregnancy had been an accident or if Devon had stopped taking her pills on purpose. Then a few years before her death, she'd admitted that she'd stopped taking them. They'd been arguing about their lack of a sex life, and she'd wanted to make him mad.

'Yes, I quit taking them. I admit it. They made me fat,' she'd said. 'You always wondered and now you know.'

'You should have told me.'

'What does it matter now?' she'd asked, and she was right. It didn't matter. It didn't matter fourteen years ago, ten years ago, or even now. Accident or no, he'd married her. She'd given him a beautiful daughter, and he'd never been sorry about that.

He shoved the carton in the refrigerator and shut the door. He loved Tiffany, but there'd never been another accident. He'd made sure of it.

The last thing he wanted was another marriage with a woman he didn't love and couldn't trust. He'd been there and done that, and it had sucked.

Friday at five, Adele put Kendra on a bus and waved good-bye. The dance team, with its six female chaperones, was headed to San Antonio and wasn't expected back until Sunday afternoon. Almost two whole days of freedom, and she was looking forward to the peace and quiet.

She watched the bus drive away, then stopped by the hospital to visit Sherilyn. Her sister had been feeling restless and bored, so Adele bought a nail file, foot lotion, some red polish, and gave them both pedicures. She stayed for a few hours, then returned to the condo and sank into the jetted tub with her friend Lucy Rothschild's latest mystery novel. A few years ago, Lucy had been the number one suspect in a serial-killer case. The detective assigned to investigate Lucy had fallen in love with her, and they'd married.

Adele sank lower into the tub and cherry-blossom-scented bubbles slid across her shoulders. She'd pulled her hair up onto the top of her head with a dreaded scrunchie. Sometimes there was nothing better than a good hot soak and a wonderful book. She stayed in the tub until the water cooled and the bubbles disappeared, then she got out and wrapped a towel around herself.

The condo was so quiet, which was more odd than relaxing. This surprised her, since she'd lived alone for a lot of years and had never found it weird before. She dried off and dressed in one of her white T-shirts and white panties. As she pulled on a pair of fluffy pink monkey socks, the doorbell rang, and she grabbed her black waffle robe.

She didn't know who it could be, but hoped it wasn't Joe with another offer of a skin sandwich.

It wasn't. Adele looked through the peephole at Zach standing on her porch, light shining in his hair and lighting up the left side of his breathtakingly handsome face. A flush of prickling heat traveled up her spine and settled between her shoulders. She knew without a doubt, opening the door would be a very bad idea.

He reached forward and rang the bell again. He hit it three times in a row and she reached for the dead bolt. She swung the door open, and Zach stood before her, wearing a blue fleece REI jacket and a pair of worn jeans. His gaze lowered from her face, down her black robe, to her feet.

'Nice socks.'

'Thanks.'

His gaze climbed back up her body. 'Are you alone?'

'Yes.'

'Then what took you so long to answer the door? Were you deciding whether or not to let me in?'

'I'm still deciding.'

He smiled with one corner of his lips. 'Invite me in.'

That was not a good idea.

'I have something for you, and I don't want to pull it out right here.'

Her mouth dropped open. 'If you reach for your fly, I swear to God I'm calling the cops.'

He rolled his eyes. 'Jesus.' He reached into the pocket of his fleece and pulled out her white bra. 'I believe this is yours.'

She reached for it, but he held it up just out of her grasp. 'Where did you get that?'

'Floor in the girls' bathroom. I thought you might want it back.'

She held out one hand. 'I do.'

'You have something that's mine. We'll swap.'

'What?'

'My coach's hat.'

She pulled her robe tight around herself and crossed her arms beneath her breasts. 'You don't have another hat?'

'Sure, but that one's lucky. We're thirteen and oh, and I'm not going to screw that up tomorrow afternoon against Amarillo by wearing a different hat.'

'If I let you in, are you going to behave?'

He held up his hands like he was as harmless as a Boy Scout. Her bra hanging from his fingers by one strap ruined the picture of innocence.

She swung the door open, and he stepped inside. 'You couldn't have called first?'

'Don't have your number.'

That was true. 'Your hat's in the baby's room.' She turned, and the heavier thud of his boots on the wood floor followed close behind her. They walked into the room filled with the small desk, her laptop, and boxes of baby furniture.

'How's your sister?'

'Today she's good.' She plucked the hat off her desk and turned to him. 'Each day she carries the baby is a good day.' She handed him the hat, and he handed her the bra.

He glanced about the room. 'Looks like you have a lot to do in here.'

'Yeah.' She tossed her bra on the desk and looked around. Anywhere but at him and his big shoulders and wide chest. She'd always known the room was small, but with Zach in it, it felt like a cubicle. 'I have to put all this furniture together, and I was thinking about painting the room blue. Maybe painting clouds on the ceiling.' She shrugged, and with the room being so small, she could smell the scent of his soap on his skin, and it was giving her a dangerous urge to take a few steps forward and bury her nose in his neck. 'I have to go to the hardware store. I don't even have a screwdriver.'

'Every girl should have a few tools around.'

She smiled.

'Don't say it,' he warned. 'When I packed for my visit, I left my tool belt at home.' Now it was his turn to smile.

'You have a tool belt?'

'Well, it's more like a toolbox that has a cheap belt that came with it.' He raised his gaze to the top of her head. 'Were you going for some sort of crazy afro?'

'No.' She reached up and pulled out the scrunchie. She shook her head, and hair fell down her back. She wondered if and when he was going to try one of his slick moves on her. 'I was in the tub.'

'The first thing I ever noticed about you was your

hair.' He tapped his hat against his leg. 'I saw you, and I thought you looked like a wild jungle girl. The ones you see in movies and cartoons running around the Amazon in leopard-skin bikinis. Growing up, I had fantasies about those wild girls.' He looked from her hair to her eyes. 'I don't think I ever told you that.'

'No. You never did.'

'Then I looked into your eyes, and I had a hard time looking away. I remember waiting around the little pizza place you worked in so I could walk you to your dorm.'

'Yes.' Her stomach fluttered, and her urge to bury her face in his neck got stronger. 'And you bought me a book about flower fairies.'

'Did I?'

'You don't remember?'

'Honey, I've had more concussions than I can recall.'

'Well, it was really thoughtful and sweet.'

'While I hate to blow your illusions of me,' he said, as a self-deprecating smile curved his lips, 'I'm sure I did it to get into your pants.'

'What?' She laughed. 'It wasn't because you liked me?'

'Oh, I liked you.' He ran his fingers through his hair and slid his hat on his head. 'I liked you a whole lot, and I wanted to have sex with you.'

She waited for him to say something about still wanting to have sex with her. About the two of them getting naked and getting it on.

Instead, he moved toward the door. 'I got a big game tomorrow. Good night, Adele.'

That was it? He really *had* come for his hat? 'You're leaving?'

He paused in the doorway and looked back at her. 'Are you going to ask me to stay?'

He wasn't going to kiss her and touch her and overload her senses and take away her ability to say no to him? She opened her mouth, but the words got stuck in her throat.

'That's what I thought.' He continued toward the door and reached for the handle.

'Don't go!' she blurted. She hadn't expected him. Hadn't expected to want him to stay, but she wasn't sorry.

'If I stay, you know what that means.'

'Yes.' The minute she'd opened the door to let him in, she'd known what would happen.

'You say yes, but you give off more mixed signals than any woman I've ever known. And frankly, sweetheart, I don't want to leave here with a hard-on.'

Her gaze lowered to the big bulge behind his button fly. 'Too late.' She wanted it to happen. 'Do you have a condom?'

Instead of opening the door, he leaned back against it. 'Always.'

'Then stay.'

He held out his arms, still giving her the choice. She raced across the floor before she could overthink her decision. Her hands slid up the front of the soft fleece to his shoulders, and she buried her nose in his neck. She breathed deep, and the scent of his skin reignited all the places he'd heated up last week. 'Make it good so I don't regret this tomorrow.'

He cupped the sides of her head and looked into her eyes. 'That's a lot of pressure.'

'Can you handle it?'

He lowered his face to hers. 'Darlin', I do my best work under pressure.' Her lips parted, and he gave her a slick, wet kiss that lifted her stomach and raised her to the balls of her feet.

Beneath the soft glow of the entryway light, she opened her mouth and touched her tongue to his. One of his hands moved from her thick hair and down her back to her behind, drawing her close until the hard bulge of his erection pressed into her. Her robe parted, and he was rock-hard against her belly, covered in a thin T-shirt. She wanted Zach. If just for one night. She wanted his touch. His kiss. She wanted him deep inside her.

His hands moved to her shoulders, and he pushed her robe down her arms. It fell and pooled at her feet, and he slid her T-shirt up and grasped her nearly bare behind in both hands. A drugged moan came from her throat as she kissed him back and surrendered to the desire bigger than her ability to hold it back. Not that she even wanted to try any longer.

The kiss caught fire, turning into a hot and greedy free-for-all of slick mouths and deep, consuming pleasure. He plunged his tongue into her mouth as if he were inside her body, and her body responded with a hot, liquid ache between her legs that left her clinging to him and wanting more. Her greedy hands moved over him, his fleece, the T-shirt beneath, and the back of his head. She pushed Zach's hat from his head and his jacket from his shoulders, and he shook it from his arms. Their lips parted long enough for her to pull his T-shirt over his head, then her hands were all over his bare chest. She ran her finger over his defined muscles and hot skin, then pulled back to look at him. She recognized the double-z tattoo circling his big biceps and studied the newer tattoo on his forearm. She slid her gaze over his hard chest muscles covered in blond hair, down his six-pack abs and the darker blond happy trail that circled his navel and disappeared into the waistband of his jeans.

'Do you like what you see?'

Only a man confident of the answer would ask that question. 'I do. Yes.' She took a step back and reached for the bottom of her T-shirt. She lifted it over her head, and her thick curly hair settled down her back. She tossed the shirt to one side and stood before him in pink monkey socks and white panties. He leaned his head back against the door and looked at her through hot, hungry eyes.

She raised a brow, and he smiled, a predatory lift of the corners of his lips. 'I love what I see.' He reached for her and pulled her to him, settling the heavy weight of her bare breasts against his chest. Her nipples pressed into his hot flesh and turned up the heat in her liquid, achy places.

He lowered his mouth to hers once more. The kiss was wild and chaotic, like nothing she could remember experiencing before. It was harsh and sweet and drugging, two people giving in to a purely physical and consuming need until he groaned deep in his throat and pulled back. His breathing was heavy when he said, 'Adele.' The desire burning in his brown eyes made her feel beautiful. 'Where's your bed, honey?'

She leaned forward and kissed his throat as she slid her hand into his. 'Come with me.' She led him into Sherilyn's bedroom.

'Turn on the light,' he said, and pulled her back against his chest. She felt the vibration of his voice against the back of her neck. 'We're not going to do this in the dark.'

He let her go, and she turned on a lamp on the bedside table. She watched him unbutton his pants and peel them down his big legs. He wore gray boxer briefs with a white elastic waist and stitching around the pouch. As he kicked his pants aside, she moved to him and slid her hand down his belly and beneath the waistband. She reached inside and took his thick shaft into her hand. He'd been her first love. Her first lover. Time had diluted her memory, but it came back to her now. The solid weight of him as she slid her palm up his hot, velvet penis. He groaned deep in his throat and covered her hand with his, stroking it up and down until he couldn't take it any longer, and he moved her hand to his shoulder. He pushed her down onto the bed and followed.

He murmured something against her throat, sweet words telling her how much he wanted her, how hard she made him, and how good her hands on him felt. He dragged his mouth across her shoulder, tasting her skin as he moved lower and kissed her breasts. The tip of his tongue licked her nipple before he sucked it into his hot mouth.

She moaned his name and arched her back with mindless need. She ran her fingers through his hair, watching through heavy eyes as he kissed her breasts and sucked her puckered nipple. He worked her over until her breath was choppy, then he worked his way down her body. He kissed her belly and just below her navel, his warm, moist tongue leaving a trail of fire.

'What are you doing?' she asked, as he left the bed to kneel between her thighs.

'Getting reacquainted with your fairy.' He pulled her panties down her legs and past her monkey socks before he placed his hands beneath her thighs and lifted until her knees rested on his big shoulders. Then he leaned over her and kissed the fairy tattoo on her belly. His hot breath brushed across her skin as he asked, 'You don't mind if I give her a sugar bite, do ya?'

She swallowed hard and shook her head. He kissed her stomach and bit the inside of her thigh as he placed his warm palm between her legs, then slid his hand up until his thumb brushed her clitoris.

She moaned deep in her throat and felt his satisfied laugh against the inside of her thigh. He parted her slick flesh and placed his hand beneath her bottom. He raised her like a feast and brought his mouth down.

Fourteen years ago he'd kissed that same spot. Only he was better at it now. Better at knowing how to use his tongue and how hard to draw her into his mouth. He teased and sucked until she almost came apart, then he slid a finger inside and touched her g-spot. He hadn't known that trick fourteen years ago, and she came apart. 'Zach,' she called, as a fierce orgasm clenched her insides and spread across her body. Her spine arched off the bed, and he stayed with her until the last shudder shook her body. Then he brushed his mouth across her inner thigh and stood.

'I've wanted to do that for a couple of weeks now.' He reached into the back pocket of his pants and pulled out a condom. 'Are you ready for more?'

She felt boneless as she looked up at him. She should have been sated, ready to roll over and go to sleep, but as she stared at his beautiful body and powerful erection, she wanted more. A lot more, and she knew she would not be truly sated until she got it.

She sat up just enough to grasp his hand, pulling until he landed on top of her. His thick penis burned into her belly as she kissed his throat and shoulder and pushed him onto his back. Their heated skin stuck together where it touched, and she took the condom from his hand and opened it. He was more than ready, and she fit the latex over the plump head and unrolled it down the long, hard length of him.

'I think you're going to like this.' She straddled his hips, positioned herself, then slowly sat. He was big and extremely hard, and she took her time, feeling every bulge and ridge through the thin latex until the head of his penis bumped her cervix.

His breath hissed from his lungs as his hands slid up her thighs and hips to her waist. 'You look good up there. I like it already.'

'It gets better.' Slowly she raised herself, rocking her hips and sliding back down. She teased him with her body, clenching her muscles around him, drawing his flesh deeper, using him to build and stoke the sexual fire burning through her.

'You've learned a few things,' he said, his grip on her waist tightening.

She rolled and rotated her hips, feeding his need and hers, and looked into his drugged eyes as he watched her. She bent forward to kiss the side of his neck. Her breasts pressed into his chest, and she whispered into his ear, 'You feel good. Hard. Huge.'

He rolled with them until she was on her back looking up into his face. His fingers curled with hers, and his mouth came down hard. His tongue drove into her mouth as he drove into her body. She felt light-headed like she might pass out as he pushed her up the bed with the powerful plunge of his hips. She tore her mouth from his, wrapped one leg around his waist, and matched him thrust for thrust. He propelled them toward orgasm, pushing again and again.

'Don't stop. Don't stop,' she whispered with each hard stroke, until the first wave grabbed her and wouldn't let go as it rushed across her over and over for an eternity. It curled her toes and clenched her fists, and she opened her mouth on a silent scream.

He groaned words of pleasure and praise. He told her she was beautiful and how good she felt inside. With one last powerful drive of his hips, he shoved into her and stopped. His grasp on her fingers tightened, and he buried his face in the side of her neck. His release turned his back and shoulder muscles to stone and elicited a final groan that seemed to come from the pit of his soul.

His breath whispered across her cheek, and he kissed her ear. 'Are you okay?'

'Mmm-hmm.'

'I didn't hurt you?'

Hurt her? She laughed. 'No.'

He raised his head and looked into her eyes. A totally unrepentant smile tilted his lips. 'I got kind of rough there at the end. Sorry.'

She ran her hands up his shoulders and down his back. She looked up into Zach's familiar brown eyes. Nothing about the sex she'd just had with Zach reminded her of the boy she'd once known. He was different now, and so was she. The biggest difference was that she didn't love him. He'd just given her great sex. Incredible sex, but it wasn't love. It had nothing to do with love, and that was just fine with her. The last thing she needed was to fall in love with the man who'd once broken her heart.

'Are you hungry?' He pressed his forehead into hers and ran his hand up her thigh. 'Could you eat some pizza?'

Nothing had reminded her of the boy she'd once known until that moment. He'd always been ravenous right after sex. 'How about a sandwich instead?'

'That's really sexy.' Zach ran his gaze up Adele's legs as he scratched his bare chest. He'd pulled on his jeans and appeared totally relaxed and at ease, sitting on a stool at the kitchen bar.

'What?' She handed him a glass of sweet tea and took a seat beside him.

'What you're wearing.'

'This?' Adele glanced down at her white T-shirt, pinched the fabric, and held it away from her stomach. She was a little embarrassed that she didn't have anything truly sexy to wear, but when she'd packed for her visit, she hadn't exactly packed with sex in mind.

'Yeah.' He took a big bite of his ham-and-Swiss sandwich and washed it down with the sweet tea.

'It's an old T-shirt.'

'But that's what I always liked about you. You're sexy without even trying.'

She was? She didn't feel sexy these days. Between her work and her sister and Kendra, she mostly felt tired.

'If you think this T-shirt is sexy, you don't get out enough.'

'Honey, I have a teenage daughter.' He set his glass on the bar. 'I don't get out at all.'

Adele found that hard to believe. 'At all?'

'I haven't been in the same room with a naked woman in a long time.'

'How long?' She took a drink of her tea.

'Let's see. It was since before Devon died. I know that. Probably about four or five months before I served her with the divorce papers.'

The tea went down the wrong pipe, and she sputtered and coughed. 'You were divorcing Devon?'

'Yeah, but don't let it get out. Tiffany doesn't know, and I'd like to keep it that way.'

'Okay, but . . .' She set the glass on the bar. 'Never mind.'

He took a bite and chewed thoughtfully. 'Never mind what?'

'It's none of my business, but if you were divorcing Devon, why is your house practically a shrine to her?'

He set his sandwich on the plate and turned on the stool to face her. 'We really haven't changed much in the house since Devon died. The furniture in my bedroom and in the media room are new, but Tiffany likes things left the way they are.'

'Oh. That explains the big spooky portrait of Devon.' But sooner or later they would have to change. Keeping things the same couldn't be healthy for either of them.

'You think it's spooky?'

'Oh, yeah. You don't?'

He shrugged. 'I'm used to it I guess. I don't really even see it anymore.'

'The first time I was in your house and saw that portrait of Devon, I about had heart failure.'

'I bet.' He laughed and scratched his bare chest. 'When I came home and saw you standing under the portico, I thought maybe I was hallucinating. You were standing there with your wild hair and white sweater, and you didn't look very happy to see me.'

She turned to face him, and her bare knees slid between his denim-covered ones. 'I was shocked. First by that enormously freaky portrait of Devon, then by you.'

He reached for her hand and kissed the backs of her fingers. 'I couldn't stop thinking about you after that day.' He flipped her hand over and kissed her wrist, sending warm tingles up her forearm to her elbow. 'I know you're only in Cedar Creek to help out your sister, but I'm glad. I'm a selfish bastard, and I'm glad you have to stick around for a while yet.'

After he finished eating, he made love to her again. He didn't demand food afterward, and Adele drifted to sleep wrapped up in his arms. When she woke the next morning, she was alone.

Like all good one-night stands, Zach had left without so much as waking her. No empty promise to call her later. No awkward good-bye.

Those were the rules of sex without love. Those were the rules of two people hooking up. She was fine with it, even if it did feel a little hollow.

She turned onto her back and looked up at the patterns on the ceiling. Yes those were the rules, but she couldn't help wondering where Zach was and what he was doing.

For some reason, the curse didn't seem to zap him. At least not yet, and she wouldn't mind using his body a few more times before the curse kicked in, and she had to kick him to the curb.

From across the shoe aisle, Devon Hamilton-Zemaitis eyed the new shipment of Metro7 dresses. From where she stood, she could see the choices were black, gray, and hot pink. Devon would never be caught dead, even when she was dead, in hot pink. Hot pink was vulgar, and gray washed her out.

To her left, she caught sight of her competition for the black jersey dolman. Her name was Jules Brussard, an upstart Junior Leaguer from New Orleans.

Devon jumped over a stack of shoe boxes, did a roundoff into a back handspring, and finished with a left-side hurdler, accidentally landing her foot in Jules's ample chest. Jules flew backward and knocked over a rack of Hanes Her Way thigh slimmers.

'Sorry,' Devon said, hardly winded as she grabbed the black jersey from the rack.

Since getting sentenced to Walmart three years ago, Devon had learned a few things. First, that just because she'd been reduced to wearing Walmart couture didn't mean she had to let herself go. Being dead hadn't changed her fashion sensibilities. Naturally, she was envied by the other associates.

The second thing she'd learned was that she had the

energy and stamina of a teenager. She could do herkies and pikes and back handsprings like no one's business, just like when she was on the UT squad. Unfortunately, she wasn't the only one with her former body. There was a woman in Beauty who delivered a mean karate chop to the throat if you got too close to the lip liner.

The third thing she'd learned was that behind the smiley face logo, lived a lot of severely pissed-off dead people who, like herself, had been unjustly charged, unfairly sentenced, and doomed to a life of Muzak.

She'd been assigned to an eternity of shelving shoes. Which should have thrilled her, but just made her long for the days when she'd sunk her feet into Prada, Manolo Blahnik, and Valentino. Cheap shoes just didn't smell like Fendi.

She supposed it could have been worse. She could have been sentenced to the kitchen, where she'd have to churn out cole slaw and chicken nuggets for eternity.

She moved into the changing room and shed the print chiffon she'd wrestled from the grasp of a woman from home appliances just yesterday. She pulled the black jersey over her head, and it clung to her body. As she gazed at herself in the full-length mirror, she smiled. She was beautiful and perfect, as always.

But unlike always, the image wavered and dissolved in front of her eyes. The racks of clothes shimmered like a mirage, then disappeared. She stood in a gray mist, and her skin tingled. She looked down at herself and gone was the black Metro7. In its place was her Chanel bouclé tweed and Mikimoto pearls.

'There you are. You never did stay where you were supposed to.'

She looked up. 'Mrs Highbanger?'

'High*barger*,' her sixth-grade teacher corrected. 'You were supposed to be in shoes. Not apparel.'

Devon shrugged.

'Come along.' Without moving her feet, Devon slid along through wispy clouds behind her old teacher. 'You have earned another chance to move up.'

'I have?'

Mrs Highbarger inclined her head slightly. She still wore that hideous purple suit with the gold buttons, but Devon supposed it wasn't her fault someone had buried her in that fashion-hell-no. Although it must have been hanging in her closet when she'd died.

'I'm going to heaven now?' she asked.

'The choice is yours.' As if they stepped onto an invisible escalator, they moved up through the clouds.

'Okay. Let's go.' After the hell of Walmart, she was ready for heaven.

'Not yet. The gift you granted the woman you wronged in your life has righted some of the harm you caused while you inhabited your earthly body.'

'Huh?'

Mrs Highbarger looked back over her shoulder at Devon. 'In the long run, your gift actually helped more than harmed.'

'It did?'

'Surprised?'

Shocked. Hadn't she cursed what's-her-name with bad dates? Which the woman had richly deserved for trying to steal Devon's man. 'Of course not.'

God knows when you lie.

Oops. 'Did she find someone?'

They stopped, and the clouds gathered and formed a filmy television screen. Images of a football game played out across the surface, and Devon recognized Zach standing on the sidelines. He looked as handsome as she remembered.

'What's he doing?'

'Watch.'

He called a few plays, made some hand signals, then stood on the sidelines as the Cedar Creek Cougars snapped the ball. 'Is he a coach at my old high school?'

'Yes.'

'I thought he took a job with ESPN.'

'He stayed in Cedar Creek for your daughter.'

'Oh.' Devon was glad. Tiffany loved her home and her friends.

The image cleared and re-formed and a silver Cadillac Escalade's headlights cut through an inky night and burned up the flat Texas highway. Zach sat inside, his thumbs tapping the steering wheel. She recognized the impatient gesture and smiled.

In her way, she'd loved Zach. He'd given her what she'd wanted and cared about most. Money and position. Their child.

'How's Tiffany?' she asked her old teacher. She really didn't worry about her daughter. She knew Zach would take care of her, but she missed her baby. Death changed a lot of things, but it didn't change that.

'She's well.'

The Escalade pulled up to a curb, and Zach got out and walked to the front door of a condo. He knocked, the door opened, and what's-her-name stood in the threshold wearing what looked like a black slip that hugged her body. Devon gasped as Zach stepped inside and wrapped her in his arms.

'Oh hell, no! This can't be happening.' Death

changed a lot of things, but not a strong emotion like hatred. She watched Zach devour the woman's mouth. Over the course of their ten-year marriage, he'd been with other women. She'd known and hadn't cared. The day she'd decided to move back to Cedar Creek while he had to live in Denver, she'd known he'd fill his needs with someone else. She'd expected him to, and as long as he avoided getting caught in a sex scandal, she was happy with the arrangement. He could sleep with whomever he wanted – except *that* woman.

'How did this happen?' Devon stepped forward and waved her arms and hands until the image dispersed.

'Every date she'd gone on for the last three years has kept her single.'

'Why hasn't the curse – or gift, I mean – worked on Zach?'

The old teacher shrugged. 'God works in mysterious ways. Perhaps it is fate.'

'So they're together?'

'The relationship is new, but yes. In part due to you. If not for your hand in things, she might have married someone else.'

Devon folded her arms across her suit. This could not be happening. Some people didn't understand what it was like to have things that belonged to you taken away. To watch your momma's car repossessed, your furniture removed, and your house foreclosed. Her momma's second husband had cleaned out her bank account, and they'd lost everything. Like beggars, they lived off the kindness of relatives until Momma had found a rich man to marry and replaced it all. Devon had hated living like that, but she'd learned a valuable lesson. Win at all costs and don't let anyone or anything take what belongs to you.

Ever.

'You said I've earned another gift.' She unfolded her arms. 'Right?'

'Yes, but you don't have to use it on the woman you wronged this time. That wrong has been corrected, and you can use this gift to serve mankind. You can do wonderful things. Help end poverty or aid in the research to find cures for diseases. I suggest you use this gift for the greater good.'

Greater-schmater.

I suggest you don't do what you're thinking.

She'd never listened to Mrs Highbarger, and she wasn't about to start now. There was one thing to do. One thing that Zach had always resented and hated her for. One thing he would hate what's-her-name for, too. She closed her eyes, and said, 'There. It's done.'

Mrs Highbarger shook her head, highly disappointed yet again. 'You still don't learn,' she said, as her image began to shimmer.

'She can't have him!' Devon hollered. 'What's-her-name was always jealous of me. In the sixth grade, she took Tinkerbell away from me. Then she tried to take Zach, but he was mine!'

As before, the teacher took a step back through sliding glass doors that suddenly appeared. The doors whooshed closed, and the gray mist formed solid walls. Devon's skin tingled as her beautiful Chanel suit warped and faded into a horrible polyester floral-print dress with a big lace collar. The hem hit her just below the knee and she looked like an escapee from 1983.

She looked beyond racks of clothes, shelves of

towels and sheets, to a big wall of automotive tools. 'Where the hell am I?'

A gentleman with a friendly smile and the name Norman sewn above the pocket of his polo walked toward her.

'Hello,' he said. 'Welcome to Sears. Home of fine Craftsman Tools.'

12

Zach lifted his face and watched Adele's eyes turn a shade darker. 'Are you going to invite me in?'

She nodded and took a step back into the house. 'Did you win your game?'

'Yes.' He followed.

'What was the score?'

'I don't know.' He brought his mouth back down to her soft lips. He tried to keep it gentle, to ease into it, but Adele wasn't playing around. The kiss she gave him sucked away any thought of gentleness. It was all slick tongues and carnal implications. Which was fine with him. Sometimes you had to go at it hot and hard and get the first one out of the way.

He kicked her front door shut and brought her body against his, so close he felt the imprint of her against his chest. Her hands slid over his arms and back, greedy as if she couldn't get enough. He liked knowing he did that to her. God knows he couldn't get enough of her.

He'd left her at four that morning, and sixteen hours later, here he was again, back for more. He'd driven like a madman from Amarillo to get to her, and he hadn't even known if she wanted to see him.

Her hand slid down his waist to the front of his

pants. She squeezed his erection and caressed him through the denim. Desire, hot and gripping, tightened his scrotum, and he had to lock his knees to keep from falling.

He lifted his face and came up for air. 'I couldn't stay away.'

'I'd hoped you'd stop by. I went to the E-Z Mart.' She slid two fingers inside the top of her slip and pulled out a condom wrapped in black plastic. 'When I set the box of magnums on the counter, the clerk's eyes bugged out of her head.'

God, he loved that she was prepared. He took the condom from her and stuck it in his back pocket. 'What would you have done if I hadn't shown up?'

'Tracked you down.' She pulled his green-and-black sweatshirt over his head and reached for his belt. 'I don't have your phone number, so I couldn't call and ask you to come over.'

'We'll fix that.' He grasped the bottom of the little black slip she wore and drew it up to her waist. 'Later.' His hands found her bottom covered in the small silk panties. As she pulled at his belt, he lowered his face to the curve of her neck and opened his mouth against her soft skin. 'I like this.' She smelled of flowers and he kissed his way across the top lace of her slip.

'I bought it this afternoon. It's sexier than the old T-shirt.'

'I like the T-shirt.' He grabbed her wrists to keep her frantic hands from finishing things before they started and pinned them behind her. 'Not so fast.' Her back arched, and he buried his face in her cleavage. He rubbed his cheek against her breasts and sucked her hard nipples through the slick, silky fabric. He loved her breasts. In his hands. Mouth. Against his chest.

'Let go. I want to touch you.' She fought against his grasp, but he wasn't ready for her to touch him. Not ready for it to be over. He might not remember a book he'd once given her, but he remembered this. At least his body did. He felt twenty-two again. As if they were picking up exactly where they'd left off.

He let her wrists go, and she reached for the front of his pants. She pulled and unzipped and shoved her hand inside. Her soft palm wrapped around his dick, and he nearly lost control before he was inside her.

'Baby, you have to slow down.' He turned her and pulled her back into his chest.

'No,' she whispered, raised her hands, and brought his mouth down to her. 'Later.'

She gave him a long, wet kiss, drawing out his will to slow anything down. He loved the way she touched him. How she let him know how much she wanted him. He'd been with women who'd done anything and everything to fuck a football player, and he could always tell if a woman was feeling it or just trying to impress him. Adele wasn't putting on an act. She wanted him every bit as much as he wanted her. And he wanted her. In every savage beat of his heart. In the dark place in his soul that wanted to push her down and rub his face against her, lick her up one side and the other, and plunge deep into her hot, wet body.

He reached for her hands, which were on the back of his head, and brought them down in front of her. Then he bent her over, and she grabbed the edge of a table in the entryway. He pushed her panties down her legs and palmed her smooth behind. He loved her round butt almost as much as her breasts. He pulled the condom from his pocket as his pants slid down his legs, and the belt buckle hit the floor with a thud. 'Spread your feet a little bit for me,' he said as he pulled himself out of his underwear and rolled the condom down his shaft.

She did, and he slid his hand over her bottom and between her legs. She was wet and ready, and moaned deep in her throat as he parted her and teased her slick flesh. Her back arched as he positioned himself and slid into the hot, gripping pleasure of her body. She was incredibly tight around him, and he pulled almost all the way out, then sank into her. He pushed her hair to one side and lightly bit the side of her neck. *Mine*, he thought, his body covering hers. She pushed her bottom against him, wanting more. He gave it to her in long, powerful thrusts. He drove inside again and again, his heart pounded in his head as he felt the first tightening pulse of her orgasm. It milked him, pulling a release from deep in his belly that went on forever. He thrust into her, hard, and the thin condom barrier burst. A gush of fiery liquid heat surrounded him, pulled him deeper, and sucked him dry. The most intense pleasure he'd ever felt in his life rippled through his body, and he closed his eyes. It spread fire across his skin, grabbed his insides, and stole his breath. His heart pounded in his head, and he thought he just might have died and gone to heaven.

'Fuck.'

Adele tied the black robe around her waist and walked out of the master bathroom and headed toward the sounds in the kitchen. Zach had just given her the best quickie of her life. It had been hot and intense – then he'd slipped from her body, pulled up his pants, and moved to the bathroom down the hall without a word.

He stood at the kitchen sink, filling a glass with water. His back was to her, the light overhead picked out golden strands of his hair and poured over his bare shoulders, the hard planes of his back, and the indent of his spine. His pants hung low on his hips.

He turned and lowered the glass. His pants were zipped, but he hadn't buckled his belt. 'The condom broke.'

'I know.' He'd been an athlete. His marriage hadn't been good, and she figured he'd been with more than his share of women. She grabbed his glass and drained it, wishing that it had been something a bit stronger. Like a Limoncello or a snakebite. She would not freak out, she told herself. Not yet. 'Let's talk about that.'

As he refilled the water, he looked at her across his big shoulder. 'I haven't had sex without a condom since the night Tiffany was conceived.'

Relief eased the tension in her back, and the knot in her stomach and brought a smile to her face. 'Seriously?'

'Seriously.'

'Then I don't think we have a problem.' She took the glass from his hand, and confessed, 'I haven't had sex for a really long time.'

'How long?' He turned toward her and shoved his hip into the counter.

She took a drink and handed it back. 'Three years ago, when I broke up with my boyfriend. He started acting so weird that I had myself tested, and I'm clean. We don't have a problem.'

He lowered his gaze to her belly. 'My guys are

swimming upstream searching for your egg, and you don't think that's a problem?'

She shook her head. 'I have an IUD.'

'What's an IED?' He took a drink, and his brown eyes watched her over the bottom of the glass.

'IUD. Intrauterine device. It's a form of birth control.'

'How effective is it?'

'The IUD has a failure rate of one percent.'

'Are you sure?' He set the glass on the counter, and a frown wrinkled his forehead. 'I don't want another child.'

Adele knew she shouldn't feel insulted, but she couldn't help it. He was suddenly looking at her as if she was the enemy. 'I'm sure. I had one of my yearly visits to the doctor a few months ago, and the IUD was right where it's supposed to be. Believe me, Zach, I don't want a child right now. That's why I have birth control implanted in my body.'

'Devon said she was on the pill when she got pregnant, but she lied.'

She crossed her arms beneath her breasts. 'Do you think I'm lying to you, Zach?'

'You wouldn't be the first woman to lie about something like that.' He tilted his head to one side and studied her.

She'd never been accused of lying about birth control. And being compared to Devon made her want to punch him. 'Then you need to leave.' Instead of hitting him, Adele walked out of the kitchen and moved to the front door. She wondered if this was part of the curse. Zach was normally a rational guy, but at the moment he was being crazy. He'd turned into a jerk, but unlike the latest victims of the curse, she was not so forgiving.

She picked up his sweatshirt from the floor. What kind of woman lied about birth control, she fumed.

Apparently Devon.

Adele tucked that bit of info away to think about it later. 'Don't compare me to other women. *I* wouldn't lie about something like that,' she said as she held the shirt out to him. 'It's insulting even to think I would.'

'I've never had a condom break before.' He took the shirt and pulled it over his head.

'So?'

'So why now?' He shoved his arms in the sleeves and pulled the sweatshirt down his chest and stomach.

Adele's brows lowered over her eyes, and she tried to control her anger. 'I don't want your child, Zach. I'm leaving as soon as Sherilyn has her baby and is able to take care of herself. I'm not ever coming back, and the last thing I want is to be some jock's baby-momma and raise a kid by myself.'

'But you wouldn't raise the kid by yourself.' He pulled his keys from the front pocket of his pants. 'I wouldn't allow that to happen, and I think you know it.'

That did it. 'You're the one who showed up at my door tonight, and now you're acting like the broken condom is my fault! As if I did something to it.'

'It was your condom. Any man would wonder—'

'Leave!' she interrupted as she opened the door and pointed out into the dark Texas night.

'Jesus, why are you so mad?'

She pushed on his chest until he stood on her porch. 'This may come as a shock to you, Zach Zemaitis, but not every woman in this world is lyin' and dyin' to birth your baby. Some of us actually find the thought horrifyin'.'

'There it is.' He actually smiled. 'When you're mad, your accent comes back.'

'Good, then you should be able to understand this. Go fuck yourself, and don't ever show up on my porch again!' She slammed the door as she heard the last few words of her own voice in her ears flattening all the vowels as if she were a Texan. Only her momma hadn't raised her to swear. Her momma hadn't raised Sherilyn to swear either, but both of them seemed to be cursing with alarming frequency. For that she blamed Zach and that jerk William. She'd like to blame the curse for turning Zach into an idiot, but couldn't. No, Zach hadn't needed any outside help. He'd turned all on his own.

Zach paused as he moved through the living room and glanced at the portrait of Devon hanging above the fireplace. Adele thought it was spooky. He tilted his head to one side and looked up into Devon's green eyes staring back at him. He didn't think the portrait was spooky. The special soft light hit it, as if it were hanging at the Met, making it more narcissistic than spooky. Not that he really thought about it one way or the other. It had been more than three years since Devon had died, and unless someone brought her name into the conversation, he didn't really think about his dead wife all that much.

'. . . *why is your house practically a shrine to her?*' Adele had asked the night before. Was his house like a shrine to Devon? Had he allowed his daughter's grief and his own guilt over Devon's death dictate how they would live in their home? Maybe. And maybe when

Tiffany got back, they'd talk about taking the portrait down.

He walked down the hall to his bedroom and flipped on the light. *This may come as a shock to you, Zach Zemaitis, but not every woman in this world is lyin' and dyin' to birth your baby. Some of us actually find the thought horrifyin'.* He smiled as he shucked his clothes, then moved to the bathroom. He'd overreacted. Clearly he had, but the condom breaking had thrown ice water on his amorous mood, chilled him to the marrow, and twisted his gut into a knot. When it came to birth control, he didn't trust women. He only trusted himself. But did he think she was lying?

Zach turned on the shower and stepped inside. No, he didn't think she was lying. Not only because until the night before, she'd been running from him instead of to him, but because he really didn't believe Adele would lie about something so important.

He thought about the football game earlier that day. They'd eked out a win in the last four minutes of the game, and he knew he was partly to blame. He hadn't been able to give the boys his full effort. His mind had been split between the playing field and Adele. While his tight end had been having difficulty running his pass patterns, Zach had been having difficulty keeping his mind in the game and off Adele. While he should have been watching the tight end more closely to make sure he was getting his hands up at the snap, he'd been wondering what Adele was doing with her hands and calculating the distance back to Cedar Creek.

He'd been distracted. Impatient to win and get back to Adele. That had never happened to him before. He'd always been able to wrap his head around the game and leave his personal life off the field. Nothing ever affected his game. Especially not a woman.

Perhaps it was because he'd gone without sex for three years that he was having a hard time concentrating on anything but seeing Adele again. Of pulling her up against his chest and getting her naked. His team had noticed, and Joe had even commented on it.

'Is something wrong, Z?' he'd asked, as they'd walked from the locker room after half. 'You seem distracted.'

'Nothing's wrong,' he'd assured his defensive coach, and had done a little better during the second half of the game.

He asked 110 percent of his boys, and they deserved no less from him. He needed to put the brakes on his relationship with Adele; to slow things down before it really got him in trouble. That wasn't going to be a problem since she'd kicked him out of her house and told him not to show up on her porch again.

Sure, he'd been wrong to get crazy and accuse her of lying, but a broken condom made him crazy. There was a one-in-a-hundred chance that she'd get pregnant, but he didn't like those odds. Then again, maybe the broken condom was just one more distraction that he didn't need. He had one more game to win before the state championship next month, and he needed to concentrate all his energy on bringing home the trophy.

Adele was beautiful, and he'd like to get to know her all over again. He'd like to get reacquainted outside of bed and reconnect a lot more in bed, but the last thing he needed was a woman distracting him. Especially one who touched him in hard places with soft hands and made him want to forget about everything but being with her.

Ignoring Adele completely wasn't an option. One, because he didn't want to, and two because it was impossible. He'd tried that, and it hadn't worked, but he did need to slow things down. At least until after State.

He thought of the look in her eyes as she'd slammed the door in his face. State was a few weeks away, and she might need that time to cool off.

'**A**unt Adele, do you know the square root of sixteen?'

She thought a moment as she buttered a piece of toast. 'I think it's four.' She looked over at Kendra, who was doing her homework at the kitchen table. It had been a long time since she'd had to figure out the square root of anything. 'Or maybe it's thirty-two.' She cut the toast and put it on a plate next to scrambled eggs. 'No, it's four. Maybe.'

'Never mind,' Kendra said through a sigh, and pulled a calculator from her backpack. She punched in a few numbers and wrote on a lined piece of paper.

'What is it?'

'Four.'

Kendra had been in a blue mood for three days since her return from the dance competition on Sunday. The team had come in third, and she'd come in tenth on her solo routine.

'I couldn't concentrate,' she'd said. 'I was worried Momma would have the baby, and I'd be gone.'

'Tenth out of all the other girls from all the other teams isn't so bad,' Adele had told her, but it was like talking to a wall. 'Look, all you can do is your best on any given day. If it isn't good enough, then try to do better next time.'

'That's what Momma told me.'

'Your momma's a wise woman,' Adele heard herself say, and was shocked.

'Tiffany says she'll help me with my attack movements.'

'That's sweet of her. Is she going to help you here?' Adele hadn't seen Zach since the night she'd pushed him out her front door, and that was just fine with her. She was busy and didn't have time in her life for a man who freaked out like that over a broken condom, especially after she'd explained to him that the failure rate of her birth control was one percent.

'Probably her house since it's so much bigger.' Kendra punched a few more numbers into her calculator.

'I'll drop you off after school and pick you up at five,' Adele said as she slid the plate in front of her niece. 'I'd really appreciate it if you could be outside waiting for me.'

'Why?'

Because Tiffany's daddy is a jerk, who thinks women are dying to have his baby. 'We just have a lot to do.'

'Okay.'

After Adele dropped Kendra at school, she jogged her usual five miles then took a bouquet of star lilies to Sherilyn. The flowers smelled wonderful, looked gorgeous, and were sure to cheer up her sister.

When Adele walked into the room, Sherilyn wasn't there, and for a few terrifying seconds, she thought they might have taken her to delivery. Across the room, the toilet flushed, and the door to the bathroom swung open. Sherilyn shuffled toward the bed, her pink nightgown wrinkled, her hair in a scraggly ponytail, dark circles beneath her eyes.

'I thought something had happened to you.' Adele put a hand on her racing heart. 'I about had heart failure.'

Sherilyn grabbed some old roses from a vase sitting beside the sink and threw them away. 'I'm so bored, I'd welcome the excitement of a little heart failure just to liven things up.' She rinsed the vase and filled it with water.

'Bad night?' Adele took the lilies to the sink and stuck them in the vase.

Sherilyn pulled them back out, and trimmed the stems. 'I had insomnia again. I don't think I slept at all.'

'Isn't there anything you can take?'

'No.' Sherilyn stuck one lily, then another in the vase. 'I even watched the *Flavor of Love* marathon on VH1. Season one *and* two. I thought that would put me to sleep.'

Adele was fairly certain *Flavor of Love* was on Kendra's banned television list and could not have been more shocked if Sherilyn had said she'd been watching a *Chucky* marathon.

'Instead of making me tired, I had to stay awake to see which "fake ass bitch" got booted and who got a clock.' Sherilyn snipped a stem and shoved a lily into the vase.

'Excuse me?'

A frown wrinkled her sister's forehead. 'Did I just say "fake ass bitch?"'

'I'm afraid so.'

'I'm so bored,' Sherilyn said through a long sigh. 'I'm obviously going out of my mind.'

Sherilyn wasn't the only one who'd lost her mind. Adele had been crazy to have ever had sex with Zach Zemaitis again. It was never a good idea to start things up with an old boyfriend. She knew that and wished she was back home in Boise. If she were home, she'd call her friends and set up an emergency lunch. She'd tell them about Zach, and they'd tell her she was great and he was a jerk. Even if it was a lie. They'd give her advice that she'd probably ignore, but at least they'd cheer her up.

'Tell me something interesting. Anything,' Sherilyn pleaded, and carried the vase to the bedside table. 'I'm so tired of staring at the same walls. I could scream.'

Adele thought about opening up to her sister. Of telling her about Zach, but in the end she didn't. She and Sherilyn had never had that kind of relationship. Her sister had always been too judgmental, and Zach had been a one-night stand – well, a two-night stand – that had taken place in Sherilyn's house while her daughter had been out of town. Adele didn't know what her sister would think about that. Hell, Adele wasn't sure *she* knew what to think about that.

'Go wash your hair and I'll curl it for you,' she said to her sister. 'Then maybe we can walk to the sitting room down the hall and watch while the big fish eat the little fish in the aquarium.'

'That's sadistic and sad.' Sherilyn pulled out her shampoo. 'But the best offer I've had in a long time.'

While Adele curled Sherilyn's hair, they talked about Kendra and the baby and about Sherilyn's divorce proceedings. By the time Adele finished with her sister's hair, Sherilyn was tired and ready to sleep. They made a date to watch the cannibalistic fish the next day, and Adele left just before noon.

She had a full day's worth of work. A whole three hours of alone time to get things done before she had to pick up Kendra from school, but when she pulled onto her street, Zach sat on her front porch. From half a block away she knew it was him. There was no mistaking the Cadillac parked at the curb. No mistaking his long legs and wide shoulders, his blond hair or the intense gaze he leveled on her as he watched her roll up the driveway. No mistaking the little flutter in her stomach and the jump of her pulse. Neither of which was welcome.

Instead of parking in the garage, she got out and moved across the lawn toward him. Beside his big cowboys boots rested a box about the size of a loaf of bread. It was wrapped with a huge pink bow and was covered in shiny pink paper.

'I'm sorry about the other night,' he said as he stood.

She crossed her arms over the front of her jacket. 'What exactly are you sorry for?' If he thought he could come here with lingerie, and she'd forgive him, he'd better think again.

'For being an ass about the broken condom. I know you said not to show up on your porch, but I think you should reconsider.'

'Why?' Unless it was La Perla. She could forgive a lot for yummy undies. It had been a while since she'd worn fabulous underwear, but the box was too big for tiny scraps of lingerie.

A cool breeze brushed the ends of his short hair. 'I have something you need.'

Once a boyfriend had given her a naughty nurse outfit, and another had given her cuffs and a leather whip. 'What?'

'Invite me in, and I'll show you.'

'It better not be crotchless.' She moved up the steps until they were on eye level. The flutter in her stomach spread up her chest. 'And don't think for a second that you can come here with an apology and a gift, and I'll forgive you.'

He seemed to consider that before he shrugged. 'Fair enough.'

'And don't think you can pull your slick' – she poked a finger at his chest – 'sneaky moves, and I'll get naked either.'

Humor creased the corners of his eyes. 'No, ma'am.'

'Your old broken moves may work on weaker women, but I'm not that easy.'

'I never thought you were.' He pushed her hair behind her ear, and his cool fingers brushed her cheek. Even after he removed his hand, she still felt his touch. 'That's why I've got new slick moves just for you.'

She almost smiled, but she wasn't ready to forgive him. Not only had he behaved badly, it had taken him three days to apologize. She gave him a hard look and continued up the steps. She opened the front door, and once inside, he closed it behind them. She hung their jackets in the hall closet, and he handed her the gift he'd brought. It was heavy and her gaze slid down his black Ralph Lauren polo to the box in her hands. She set it on the entry table and pulled off the bow. It obviously wasn't underwear, not that the box was the right shape, anyway.

She ripped it open and pulled out a leather tool belt, complete with screwdrivers, hammer, and a tape measure hanging off it.

'A tool belt,' she said through a smile. No man had ever given her something she'd actually needed.

'Sorry, it's crotchless.'

'So it is.' She put it around her hips and buckled it over the top of her jeans. 'Should we try it out?'

'I'm willing.'

She had a feeling he wasn't talking about trying out the tools, but she was too excited to care. The hammer slapped the outside of her thigh as she moved into the baby's room. It was just a tool belt. A strap of leather with metal hanging off it, and she tried not to read more into the gift. Like the thought and effort that went into driving to the hardware store and picking out her tools just for her. Of wrapping it up and waiting on her porch for her to return home. It was probably one of his slick and sneaky ways of getting her naked, but she had to give him serious points for it.

He stopped in the middle of the room and looked at the boxes shoved up against the walls. 'What do you want to tackle first?'

'The crib.'

He grabbed a flat-head screwdriver from her belt and popped the big staples from the carton as if they were nothing. It would have taken her forever to work them out. The big hands that had fired footballs downfield for most of his life worked with such ease that she was reminded that sometimes a man was handy outside of the bedroom.

'You don't have to help me do this.' Watching him started a hot little spark at the top of her stomach. Her body seemed to remember the skill of those hands on her, and the little spark spread through her veins. 'I'm sure you have other things to do.'

He lifted his gaze to hers. 'I have a lot of other things I should be doing, but I'm here.' He stared into her eyes for several heartbeats before he returned his attention to the big box. 'I've tried to stay away. After you threw me out of the house, I thought it was probably for the best. You're a distraction, and I don't need a distraction right now.' He handed the screwdriver back to her and ripped the box open with his big hands. 'I've got tapes I need to review, and plays I need to go over in my head before today's practice, yet here I am. Putting baby furniture together for you because I can't get you out of my head. I plug in a tape, and all I do is think about you.' He peeled back the cardboard and reached for the instruction shot that had fallen to the floor. 'But the thing is, Adele, I'm not really sure whether you want me to be here or not.' His polo shirt pulled out of the waistband of his Levi's and slid up the tan muscles of his back. He straightened and looked at her over the top of the instructions. 'I don't know what you want.'

She looked at him, standing there, filling up more than his fair share of space, with his long legs and wide shoulders, offering to put the baby's crib together so he could be with her, and she didn't know either. After the dry spell she'd been living in for the past three years, having a man around again was nice. But having this particular man around wasn't a good idea for many reasons.

'Do you want me to leave?'

'No.'

'You don't sound convinced.'

'I want you to stay. It's just that . . . I don't want to want you to stay.' She took a breath and let it out slowly. 'I don't know if it's ever a good idea to get together with someone from the past. There's just too much . . .' She lifted one hand and let it drop to her side. 'Usually what broke the relationship up is still there, unresolved.'

'She's not here.'

'No, but I'm not sure it's ever a good idea to pick up something that was broken to pieces.'

He tilted his head to one side and looked across at her. 'Yesterday, when I was watching my football players run drills, I remembered giving you that fairy book in your dorm room fourteen years ago. One second I was yelling at the tight end, and in the next, I remembered the look on your face when I gave you the book. I remembered how much you loved it.'

'I did.'

'Then I remembered the night I told you Devon was pregnant.'

She remembered that, too.

'I remember the look in your eyes.'

Adele glanced down at the toes of her velvet flats. 'This is what I mean by not picking up broken pieces.'

Silence stretched between them for several long moments before he said, 'I went to your dorm room a few days later, but you were gone. No one knew where you'd run off to.'

She looked up. 'You asked?'

'Yes.'

She shook her head. 'Maybe we shouldn't talk about this.'

'I think we should.' He tossed the instructions on top of the crib pieces. 'I always regretted how much I hurt you.'

'That was a long time ago. I'm over it.'

'Are you?'

'Yes.' It was true. But that didn't mean she was stupid enough to make the same mistake twice in one lifetime. She was older and wiser. She didn't want to develop feelings for Zach. For one thing, he lived here in Texas. Her life was over a thousand miles away, waiting for her return.

'I hope so because I had to do what I felt was right. At the risk of getting told to go fuck myself and the door slammed in my face again, you have to know that if given the exact situation, I'd have to do it all the same. I had to step up and take responsibility for something I'd done. It wasn't easy, but I didn't have a choice.'

'I know you didn't. I always knew you had to do the right thing. It was one of the things I loved about you, but that didn't mean it hurt any less.' She looked into his brown eyes, and said, 'Or that I'll ever let you hurt me like that again.'

'I'm not going to hurt you.' He reached for her hand and pulled her against his chest. 'I like you, and I think you like me. We're adults. Let's just have fun together while you're here.'

His fingers brushed her back and sent hot tingles up her spine. Through his clothes and hers, his chest warmed her breasts, and she didn't want to give up the tingles. Not yet. She wouldn't be here long enough to develop deep feelings for him. Not this time.

'Okay, but just don't ask me out on a date,' she said, fearing that if they ever actually dated, the curse would make sure things went straight to hell.

'What? Of course I'll ask you out.'

She shook her head. 'No don't. It will ruin everything.' She wrapped her arms around his neck and raised her mouth for his kiss. She liked him. After a three-year dry spell, he made her feel wanted. Like a desired woman, but that wasn't love. It wasn't the heart-pinching, stomach-aching love she'd had for him so many years ago. It wasn't even the easy kind of love she'd felt as an adult for some of the other men in her life.

This time it was simply heart-pounding, stomach-tightening lust. She was old enough not to mistake the two. To know the difference and not confuse it with deeper emotions. Not even when he made love to her on the floor and gave her an orgasm that left her weak and gasping. Not even when he came over the next two days for repeat performances.

Over the Thanksgiving holiday, he and Tiffany left town to visit his family in Austin, but he turned up on Adele's porch bright and early the following Monday morning. They ran five miles together, and he told her about his mother's corn-bread stuffing and ambrosia.

'You *like* ambrosia?' Adele managed to ask as they ran. Usually Adele didn't like to talk while she huffed and puffed along, but Zach didn't seem to have the same problem. In fact, a few times he turned and jogged backward.

Show-off.

'You don't?'

Adele shook her head. 'Too much going on all in the same bowl.'

'Are you sure you're from Texas?'

Sometimes she wondered that herself.

Over the next two weeks, they jogged together most weekday mornings. When they returned, they soaped each other up in the shower or in Sherilyn's spa tub and worked out in a whole different way. Zach always made sure he brought his own condom, and she always made sure she had granola bars or croissants for afterward. Together, they even managed to put up the baby's crib and swing.

He always parked his Escalade by the curb and didn't seem concerned that anyone would see them together out on their run, but she knew Tiffany wasn't aware that her father was spending a lot of time with Adele. Adele did not kid herself into thinking Tiffany would be okay with it.

'Daddy wants to take down the portrait of my momma,' Tiffany mentioned as Adele took her home one day after school. 'He says it's time, but that makes me mad. When your momma died, did your daddy make you take all the pictures out of the house?'

Somehow, Adele figured 'all the pictures' was an exaggeration. 'Not all of them. Just the ones that made him sad.' She looked into the rearview mirror into Tiffany's green eyes. 'Maybe you could find something to hang up there that would make you both happy.'

A frown appeared between Tiffany's brows, and Adele returned her gaze to the road. 'Do you think the picture of Momma makes my daddy sad?'

No. 'Talk to him about it.'

'Right,' Tiffany scoffed. 'All he wants to talk about is the game Friday night.'

That particular game was the state championship, and it was being played across town at the Warren

P. Bradshaw Stadium. The whole town had been celebrating for a week. The local newspaper had written about the impending game and about Zach, and the story had been picked up in papers across the state. The *Dallas Morning News* and *Austin American Statesman* had interviewed him. A former NFL star turned high-school football coach in a small Texas town made great ink.

She asked him if all the pressure got to him and made him nervous. He'd shrugged. 'Everyone gets nervous right before a game. L. C. Johnson used to puke before every game. A lot of guys do.'

'Did you?'

'Nah.'

'Who's L. C. Johnson?'

He'd chuckled and kissed the curve of her neck. 'Only the biggest dual threat in the NFL. The last year I played for Denver, he put up some crazy stats. He rushed for over sixteen hundred yards and caught damn near everything I threw to him.'

She'd moved her hair to give him better access. 'Do you miss it?'

'Playing ball?' He'd run his finger across her bare shoulder and pushed her bra strap down her arm. 'Sometimes, but not as much as I used to. I miss throwing the perfect pass. I miss winning the battle, but I don't miss trying to get out of bed the morning after a game. Or playing through the pain and nausea right after getting hit by a guy determined to kill me.'

She'd pulled back and looked into his face. 'That's horrible.'

'It's part of the game. Besides, I had a live-in masseuse.'

She laughed. 'I can't see Devon playing masseuse.'

'Honey, Devon didn't live in Denver with me.'

'Ever?'

He shook his head. 'For most of our marriage she lived here. Across town in the big house she built. I'd come and see her and Tiffany as much as I could.'

Adele couldn't imagine being married to Zach and living so far away him. 'That doesn't sound like much of a marriage.'

'It wasn't.'

She stared into his brown eyes and asked a question that was none of her business. 'How could you be faithful to each other if you lived in different states?'

'I wasn't.'

Adele had guessed that he'd been a typical jock, and it disturbed her more than it should. Bothered her more than she had a right to be bothered, and she looked away. 'Oh.'

Zach's hand of the side of her face brought her gaze back to his. 'Devon didn't give a shit who I slept with. I can tell by the look in your eyes that you don't understand that.'

He was right. She didn't.

'You're a woman who'd want her man's body and soul. Devon didn't want me body and soul.'

'What did she want?'

'Money and status. As long as Devon got what she wanted, she didn't care what I did.'

'What did you get?'

He looked at her as if he'd never thought to ask himself that question. He shook his head slowly. 'How did we get on this topic?'

'Football.'

'Ahh.' He put his arms around her waist and pulled her to him. 'Are you coming to the game?'

She looked up into his beautiful face and almost said yes, but something held her back. Something deep inside that kept her heart safe. Something that kept her from falling completely in love with him again. 'I need to spend time with Sherilyn,' she said, and looked away from the disappointment in his eyes.

The second Saturday in December, the Cedar Creek Cougars squared off against Odessa for the state championship at Warren P. Bradshaw Stadium. Twenty-five thousand fans from around the state packed the seats, chanting and cheering and stomping their feet.

At the half, the score was tied at fourteen all, and Zach stood in the home team's locker room with his arms crossed over his chest. His boys had played near-perfect ball. They'd played in sync, hitting and sticking and moving the ball down the field. They were doing everything he asked of them, and he feared it might not be enough. Odessa had come to play, and they were bigger and faster than the Cougars.

Joe stood in front of the boys going over defensive plays, and for once, he wasn't ballistic. He went over the strategies and what the boys should do depending on how Odessa lined up on the offense.

Zach knew the pressures of the game, had lived it most of his life. The last time he'd felt pressure like this was when he'd played in the Super Bowl. When Joe finished, Zach stepped to the front of the team. He looked at them all sitting there, beat-up, bloodied, and grass-stained. He'd never been prouder.

'You boys have given me everything you have to give. You've left your blood and sweat out on that field. You haven't held anything back, and the other coaches and I thank you.

'I'm not going to lie to you guys, you're too smart and deserve the truth. Those Odessa boys are bigger and faster than we are. We knew that going in, but we're hanging in there. Going toe-to-toe. Hit for hit, just like we talked about. Y'all should be proud of what you've accomplished so far today.

'But now every one of you is going to have to pull something extra from somewhere. Something that's gonna make you play better than you have your whole lives. You're going to have to seize every opportunity. Take every advantage. When you step onto the field, you go balls out. You stick every play and don't give them anything. I know you can win this thing. They might be bigger and faster, but you're smarter. It's going to come down to who wants it more.'

He looked into the faces of his young warriors, their hair sticking up at odd angles or plastered to their heads.

'This is it, gentlemen. This is what we've been playin' for all season. Some of you are going to go on to play college ball. Some will go on to different lives, but I guaran-goddamn-tee every last one of you will remember this night. You will either look back on it with glory or regret. The choice is yours. You play with your hearts and guts, and you'll get the glory.'

He gathered the team around him. 'So let's hear it together: hearts, guts, glory.'

'Hearts, guts, glory!' they yelled, butting chests and

helmets. Then they raised a battle cry and ran toward the field and the destiny that waited for them.

Zach lined up with the other coaches, and they followed the players out of the tunnel to the blare of horns and boom of drums as the Cedar Creek band played the school fight song.

During the third quarter, both teams played textbook ball, but in the last five minutes, Odessa's size and speed finally gained them an advantage, and they scored on a thirty-eight-yard drive.

Zach stood on the sidelines, his heart in his stomach, and studied both teams' offensive and defensive formations. He looked at how they lined up, and five minutes into the fourth quarter, he finally saw what he'd been looking for: a crack in the Odessa defense. Something he hadn't seen in the hours of game tapes he'd watched. If the Cougars could take advantage of it, exploit it, they just might turn the game around. He called a time-out, and walked out to meet his quarterback. He told him to start playing the left side. Then he turned toward the sidelines and something made him look up. Maybe it was the blast from an air horn or someone waving silver pom-poms, but he looked up and saw her. She sat on the second deck, a few rows over from the fifty. Perhaps it was her wild blond hair that drew his gaze, or maybe it was her smile. Whatever it was, it had always been that way. Wherever she was in a crowd, his attention had always been drawn to Adele.

He turned back toward the game, pulled the brim of his hat lower, and smiled. She'd come. He guessed he'd better win this thing.

*

Growing up in Texas, Adele knew the basics of football. There are four quarters and each team tries to score a touchdown when it got the ball. Watching Zach, she had a feeling that the game was a lot more complicated than that. At first glance, he appeared just to be standing there, but the more she watched him, the more she noticed his hands move. He'd point to the left or the right, make some sort of signal with his fingers, or send one of the players out to the huddle. He talked into his headset and raised a clenched fist into the air when the Cougars made a good play. He was like a general, directing his troops, and her heart warmed a little as she watched him. He turned and glanced up at her, and her stomach got light and fuzzy and took a tumble.

She pulled the collar of her wool peacoat up around her cheeks and looked over at Kendra, sitting two rows down with Tiffany and some other girls. Adele was really glad Kendra had made good friends since she'd moved to Cedar Creek. Otherwise, the upheaval in her life would have been so much harder on the thirteen-year-old.

The crowd around Adele cheered, and she looked toward the field. One of the Cougar players intercepted the ball on the Odessa fifteen. With four minutes left on the clock, the Cougars got the ball and steadily moved it down the field. If Adele had been a nail biter, she would have chewed off her fingers as they moved it yard by painstaking yard. With less than thirty seconds to go, tension buzzed the air and grabbed the back of her neck as the Cougars' quarterback dropped back, looked to his right, then threw the ball to the left. The ball sailed through the air into the hands of a receiver, who ran the ball into the end zone from the ten-yard line. The crowd went wild, jumping to their feet and screaming as six points were put up on the scoreboard. Odessa still led by a point with five seconds left in the game.

'It's goin' into overtime,' said the man next to her. He'd painted his face green and black and wore a Cougars jersey.

Overtime? Adele didn't think she could take the excitement of overtime. She wondered how Zach could handle it. He called a time-out, and she looked down at him in his dark green Cougars jacket, surrounded by his players, pointing as they nodded their helmets. Then he moved back to the sidelines and put his hands on his hips. As he watched his team line up, he pulled at the brim of his hat as if he couldn't find the right spot on his head.

'They're going for the two points,' the guy beside her said, his voice serious as a heart attack. 'I hope like hell they don't screw the pooch on this one.'

Adele's attention returned to the line of scrim-mage as the ball was snapped. The quarterback took the snap, fell back and brought the ball behind his head for a pass to the left. The defense anticipated the pass and crowded the end zone, leaving a gaping hole on the right for the Cedar Creek running back to sprint through. By the time Odessa saw the ball hadn't been thrown but handed off, it was carried into the end zone.

'They ran the Statue of Liberty,' the guy beside her yelled, as half the crowd screamed, and the other half groaned. Two more points flashed up on the Cougars side as the time clock read double zero. Game over.

'We won?'

The guy nodded and wrapped his arms around her shoulders.

'H-h-how?' she managed, as he jumped up and down while she was trying to avoid all that paint on his face. How had the quarterback handed the ball off when everyone thought he'd passed it? Was that legal?

'That was goddamn brilliant.' Then he let out a holler that made Adele's ears ring. He sat her back down on her heels, then leapt over a few rows and moved toward the field. Adele couldn't see Zach at first, but then she spotted him out on the field, in the center of his team. The boys were all jumping on top of each other and flashing the hook 'em horns sign. Two of the players ran onto the field with a big ice chest and dumped its contents on top of Zach's head. He turned as ice cubes bounced off his shoulders and the top of his hat. He laughed and shook his head.

Kendra made her way to Adele and together they sat for the award ceremony. Adele watched the Cougars hoist their big gold trophy and pass it around. They named the most valuable players, and Zach gave a little speech about the team. He was interviewed by news organizations from as far away as Austin and Dallas, and as the crowd moved from the stands, Zach and the players headed into the tunnel.

'You ready?' she asked Kendra as she pulled out one of Sherilyn's lists from her coat pocket. She had to get two Christmas trees. One for the hospital and one for the condo, as well as ornaments and gifts. 'We've got a lot to do before Christmas. We have to decorate the condo and your mom's room,' she said, and looked up, catching one last glimpse of Zach and the lucky hat she'd rescued from a couple of cheerleaders that day last month inside the girls' bathroom.

Tiffany stood at the back of the crowd and waited for her daddy to make his way toward her. She could see his head above everyone around him as he shook hands with the people who waited for the coaches and players at the gates to the stadium. She could see his ball cap and his great big smile. Her heart got big as a balloon when she saw him. She loved him and was so proud that she was his daughter. Sometimes she got scared when she thought about something happening to him like it had Momma. When she thought about losing her daddy, her stomach hurt, and her chest got tight.

A man in a big cowboy hat shook her daddy's hand, then wrapped his arms around him in a big hug. The man looked like he was crying.

Tiffany liked football, but gee, it wasn't like dance-team competition. Dance team was tough.

She continued to wait for him as the crowd filed past, shaking his hand and patting him on the back. She looked at her pink wristwatch. It had been about forty minutes. Sheesh, that was a really long time to wait, and the crowd didn't seem to be thinning. Tiffany didn't mind sharing her daddy sometimes, but this was getting ridiculous. She was supposed to have gotten a ride from Becky Lee and her mom, Cindy Ann, but she'd rather wait and ride home with her dad.

Finally, after a few more minutes he looked over in her direction. He smiled and lifted a hand to wave. She waved back, and his smile got bigger. Something in his eyes made her slowly lower her hand and turn at the waist to look behind her. Her gaze landed on Adele and

Kendra standing a few feet away. She turned back, and her dad motioned for her to join him. She picked up the green-and-black stadium chair by her left foot and weaved her way through the crowd. Just before she got to him, he reached out his hand, but he didn't reach for her. A few feet from Tiffany's face, her daddy grasped Adele's hand and he pulled her toward him.

'Excuse me,' he said to someone who was chatting at him. He put one hand on Adele's waist and one on the side of her face, and right there in front of the whole town, he kissed her.

Tiffany's heart pinched, and fear stole her breath. 'Daddy,' she gasped, but he didn't hear her. He was too busy sucking face with Adele.

'Congratulations,' Adele said against Zach's mouth. His shoulders were wet beneath her hands from the big chest of ice water his players had dumped over his head.

He kissed her hard, then pulled her against his chest. 'We'll celebrate later,' he spoke next to her ear. 'When we're alone.'

'It's Christmas break. School's out,' she reminded him. 'That might be tough.'

He groaned. 'I'll figure some way to get you naked.' He leaned back and looked into her face. 'Thank you for coming.'

She stared up at him. Into his shining brown eyes with the smile lines in the corners. Her heart swelled with pride and joy and something else. 'I'm glad I came.'

'Coach Z!' someone called out, and he looked over her head. He smiled and dropped his hands to his sides. He looked back into her face. 'I'll see you soon.'

'Soon' turned out to be Monday morning. Tiffany and Kendra were at a dance camp in San Angelo for the day, and Zach showed up on her porch bright and early. He wore a pair of shorts and a sweatshirt, and they set off on their usual jog. Only this time, he stopped about every few blocks and kissed her. His big body warmed her up, and she wrapped her arms around his waist. On the corner of Fifth and Yellow Rose, his mouth opened over hers and he fit his pelvis against hers. She rocked against the hard length of his erection and the usual five-mile run got cut short, and they ended up in Sherilyn's spa tub, surrounded by hot water and rose-scented bubbles.

'You looked kinda studly down there on the sidelines Saturday,' she said. Zach sat across the tub from her, and she ran her toe up the outside of his bare calf. 'I can see why all the Junior League girls think you're so hot.' She lowered her face and hid her smile amongst the bubbles.

He lifted a brow and reached for her foot. 'Only the Junior League girls?'

'Maybe a few others.' She shrugged. 'You're much more fun to watch than the game.'

'When I looked up into the bleachers and saw you, I couldn't believe you were there.' He pressed his thumbs into her arch and massaged little circles. 'I'm glad I didn't see you until the second half.'

'Why?'

'Seeing you added about ten times more pressure to the game.' He lifted her foot and kissed her instep. 'I didn't want to screw it up and lose in front of you.'

Soap bubbles slid down the side of her foot and ankle. She looked at him, sitting across from her and kissing her foot, and something warm and bubbly slid next to her heart. 'You mean, you didn't want to lose in front of the whole town.'

'That too, but mostly I didn't want to embarrass myself in front of you.' His thumbs moved over her heel and he pressed his lips to her arch. He turned his head to one side, and said, 'When I used to play football, I didn't have to worry about impressing women. Hell, I think you're the only woman I've ever tried to impress.' He softly bit her instep. 'First at UT, and now here.'

Her eyelids suddenly felt heavy. 'Are you trying to impress me right now?'

'Why else do you think I'm sitting here, smelling like a rose garden and surrounded by girly bubbles.'

' 'Cause you like girly bubbles?'

He shook his head. 'I like you. Ever since I saw you in the gymnasium over at the junior high, I've wanted to be with you again.'

Wanting to be with someone wasn't love, but tell that to the warm feeling next to her heart. Her stomach lifted like she swallowed a mouth full of 'girly bubbles.' She was in trouble. Big bad trouble with blond hair and hot brown eyes looking back at her over the tips of her toes.

'What are you thinking?' he asked just above a whisper.

She shook her head. 'Nothing.' He didn't want to know. Hell, she didn't want to know. Somehow, she was falling in love with him all over again. She could feel it happening with every touch of his mouth and beat of her heart. Sometime between the night they'd kissed in the girls' bathroom and today, her feelings had grown and gotten stronger.

'Then why are you frowning?'

She hadn't realized she'd been frowning until he mentioned it. She forced a smile. 'Because I'm going to miss you when I leave,' she said, which was true, but hadn't been what she'd been thinking.

'That's not for a while yet. Who knows. Maybe by then, you won't want to go.'

She waited for him to say more. To say that he wanted her to stay in Cedar Creek. Stay and be with him, but he didn't. Instead, he softly bit the ball of her foot. She should get out of the tub. Get as far away from him as possible before she fell in love with him completely.

That would have been the smart thing, but she reached for his hand, and he dropped her foot. He pulled her toward him as he reached for the condom on the side of the tub. He stood, and she took the black square package from his hands. She knelt before him as rose-scented bubbles swirled about her breasts and jets of hot water tickled her thighs. She wrapped her free hand around the long ridged length of his erection and looked up into his face. His lids were lowered over his hot brown eyes, and she parted her lips and took him into her mouth.

He groaned deep in his chest and pushed her hair back from her face. She slid her hand up and down his hard shaft and pressed her tongue into the corded vein just beneath the plump head. 'That feels good,' he said just above a whisper, watching her from eyes glazed over with lust. She worked him over with her mouth and his fingers tangled in her hair. He didn't push or shove the back of her head, as some men tended to do. Just held her hair and watched as she had her way with him. He told her how much he loved what she did to him, then he tilted his head back and came in her mouth.

When it was over, he wrapped his hands around the

tops of her arms and pulled her to her feet. 'Thank you,' he said, and pulled her tight against his chest. 'I remember the first time you did that for me.' He ran his fingers up and down her spine, then grasped her bottom in both of his hands.

'I remember.' She reached between their bodies and wrapped her hand around his penis. It wasn't as hard as it had been moments ago, and she stroked it until it was stiff. 'And I remember how fast you could get it up again. You still can.' She rolled the condom down his shaft and pushed his shoulders until he sat submerged in bubbles halfway up the defined muscles of his chest. She straddled his hips, placed her palms on the sides of his face, and kissed him. The tips of her breasts brushed his warm skin, and she ran her fingers through his hair. She kissed his neck and his throat, and her hands ran all over him, touching as much of him as she could reach. It wasn't just sex now. There was more involved than just body parts, and when she took him deep into her body, her hands returned to the sides of his face and she stared into his eyes. His labored breath brushed her cheek as she moved and rocked her hips.

'Zach,' she whispered, her voice heavy with desire and emotion. Within minutes an orgasm rushed across her skin and gripped her heart. Her vaginal walls tightened around him, and his fingers dug into her behind. As he came into her body, she kissed his mouth, filling the kiss with the new and conflicted feelings she felt in her heart.

When it was over, he pushed her hair from her cheek. His gaze searched her face as if he were looking for something. 'I didn't think sex could get better than it was last week. I was wrong.'

She wrapped her arms around his neck and kissed the side of his head. What was she going to do now? Now that she was falling headfirst in love with him – again.

He softly bit her shoulder. 'The next few weeks are going to be hectic,' he said against her skin. 'With the girls out of school until after New Year's, but I want to see you. I want to be with you all I can before your sister has her baby and you move back to Idaho.' He kissed the crook of her neck. 'I'm going to miss being with you.'

There was a lot she could have said. Like she was going to miss being with him too, but she didn't. Her feelings for him were too painfully new. Or perhaps they were old hidden feeling from the past just waiting to be reignited. She was scared and confused and didn't know what to do. 'Are you hungry?'

'Starvin',' he said as he pulled back to look into her face. 'Got any more of those waffles from the toaster?'

'Eggos?'

'Yeah. I love those.'

She smiled and shook her head. He didn't love her, but he loved her Eggos.

After Zach left, Adele got busy writing her new series. She filled her head with characters from different galaxies and an outlandish plot. She didn't want to think about falling in love with Zach. She didn't want to dissect it and analyze it and pick it apart. It was much easier to calculate space travel and invent new life-forms.

At five thirty, she left to pick up Kendra from the middle school. The moment she pulled behind the buses that had taken the dance team to San Angelo, she knew there was something wrong. Her niece stood by herself, her eyes red and her backpack slung over one shoulder.

'What's the matter?' she asked, as Kendra got into the car.

'Nothing.'

'Where's Tiffany? Doesn't she need a ride home?'

'She rode with Lauren Marshall.'

'Isn't her stepmamma Genevieve Brooks?'

'Uh-huh.' Adele was fairly certain Tiffany didn't like Genevieve.

'Why?' She pulled out into traffic and headed toward the hospital. 'We could have taken her home.'

'She doesn't want a ride from us anymore.'

Adele glanced at her niece. 'Did you two have a fight?'

Kendra shook her head, and her dark ponytail brushed the shoulders of her coat. 'She saw you kiss her daddy after the game.'

'Oh.' She returned her eyes to the road. Shit. 'So now she hates me.'

'She says you are like all the rest. That you only acted like you liked her to get to her dad.'

'That's bullshit.' They stopped at a red light, and Adele pushed her hair behind one ear. 'Do you believe her?'

Kendra shrugged. 'Not really . . . but . . .'

'But what?'

'She says I can't come to her house and practice the dance routines anymore. And if I don't practice between now and Friday, we could lose the competition against Pampas.' Tears welled up in Kendra's eyes. 'If she doesn't like me, the other girls won't like me either.'

'The other girls will still like you.'

'No, they won't.' She sniffed and wiped her eyes. 'Not if she doesn't.'

Adele thought back to the hell of junior high and cringed.

'I wish I'd never moved here,' Kendra cried. 'I miss my old school and my old friends.'

'Can you get one of the other girls to come to your house and practice the routines with you?'

'Maybe.'

'Why don't you ask, and tomorrow night we'll move all the furniture out of the living room, and you can practice in there.'

'I'll ask.'

But when Adele drove to the school to pick up Kendra from practice the next day, she was once again by herself. She'd suffered another day of Tiffany's cold shoulder and felt more alone than ever. By that Friday, when things had not gotten any better, Adele mentioned it to Zach while they put together Harris's Swing 'N Bounce. Both girls were at the local mall with the rest of the team, selling cookies to raise money for a big trip they had coming up.

'Has Tiffany mentioned anything to you about seeing you kiss me after the State Championship game?'

He looked up from the instructions in his hands. 'No. I don't think she saw it.'

'Yes. She did.'

'She didn't mention it to me.' He set down the instructions and picked up a metal leg. 'Has she said something to you?'

'Evidently, she's not speaking to me. She mentioned it to Kendra. I think she's really angry.'

'She might be a little upset right now, but she'll get over it.'

'I don't think so.' Adele opened a plastic bag of nuts and bolts.

'Why don't you think so?'

Adele really didn't want to tattle on Zach's daughter. 'You should talk to her about it.'

'I will, but why don't you tell me what you know first.'

'She's mad at me, so she doesn't want to be friends with Kendra anymore.'

He took the bag from her and fished out a long screw. 'I'll talk to her about it tonight and see what I can do. Everything will work out.' He leaned over and squinted his eyes as he read the instructions. 'Jesus, this thing is complicated.'

Adele took the little seat out of the packaging and ran her hand over the jungle-animal-print fabric. 'This is just so cute,' she said. She pulled out the music box and wound it up. 'Rock-a-bye Baby' filled the room. 'Doesn't all this make you want a baby?'

He looked up from the instructions and scowled. 'No.'

She laughed. 'You already know how to put together the furniture. When I have a baby, I'm going to hire you.'

'"When you have a baby?"' He reached for a curved bar. 'Don't tell me you're one of those women whose clock is tickin'.'

She tilted her head to one side. 'It's less of a tick and more of a tap on the shoulder. I've always wanted kids, but being around Sherilyn has made me broody.'

'Broody?'

'Like I need to nest with a chick or two.'

'Two?'

'Didn't you ever want more than one child?'

He shrugged. 'Devon was an only child and wanted Tiffany to be an only child. I didn't care one way or the other.'

'Tiffany wants a little brother.'

'I know, but she wants a lot of things she doesn't get.'

'She doesn't want us to see each other.'

He fit the tubes together. 'When Tiff and I get back from Austin after the first, I'm sure she'll be over it.'

Adele wished she could share his optimism.

'We'll take her and Kendra to a movie or something.'

It could work, or it could be disastrous. 'Okay.'

'It's a date.'

She shook her head. 'No dates.' She liked Zach, and the last thing she needed was for the curse to rear its head.

'What is it with you and your aversion to dating?'

If she told him, he'd think she was crazy.

Zach handed Tiffany a box of Christmas ornaments and reached in it for a gold-foil star. Even though they would be in Austin on Christmas Day, they trimmed the tree together every year. Devon had hired a professional, but he and Tiffany liked to pick out a tree and do it themselves. 'Why didn't you mention that you saw me kiss Adele the other day after the game?'

Tiffany shrugged a shoulder but didn't look up from the colored bulbs in her hands. 'It was embarrassing. I'm surprised it wasn't on the news. The whole city saw you make out with her.'

That was a bit of an exaggeration. Only half the city had been there, and by no stretch of the imagination could the kiss he'd given her be confused with making out. Looking back on it now, he probably should have waited until he'd gotten Adele alone. But at the time, he hadn't known Tiffany had been watching. 'I like Adele.'

'I hate her.'

'You hate her 'cause I like her.' He climbed up onto a chair. 'Which is a stupid reason.' Sometimes, Tiffany was so much like Devon that it worried him. 'I haven't noticed Kendra around here practicing this week. I hope you're not taking out your anger on your friend.'

Tiffany hung a few bulbs on the tree and pressed her lips together. She didn't speak, but she really didn't need to say anything. Zach knew her well enough to know what she was thinking. He reached out for the top of the tree and shoved the star on top. 'Is this straight?'

She looked up and nodded.

'I'm sure you would never cut off your nose to spite your face, sugar bug,' he said as he climbed down.

'What do you mean?'

'Just that you're smart enough not to let how you feel about Adele get in the way of helping Kendra out. You girls have some big competitions coming up.' He knew what Tiffany wanted to hear, but that wasn't going to happen. He wasn't going to stop seeing Adele to make her happy. 'I'd hate to see you lose because you're mad.'

'I know what you're doing.' She set down the box and picked up some tinsel. 'I'll be nice to Kendra 'cause I like her, and because we're on the same dance team. But I don't like her aunt, and I'm not going to be nice to her.'

Zach shook his head. That had gone better than he'd thought, worse than he'd hoped for. 'You liked her until you found out I liked her, too. I never thought you'd be so ornery.'

'But Daddy' – two tears spilled over her lashes – 'she took me shopping and talked about Momma, and I even gave her fashion advice about those stupid scrunchies she wears. And the whole time she only pretended to like me so she could see you.'

'Honey, I don't think people have to pretend to like you.'

'Uh-huh.'

This wasn't about Tiffany thinking people pretended to like her. That was the excuse she used. It was really about her not wanting any woman but Devon in their lives. He knew it, but he just didn't know what to do about it.

He moved into the kitchen and grabbed a bottle of water out of the refrigerator. He and Tiffany were leaving in a few days to spend the Christmas holiday with his family in Austin. They'd be gone until after New Year's. Maybe that's what Tiffany needed. A break for a while. He'd told Adele that things would settle down when he and Tiffany returned. That she'd be over her anger, and he hoped he was right. He was more than ready for some postseason downtime and a little less drama.

No. A *lot* less drama.

Christmas Day, the temperature outside Sherilyn's hospital window was forty degrees. Brightly colored paper and bows littered the floor, and stacks of opened Christmas presents lay under and beside the little tree they had put up last week. Over cocoa and doughnuts, the three of them watched *A Christmas Story* on the hospital television and took turns feeling the baby kick and move within Sherilyn's rapidly growing belly.

Adele took photos of Sherilyn and Kendra wearing Santa hats. They gorged themselves on chocolate and candy canes, and she told her sister about how hard it had been to get all the pieces of the changing table and swing together, but she didn't tell her about Zach. Not yet. Her feelings were too new and confusing, and beside, it couldn't go on forever. She was leaving when Sherilyn had her baby. She was looking forward to living in her own home again, surrounded by her own stuff and going about her own routines. Now that she was fairly certain her bad-date curse was broken or had run its course, she wanted to get back to living her life, but the thought of dating, of being with anyone but Zach, felt wrong. Her heart shied away from the idea of another man's arms around her.

In the past two days that he'd been in Austin, he hadn't called. Of course he was busy with the holiday and his family, but perhaps it was best that he was away. She needed time to herself. Time to think. With her sister in the hospital, taking care of a thirteen-year-old, and spending time with Zach, she needed a break from the emotional roller coaster that was her life here in Cedar Creek.

At four that afternoon, she and Kendra left the hospital. They ate a light dinner, and Adele went to bed. She didn't wake until seven the next morning. She still felt tired and a little nauseous and guessed all of the excitement and chocolate had caught up with her. As she rolled over to go back to sleep, the telephone rang. For a few unguarded seconds, she thought it might be Zach.

It was the hospital. Sherilyn had just been wheeled into the delivery room. Her blood pressure had skyrocketed and they were taking the baby by caesarian.

'Kendra,' Adele called out as she ran to her niece's room. 'We have to go to the hospital. Your momma's having the baby.'

They both grabbed up their clothes and dressed as quickly as possible.

'She was fine yesterday,' Kendra said, as frightened tears rolled down her cheeks.

Adele ran every red light on her way to the hospital, but by the time she and Kendra made it to the maternity ward, Harris Morgan had been born and whisked to the neonatal intensive care unit. Kendra sobbed uncontrollably in the tiny waiting room as they waited for Sherilyn to be wheeled to recovery. Adele held her niece and held it together until she finally saw her sister, covered up to her chin in a white sheet. She looked totally drained, and her eyes were red from crying. Kendra laid her head on her mother's chest, looking very young and scared.

'Are you okay, Momma?' Kendra asked through her tears.

'I'm tired, but I'm fine.'

'I'm sorry I wasn't here when you needed me,' Adele said, fighting back the tears stinging her eyes.

'You were here when I needed you the most,' Sherilyn said as she rubbed Kendra's arm. 'I don't know what we would have done without you these past few months, Dele. Thank you.'

Adele smiled. 'I'm glad I came.' And it was even the truth.

'Did you see him?' Kendra asked.

Sherilyn looked into Adele's eyes for several more seconds before she turned her face and spoke against her daughter's forehead. 'He has dark hair just like you. When they delivered him, he started crying. Which is good. He sounded just like a kitten.' She lifted her gaze to Adele, and Adele wiped a tear from her cheek. 'No more crying. I'm going to be fine. The baby is going to be fine. We're all going to be fine.'

Later that day, Kendra and Adele wheeled Sherilyn down to the neonatal intensive care unit, and the three got to stare at Harris in his incubator. He had on a blue knitted cap and the tube to his nasal cannula was taped to his cheeks. He had a temperature probe stuck to his belly and an IV in the back of his tiny hand. The three of them touched his feet and legs, and he opened his eyes to look at them. Then he yawned, as if he'd had a tiring day, which he had, and went back to sleep.

The next three days were a blur of sleeplessness and worry. Sherilyn's blood pressure slowly lowered, and Harris gained two ounces. Saturday afternoon, Sherilyn was well enough to be discharged, but the baby had to stay until he gained more weight. His lung function was good and improving every day, which had been the biggest worry.

As Adele and Sherilyn packed up Sherilyn's belongings and waited for the wheelchair to take Sherilyn to the front doors, William Morgan walked into the hospital room. He looked older than Adele remembered. Shorter. His dark hair balding. She was relieved that he hadn't brought his girlfriend with him.

'If you'll excuse us,' he said pointedly to Adele in that dismissive way she'd always hated.

Adele looked at her sister. 'Do you want me to go?'

Sherilyn shook her head. 'Not unless you want to leave.'

Adele smiled and looked at her soon-to-be-ex brother-in-law. She sat on the edge of the bed and folded her arms across her chest. 'I'll stay.'

William frowned.

A tired smile curved Sherilyn's lips. 'Have you seen the baby?' she asked as she shoved her hairbrush into an overnight case. 'He looks just like Kendra did.'

'Yes.' William dragged his gaze from Adele. 'I'd like to name him after my father.'

'Alvin?' Sherilyn shook her head. 'Perhaps that can be his middle name.'

'But my family—'

'His first name is Harris,' Sherilyn interrupted and

zipped up the bag. 'I already filled out the birth certificate.'

'Without consulting me?'

'You weren't here.'

'He's my son.'

'Whom you will see on every other holiday and one month out of each summer. When he is old enough, of course.' A nurse entered with the wheelchair, and Sherilyn smiled. 'Ah. Here's my ride.' Sherilyn waddled across the room and sat. 'Could you grab my bag?' she asked Adele.

'Sure.'

'Kendra's at home making everything nice for me,' Sherilyn told her soon-to-be-former husband. 'Give her a call. I'm sure she'd like to see you.'

The nurse wheeled Sherilyn out of the room, and Adele grabbed the bag off the bed. 'When you see Kendra, leave the dental assistant at the hotel. Your daughter's been through a lot and doesn't need to see your girlfriend.'

William's gaze narrowed on her as if he suddenly smelled something rotten. 'Don't you tell me what my daughter needs. I know how to take care of Kendra.'

'Oh, and you've done such a bang-up job lately.'

'You have no right to lecture me.'

Adele was tired and not feeling well from the stress of the past few days. She had missed the one and only call from Zach the night before, and she was in no mood to take crap from William. 'I didn't run out on my family.'

'You haven't seen your sister for five years.'

That hit a little close to home. 'I might not have visited as much as I should have, but when Sheri needed someone, she called me. I'm the one who's been holding her hand these past few months while she struggled to save her baby.' She pointed to her chest. 'I'm the one who's been taking care of your teenage daughter. Not you! You turned your back on your family for a piece of barely legal ass. So don't walk in here and think you can say diddly-shit to me.'

'You never did have any class.'

'And you never did know your position on the food chain,' Adele felt free to point out now that he was no longer family, and Kendra wasn't around to hear. 'You're a dentist, William. Not a heart surgeon. You replace molars. Not heart valves. For God's sake, get over yourself.'

Adele stormed out of the door and almost fell over her sister's feet. 'I thought you left,' she said.

Sherilyn smiled. 'I thought I should wait in case you needed rescuing from William. But I think William might have needed rescuing from you.' The nurse pushed the wheelchair, and they moved down the hall. Sherilyn reached for Adele's hand and pointed out with a hint of a smile, 'Dentistry is a noble profession, you know.'

'Yeah. I know.'

On the way home from the hospital, they dropped off Sherilyn's prescriptions at the pharmacy, then Adele drove to the condo and tucked her sister in bed.

'I'm going to go get your prescriptions,' she told Sherilyn as she shoved her arms back into her coat. 'Kendra's in the living room if you need anything.' Her stomach tumbled a bit, and she took a deep breath and let it out slowly. 'I shouldn't be long.' She grabbed her purse off the bed.

'What's wrong with you? You look white.'

'Nothing.' She dropped the purse and ran for the bathroom. She hadn't felt real great for the past few days, but this was the first time she actually threw up. When she was done, she rinsed her mouth and brushed her teeth. 'Don't drink after me,' she said as she left the bathroom. 'I think I have the flu.'

'How long have you had it?'

'A few days. It kind of comes and goes.' She picked up her purse again. 'Mostly it's bad in the morning when I first get up.'

'Could you be pregnant?'

'For the love of God, no.' She shoved her hand into her purse and grabbed her keys. 'You have babies on the brain. I'm not pregnant.'

Her sister's brow furrowed. 'It sounds like morning sickness. I know. I've had it twice.'

'Sherilyn, stop. I'm not pregnant. I have an IUD.'

'Interesting. You didn't say you haven't been having sex.'

'I didn't?'

'Have you been seeing someone?'

Adele shrugged.

'Who?'

What did it matter if Sherilyn knew? Zach would be home in a few days, and Sherilyn would see him when they jogged together. If they jogged together. 'Zach Zemaitis.'

'The football coach.' Sherilyn's brows shot up her forehead. 'The one who was in all the papers and on the news a few weeks ago?'

'Yeah.'

'Kendra's friend's dad?'

'Yeah. He kinda helped me put the baby furniture together.'

'Sounds like he did more than that.' Sherilyn frowned. 'What are you going to do?'

'Nothing. I'm not pregnant.'

'While you're at the pharmacy, get an e.p.t.'

Adele rolled her eyes and walked out of the bedroom. She counted back to her last period. She was only two weeks . . . no three weeks late. But she'd been late before and wasn't worried.

'Did you get it?' Sherilyn called from her bedroom.

'Your pills?' She set the bag on the counter and called back. 'Yeah I got 'em.'

'No.' Sherilyn waddled, hunched over with one hand low on her abdomen, into the kitchen. 'The pregnancy test.'

'Sheesh. Be quiet. I don't want Kendra to hear you.'

'William came by and picked her up.' She carefully sat down on a barstool. 'Did you get it?'

'Yes, but I only got it to shut you up.' She still wasn't worried. 'I have an IUD. He used a condom.' It had broken once, but what were the chances? One percent?

Sherilyn reached into the sack and pulled out the box. She ripped it open and read the instructions. 'Hold it in your urine stream for five seconds.' She handed Adele the plastic stick. 'It says not to put it up your vagina.'

'Gee. And I was all set to.'

Adele took the stick, went into the bathroom, and came back out a few minutes later. She set the stick on a napkin on the counter across the kitchen and got Sherilyn a glass of water.

'Did you wash your hands?' Sherilyn asked as she eagle-eyed the stick.

'Yes, Mom,' Adele answered as she made toast.

'Eat this and take these,' she said, and handed Sherilyn the toast and medication. She held the stick behind her back for the full two minutes, pulled it in front of her, and stared at a plus sign.

'What does it say?' Sherilyn asked around a bite of toast.

Adele grabbed the instructions and read them. 'This one is obviously defective. He wore a condom.'

'Every time?'

'It broke once.'

'Once is all it takes.'

The blood rushed from Adele's head, and she grabbed her coat and her purse.

'Where are you going?'

'To get another test.' Forty-five minutes later, five more e.p.t sticks were lined up on the table. All of them had positive plus signs in the round windows. Adele's fingers and toes felt numb, and she felt sicker than she had in days. Her face was hot, and she sat down next to Sherilyn so she wouldn't pass out and fall on the floor. She still couldn't believe the results. There had to be a mistake.

Sherilyn waved a hand in front of Adele's face. 'Are you in there?'

'What?' Her voice sounded weak and like it was coming from a long, dark tunnel.

'Why didn't you tell me that you're seeing anyone?'

'Because I don't know how serious it is.'

'It just got real serious.'

'You're not helping.' She covered her cheeks with

her hands. 'This is a nightmare. I cannot be pregnant.'

'What are you going to do?'

'I don't know! I just found out.'

'You have to tell him.'

'Maybe I'm not pregnant.'

Sherilyn pointed to the tests. 'You flunked six tests.'

'Maybe that was a bad batch,' she said desperately. 'It could happen.'

'No, it couldn't.'

Her mind raced and tumbled and thoughts slammed into each other. 'Maybe Zach won't notice.' She didn't have to wonder how Zach would react. She remembered the night of the broken condom and she knew.

Her sister looked at her like Kendra did sometimes. Like just the sound of Adele's voice was painfully robbing her of IQ points. 'He'll notice. You have to tell him.'

'He won't be back until Wednesday. I have until then to figure out what I'm going to do.'

Sherilyn reached for her hand and squeezed her cold fingers. 'How do you feel about him?'

'Zach?' She shook her head like she didn't know, but she did. 'I love Zach,' she whispered, saying it out loud for the first time. 'I didn't mean to fall in love with him, but I did. I could feel it happening, and I knew I should stop it. But I couldn't.'

'Maybe everything will work out.'

'No.' Tears stung the backs of her eyes. 'It won't. He doesn't love me.' And he definitely didn't want a child with her. She shook her head again as tears slipped down her cheeks. This couldn't be happening. Whatever feelings he did have for her were not going to change.

She wiped her cheeks and her hands fell to the table as a thought popped into her head. Good Lord, was this part of the curse? A bad date that ended in pregnancy? And how crazy was she for thinking it?

Sherilyn stood and patted Adele's shoulder. 'I'll take care of you like you took care of me.' She took a deep breath and her eyes rounded. 'Wow, that pain pill just kicked in, and I'm feeling funky.'

17

Zach rang the doorbell, then rocked back on his heels. He'd told Adele he'd be back in town on the second, but he'd packed up Tiffany and all her crap and returned last night. Tiffany had pouted most of Christmas Day, and he'd missed the quiet calm he always found with Adele. Tomorrow was New Year's Day. If she could find someone to stay with Kendra, he'd like to take her to the big party in the new Radisson downtown. He knew she was weird about dating, but she needed to get over it. What was between them was more than just sex.

The door swung open, and a woman in a blue bathrobe stood before him. She had blond hair, and she was hunched over.

'I'm sorry.' He started to leave, looked up at the house number, then turned back. 'Is Adele around?'

'She ran Kendra to the hospital to meet up with her father. You must be Zach.'

'Ah, yeah.' He looked into the woman's tired face and turquoise eyes. 'And you must be Sherilyn.'

She swung the door wider and he followed her inside. 'Adele will be back in a bit.'

'And you must have had your baby.'

She shut the door behind him. 'Yes.'

'Congratulations. How is he?'

'He's still in the hospital, but he's going to be just fine. Thank you for putting his furniture together.'

'You're welcome.' He followed behind her as she shuffled into the living room. 'Can I get you anything?' he asked. Coffee. Tea. A wheelchair?

'No.' She sat slowly on the couch. 'How well do you know my sister?'

Zach paused in the act of lowering himself onto a chair. 'We met at UT and then again a few months ago.' He sat and looked at the clock on the wall. 'When do you expect Adele? I'm sure you need your rest, and I'd hate to keep you from it.'

Her gaze narrowed and she waved away his concern. 'What are your feelings for her?'

He hadn't felt so scrutinized since he'd thrown five interceptions against the Bears back in '99. 'Adele's great.'

'Yes I know. What are your feelings for her?'

He hadn't been grilled about a girl since he'd been . . . Well, he'd never been grilled. 'Maybe I should come back later.'

The door to the garage opened, and Sherilyn settled against the cushions. 'I hear her now.'

Less than a minute passed, but it felt like five. The door to the garage opened and closed and Adele called out from the kitchen. 'I'm back. William was at the hospital, and the tool was wearing a toupee.'

'I'm in here.'

It had been over a week since Zach had heard Adele's voice in person, and the sound of it rushed over his skin. He'd tried to call a few times, but he'd never reached her.

'I stopped at Starbucks and got us some tea. I think the tea will help with the . . .' She stopped when she saw him and her eyes widened. She wore a big bulky sweater, jeans and held two cups in her hands.

'Hey there,' he said as he stood.

'I didn't expect you until Wednesday.'

He shrugged. 'I got bored.' *I missed you.* If Adele's sister hadn't been sitting on the couch staring at him as if he were a criminal, he would have put his hands on the sides of Adele's face and kissed her until she took his hand and led him to the bedroom. Or spa tub. Or shower. Or floor. Which brought up a dilemma. He wouldn't mind taking Adele to his house and making love to her in his bed, but Tiffany was there.

'I'll leave you two alone.' Sherilyn scooted to the edge of the couch, and Zach crossed the room to help her stand. 'Thank you,' she said, and shuffled over to Adele. She grabbed one paper cup of tea and took a sip. 'Tell him.'

'Shh.' Adele glanced at Zach then returned her attention to her sister. 'We're not even sure.'

'Dele, don't be stupid. We're sure.'

She gave her sister a very hard look, then pasted a phony smile on her face. 'Go to bed.'

Sherilyn glanced over her shoulder. 'It was nice to meet you, Zach.'

'My pleasure.' He stared at Sherilyn's back until she disappeared. There was something going on between the sisters, but first things first. He moved toward her and placed his hands on Adele's cheeks. He lowered his face to hers and brushed his lips across her mouth and waited for her to open up for him. She remained stiff and unmoving, just as she had a few months ago when she'd thought they shouldn't get involved with each other. He pulled back and looked into her eyes. 'What's going on?' He had a feeling he knew. Ever since he'd seen Adele again, she'd talked about leaving after her sister had the baby. He'd known she would leave, he just hadn't anticipated that it would be so soon nor that the thought would leave him so cold.

'Oh . . .' She shrugged a shoulder then closed her eyes and took a deep breath.

He slid his hands to her shoulders. 'What is it?' He wouldn't mind if she decided to move to Cedar Creek. He liked having sex on a regular basis. He liked his life with her in it.

She opened her eyes and blurted on an exhaled breath, 'I have something to tell you.'

His grasp tightened, and he steeled himself against the news that she was leaving. He wondered what she would do if he asked her to stay?

'I think I might be pregnant. Maybe.'

He dropped his hands and looked into her pale face. He felt the blood drain from his head and his stomach drop. 'Tell me you're kidding.'

'I wish I was.'

The floor beneath his feet shifted, opened, and the bottom fell out of his life. 'How can you be sure?'

Adele took a drink of her chai tea. The liquid warmed her throat and upset stomach. She gazed up at Zach's brown eyes and the furrow creasing his forehead. 'I took six pregnancy tests, and they all came back positive.' She loved him with every beat of her heart. She loved the way his blond hair touched his forehead and the curve of his lips when he smiled. She loved the way he made her laugh and the way he looked at her when they were alone together. But he wasn't looking at her that way now, and she wanted so badly for him to take her into his arms and tell her everything would be okay, even if it wasn't true. 'I'm pregnant.'

Instead he stepped back as if she was suddenly radioactive. 'Goddamn it.' He scrubbed his face with his hands then pressed his fingers into his forehead. 'Fuck. How in the hell did this happen?'

Adele's heart sank, but she wasn't surprised. She moved past him and sat on the couch. She was tired and sick, and she just wanted to go to sleep and wake up and have this all be a bad dream. 'I don't know. It wasn't supposed to happen.'

He dropped his hands and turned to face her. 'You said you had one of those IUDs.'

'I do. Or did. Or, I don't know.' She took a sip of tea. 'Your condom broke just that one time. Just once. I don't understand. I can't believe this is happening. I'm as shocked at you are.' She glanced over at him and her heart sank even more. He was looking at her as he had the night the condom broke. With suspicion and distrust. 'Don't say it, Zach,' she warned.

But he went right ahead and said it anyway, 'I don't think you're as shocked as I am. You gave me the condom that broke, and obviously you don't have an IUD.'

She wanted to cut him some slack for shock, but she wasn't feeling generous. She was still in shock herself, but she wasn't blaming *him*. 'You think I planned this?'

He folded his arms across the chest of his flannel shirt and didn't say a thing. He didn't have to.

'I didn't lie about the IUD, and I didn't do anything to the condom. I just didn't know you have turbo swimmers that can take out birth control.'

'You knew this was the only way that I would ever get married again.'

She set her tea on the table and stood. She loved him, and his words sliced at her heart. 'Who said anything about getting married?'

'Isn't that what this is all about?' He raised his chin and looked down at her. 'I knock you up, and we get married?'

'No.'

'Let me make this really clear. I'm not asking this time.'

Her wounded heart could only take so much. 'Leave.' She pointed toward the front door. She was tired and sick and not in the mood to put up with Zach's anger. 'I have a doctor's appointment tomorrow,' she said, her lips stiff with her own anger. 'I'll call you once it's confirmed.'

He reached into the front pocket of his jeans and pulled out his keys. 'What time tomorrow?'

She'd called Sherilyn's OBGYN, who'd had a cancellation and had been able to get her in. 'Ten thirty. I'll call around noon.'

'I'll take you.'

'I can drive.'

'I said, I'll take you.'

'Fine.' But it wouldn't change anything. They'd find out she was pregnant, but Zach still wouldn't love her. She'd still be alone and scared and wondering what the hell she was going to do.

*

On the drive to the doctor's office the next morning, Zach was unusually quiet. The scent of him filled the Escalade, his spicy deodorant and soap mixing with the smell of leather. He wore khakis and a wool coat over a blue button-down shirt. His hair was wet as if he'd just got out of the shower, and he looked tired. She knew the feeling. He'd asked how she was feeling and if he could get her anything, but that was about it.

They sat in the waiting room with other couples, the women in various stages of hugeness. While Adele filled out her medical information, Zach hung their coats on hooks by the door, then he took the seat beside her and kicked back with a golf magazine. Adele glanced up from the clipboard at the couple across from her. The man placed a hand on his wife's rounded belly and leaned to whisper something into her ear. The woman smiled and rested her head on his shoulder. A couple in love, happy about having their baby.

Adele returned her attention to her clipboard, and her heart pinched. She looked at Zach out of the corners of her eyes. She would never have that. No loving touch or comforting whisper. No strong shoulder on which to lay her head. He lifted his gaze from his magazine. His eyes were void of any emotion.

After about half an hour, a nurse came and got Adele. When she stood, Zach rose also. She turned to him, and whispered, 'Stay out here.'

He shook his head. 'Not a chance.'

The thought of her feet in the stirrups in front of Zach heated her cheeks. 'Things get a little personal in there.'

He lowered his face and said next to her ear, 'I've

had my face in your crotch. It doesn't get any more personal than that.'

Her heated cheeks caught fire. 'Fine, but if I am pregnant, you better not swear and start saying I tricked you again.'

He sat next to her right shoulder as Dr Helen Rodriguez examined her. He didn't say anything when the doctor confirmed the pregnancy, and Adele was reluctant to look at his face to see his reaction.

When it was over, the paper drape around Adele's hip crinkled as she sat up. 'Where did the IUD go? My doctor said it was there at my last exam back in June.'

Dr Rodriguez stood and pulled off her latex gloves. 'My guess is that it's in your uterus, but I can't be sure without an ultrasound.' She tossed the gloves in the garbage and picked up Adele's chart. 'Get dressed, and a nurse will take you down the hall, and we'll look for it with the ultrasound.'

So many thoughts raced through Adele's head, and none of them stuck. She was pregnant. It was real. She was going to have a baby. It wasn't until the door closed behind the doctor, that she thought to ask questions. Like what did it mean if the IUD *was* in her uterus?

'You're pregnant.' Zach frowned and handed over her panties and jeans.

She hopped down and reached for the table for support as she stepped into her panties. Zach wrapped a hand around her arm, and she wished things were different.

'Contrary to what you think, I'm not happy about this.' She felt sick to her stomach and sick at heart. She was scared, and she just wanted someone to tell her it was all going to be okay. 'I'm not any happier about it than you are.'

'I doubt that.' He dropped his hand from her. 'You're the woman whose biological clock is tapping her on the shoulder.'

She looked up at him as she stepped into her jeans and buttoned them over her flat abdomen. 'Don't turn my words around on me. Wanting a family some-day and an unplanned pregnancy are two different things.'

The arch of his brow spoke volumes. He was never going to believe that it was unplanned.

She and Zach followed the nurse to a second room, and fifteen minutes later, she lay on a table with clear goop on her stomach while the doctor ran the probe across her skin. 'I don't see the IUD anywhere,' she said. 'If it was there, I'd see the copper.'

Adele glanced up at the doctor, then returned her gaze to the monitor screen. 'It's just disappeared?'

'It's not anywhere in your pelvis.'

'That's good. Right?' she asked.

'Very good. An IUD pregnancy is very high-risk. If it was there, we'd either have to dilate your cervix and chance a spontaneous miscarriage. Or leave it in, and at seven weeks gestation, there's a twenty-five percent chance of a spontaneous miscarriage. The rate goes up to fifty percent by midterm.'

'How does an IUD just disappear?' Zach asked.

The doctor looked at him. 'About seven percent of IUDs are expelled by a woman's body. Usually within the first year of insertion.' She returned her gaze to Adele. 'Which make this case unusual because you've had yours in for three years.' She pointed at the monitor and moved the probe. 'Here's a heartbeat.'

Adele squinted at the monitor, and Zach scooted forward in his chair for a better look. 'That little white thing surrounded by black?' he asked.

'Yep. That's a baby.'

It looked like a shrimp to Adele.

The doctor slid the probe a few inches. 'And here's the second.'

Adele scrunched up her eyes. The screen looked like a television between channels except for two black circles with white images in the middles. 'The heartbeat shows up in a second place?'

The doctor laughed. 'Two babies.'

'What?'

'Shit.' Zach sat back in his chair.

'Two?' Adele heard a buzzing in her ears.

'Yes. You're having twins,' the doctor assured her.

She closed her eyes. 'Shit.'

A half hour later, Zach helped her on with her coat. Armed with prenatal vitamins, a card with her return visit on it, and a printout of the twins, Adele walked from the doctor's office. She was numb from shock as she made her way to Zach's Escalade. Her vision blurred, and she looked down at the picture. 'These fuzzy white spots don't look like babies to me.' Her voice sounded like it was coming from a distance. 'I don't want to have twins,' she said, and held up the photo. '*You* did this to me, Zach.'

'Yeah, me and my turbo swimmers.'

'That isn't funny. What am I going to do with . . .' she held up two fingers, 'two?'

He opened the passenger door of the Cadillac. 'Twins. Jesus, are you on fertility drugs?'

She hit him on the shoulder through his coat. 'You get me pregnant with twins, then act like you're the wounded party.' She thought of how big Sherilyn had gotten with Harris, then doubled it in her head. 'I'm going to be as big as a whale,' she wailed. 'My hands and feet are going to swell up, and it's all your fault!' Hot tears splashed down her cheeks as she climbed in the car. Zach closed the door, and she wiped her face with her hands. *Twins!* She hadn't known what she was going to do with one baby, let alone two. How was she going to take care of twins? One baby would be hard enough, but two? She stared out the side window as Zach got into the vehicle. He started the engine and sat for several long moments, the sound of the heater filling the silence between them.

'Just once,' he finally spoke, 'I'd like to attend my own wedding where the bride isn't knocked up.'

Adele turned and looked at him across the SUV. 'What? I'm not marrying you.'

He leaned his head back and closed his eyes. 'You're pregnant,' he said through a sigh. 'With twins. You can't take care of two babies by yourself.'

She'd been thinking the same thing but wasn't about to admit it to him. 'Which is no reason to get married.' She shook her head. 'You don't want to marry me any more than I want to marry you.'

'Doesn't matter.' He put the Escalade into gear, and they rolled out of the parking lot. 'Pick a date, and we'll go to the courthouse and do it,' he said without the slightest hint of emotion.

'I'm pregnant, not stupid. I'm not going to make two mistakes.' It was all so horribly unromantic, so loveless, that it might have been funny if it weren't so sad. 'You don't love me, and I don't want a bad marriage on top of everything else. Admit it, you don't want to marry me any more than you wanted to marry Devon.'

He glanced over at her, and he lifted his gaze to her hair. 'It probably wouldn't be that bad.'

She hadn't realized until he'd spoken that she'd been holding her breath, waiting from him to tell her he wanted to marry her because he loved her. She'd fallen in love for the second time with the same man who didn't love. Only this time it was worse. Two times worse.

'You're not Devon.' He looked into her eyes.

She laughed through the little sob that broke her throat. What irony. She and Devon had always loathed each other and yet they'd ended up impregnated by the same man, and he didn't love either one of them. The only difference was that Adele hadn't done it on purpose. And of course, Adele would demand a lot more from the man she married than money and social position. 'You're right. I'd expect more from you than Devon. Money is easy. I'd expect something that I don't think you can give.'

'What's that?'

'I'd expect you to be faithful.'

'And you don't think I can?'

She shook her head. 'A man has to have a reason to be faithful.'

'Yeah?' he said through a scoff. 'What's that?'

'He has to love his wife.'

Zach watched Tiffany push ravioli around on her plate. She'd eaten half her pasta and salad and was now making patterns through the sauce.

'Are you finished?' he asked.

She nodded but didn't look up.

'I have to talk to you about something important.'

'Is it about Adele?'

'Yes.'

'I don't want to talk about her.'

Hell, Zach didn't really want to talk about her either. Not with Tiffany. Not until he had it all sorted out in his own head, but he figured he better before she heard the news from Kendra. 'She's going to have a baby.'

The fork stopped and Tiffany finally looked up.

'Two babies, actually.'

'Your babies?'

'Yes.'

Her big green eyes rounded. 'You had . . .' she paused and spelled out the word, '. . . s. e. x?'

'That's generally how babies are made.'

She sat back in her chair and looked at him as if he'd suddenly turned into some kind of pervert. 'Yuck! That's so . . . yucky.' She gasped and her mouth fell open. 'And you're not even married.'

Lord, he felt like a sinner. A perverted sinner.

'How could you do . . . that?'

He stood and reached for the plates. 'I'm an adult, and sometimes adults do "that." You'll understand someday.'

'You're gross!'

On top of everything else, he thought as he moved from the dining room, his daughter thought he was gross. He set the plates on the counter and planted his hands on the cold granite. How had his life gotten this fucked up? Just when it had been better than it had been in a long time, the bottom falls out. God, he'd give anything to go back to his life a few weeks ago, when everything had been good. When he'd won the state championship and he could relax. When he looked forward to seeing Adele every morning, making love, and sharing a waffle afterward.

How had this happened to him again? He'd learned his lesson the first time. He'd been careful with Adele. Even after she'd told him she had an IUD, he'd always worn a condom.

He thought of her face as the doctor examined her. She'd looked so pale and tired. When she'd slid off the table and stepped into her pink panties, he thought she might pass out, and he'd grabbed her arm to keep her from falling. He'd fought the urge to pull her against his chest and tell her everything would be okay, but he hadn't. It wasn't going to be okay.

Twins. He couldn't wrap his brain around one baby, let alone two. He didn't want any more children. Hell, he didn't know what he was doing half the time with the child he already had. He didn't want a wife either. He hadn't meant to mention marriage as an option, but as she'd sat in the Escalade crying about getting as big as a whale, he'd felt responsible. She'd accused him of getting her pregnant, then acting like the wounded party, which was partly true, and for a few unguarded seconds, he'd felt like he had fourteen years ago when Devon had told him she was pregnant. Like before, he'd proposed marriage, but unlike Devon, Adele had turned him down flat. He should be congratulating himself.

I'm pregnant, not stupid. I'm not going to make two mistakes, she'd said. *You don't love me, and I don't want a bad marriage on top of everything else.* He should be doing a victory dance in the end zone, but he didn't feel like celebrating. *Admit it, you don't want to marry me any more than you wanted to marry Devon.* He hadn't given marrying *any* woman a lot of thought. Knocked up with his twins or not. He remembered how he'd felt when he'd married Devon. Responsible. Resigned. Trapped. Like fourteen years ago, he was responsible for creating new life, two new lives, and he felt like someone had kicked him in the chest and knocked the wind out of him, but he didn't feel trapped. Adele hadn't tried to trap him, or she clearly wouldn't be so upset about it herself. He should probably clear that up with her. Maybe even apologize for thinking she'd lied about the IUD. Yeah, maybe he'd do that when she wasn't so emotional.

'Daddy?'

Zach turned his head and looked at Tiffany. 'Yeah?'

'Are you going to marry Adele?'

'I asked.' He pushed away from the counter. 'She said no.'

'She doesn't like you?' Tiffany asked, as if the mere thought was impossible.

Adele refused to marry him and didn't think he was capable of being faithful. 'No, I don't think she likes me right now.'

'Do you like her?'

'Yeah.' He liked her. He liked the way her hair wrapped around his fingers and the way her cheeks got real red when she jogged. He liked that she'd moved to Texas to help out her sister. He liked a whole lot of things about her that he wasn't even going to think about with his daughter around. Mostly, though, he liked the way she made him feel when he was with her. Alive for the first time in a very long time.

Tiffany moved toward him and wrapped her arms around his waist. 'I'm sorry I said you were gross. You're the best ever.'

At the moment he didn't feel like 'the best ever.' His life was suddenly a damn mess. He'd been knocked flat. Now he needed to pick himself up and figure out the game plan.

One thing was for certain though, having Zach's twins certainly settled the question of Adele leaving town.

Adele sat on the edge of the couch where she'd slept the night before and took a careful sip of tea. She flipped on the television and watched the last segment of *Today*. Kendra and Sherilyn had already left for the hospital an hour before. This morning, little Harris was coming home to begin his life with his mom and his sister.

Adele curled up with the quilt and took another sip, hoping she'd keep it down this time. Her shoulder ached from sleeping on the pullout, and she thought of her own bed. In her own home and she felt a wave of sickness that had nothing to do with her pregnancy.

The doorbell rang, and she ignored it. It rang again, and she pushed the quilt aside. Zach. It had to be. Who else would be so pushy so early in the morning? Adele moved to the door and swung it open to stare into Tiffany's green eyes and neon blue eye shadow.

'My daddy says you're gonna have his babies,' the teen said without so much as a hello.

'Yes.' She stuck her head outside and looked around. 'Does your daddy know you're here?'

'No. Joe and Cindy Ann Baker came over. He went to breakfast with them at the Caralinda's Cozy Cafe.'

She played with the pull on the zipper of her coat. 'I think they're dating.'

'Who? Joe and Cindy Ann?'

Tiffany nodded.

Just a few short weeks ago, Joe had wanted a skin sandwich with Adele. 'Come in.' She shut the door behind Tiffany, and the young girl followed her into the living room.

'Do you know if they're going to be girls or boys?'

'What?'

'The babies.'

'Not yet.'

Her gaze lowered to Adele's stomach. 'You don't look pregnant.'

'I'm not very far along.'

She looked back up. 'When are the babies due?'

'August.'

Her eyes rounded and she pointed to herself. 'My birthday's in August.'

Adele smiled at the irony.

'My daddy said you won't marry him.' Tiffany folded her arms across her chest. 'Why?'

She really didn't how to explain it to a thirteen-year-old. So she said simply, 'Because he doesn't love me.'

'Maybe he will.' Tiffany shrugged. 'Someday. You should think about it.'

Adele wasn't going to wait for someday. She tilted her head to one side. 'I thought you didn't like me.'

'Things are different now.'

Which was a huge understatement.

'Where's Kendra?'

'She and Sherilyn are bringing the baby home.'

'Gosh. Today?'

Adele heard the car pull into the driveway. 'Right now.' A few minutes later they were all crowded in the baby's room watching him sleep in the cradle Zach had put together. Adele was the first to leave the room. She returned to her spot on the sofa and closed her eyes. She was exhausted and wanted to go to sleep for a year or two.

It was time to go home.

18

'**Y**ou're what?' Lucy Rothschild-McIntyre sat up straight in her chair, a piece of chocolate torte suspended on the fork tines in front of her face.

Clare Vaughan stared across the kitchen table at Adele, her eyes wide as Maddie Jones set down her glass of wine and lifted a brow. 'Are you shitting me?' Maddie asked.

Adele shook her head. Her three closest friends sat at her kitchen table in her home in Boise, feasting on Lucy's torte. She'd been home a day and a half, and her friends had come over to cook dinner together and catch up. Adele had waited until dessert to drop her bombshell.

'Nope,' Adele answered, and took a bite of cake. 'Not shitting you. I'm pregnant.'

'And you waited until now to tell us.'

Adele shrugged. 'I knew that's all we'd talk about, and I wanted to know what y'all have been up to first.'

One corner of Maddie's lips rose. 'Y'all?'

'How far along are you?' Clare asked.

'Eight weeks now.' Two months. The nausea hadn't let up, and her breasts were sore. She could practically feel them getting bigger, pushing against the restraint of her C cups.

The three friends all glanced at each other, and Maddie asked, 'Who's the daddy?'

'His name is Zach Zemaitis.' The sound of his name on her lips brought back memories of him and made her heart stutter. Distance had not put a dent in healing her heart.

A frown wrinkled Lucy's brow. 'Why does that name sound familiar?'

'He used to play professional football.' She remembered the day in his office when she'd read about his skilled hands. She took another bite and said around a mouthful of torte, 'He played for Denver.'

The wrinkle in Lucy's brow smoothed. 'That Zach Zemaitis?'

'The quarterback?' Maddie once again reached for her wine. 'He's huge.'

'Yep.' Lord, cake hadn't tasted so good since she'd dated stoner Doug back in college, and she tried to concentrate on that rather than Zach and how much she missed him. Like the first time she'd been with Zach, their time hot and intense and brief, and he'd left her shattered.

'I don't watch football.' Clare shook her head. 'Sorry, I don't know who he is. How did you meet him?'

'I met him years ago at UT,' she answered, then filled them in on the past. She told them that Zach was the first guy she'd had sex with and she told them about Devon. 'Now he lives in Cedar Creek with his daughter,' she finished. She took a drink of her decaf coffee and wondered what he was doing; if he even knew that she'd left two days ago. She'd left without telling him. Not out of hurt or spite, but because he'd want to know when she'd be back, and she didn't know the answer to that herself. Or maybe he wouldn't want to know. Maybe he didn't even care. He hadn't called, so her guess would be that he didn't care. He was probably out celebrating her refusal to marry him.

'I guess it's too late for my safe-sex lecture,' Maddie said.

'We used two forms of birth control.' Or at least she'd thought she had birth control.

'What's he do now?' Clare wanted to know.

'He coaches high-school football,' she said, and recalled they way he pushed and pulled at his hat as he stood on the sidelines. Her chest ached, but she wouldn't cry. Not now. Her friends were here. She didn't want the sadness to swamp her like an incoming tide. Not yet.

'What does he think about the baby?'

Adele held up two fingers. 'I'm having twins.'

'What?'

'No!'

'Yep. Twins, and Zach believes I got pregnant on purpose to trap him into marriage.'

'Jerk.'

'Ass.'

Clare reached for Adele's hand. 'You would never do that. If he thinks so, then he is unworthy of you.'

Adele smiled and squeezed Clare's fingers. 'Thank you.'

'What are your plans?' Lucy asked.

Adele shrugged and lifted her gaze to the dark windows above Lucy's head. Outside, fat snowflakes floated toward the ground and blanketed the earth in virgin white. It was the first weekend in January. New Year. New snow. New life.

'You know we'll help you in any way that we can.' Lucy spoke for all of them.

'I know.' She looked at her friends who were so important to her. The four of them were as close as family. They'd been through a lot together and shared their writing and heartache and joy. She loved them like they were her family, but a big chunk of her heart, her life, wasn't here anymore. It was more than a thousand miles away. With Sheri and Kendra and Harris. And Zach. She wouldn't raise two children so far away from their father. It wouldn't be fair to them. Zach might be fine with having his children live several states from him. That's how he'd raised Tiffany until three years ago, but it wasn't okay with Adele. She hadn't gotten pregnant by herself, and she wasn't going to raise these babies by herself. Once the babies were born, she and Zach would have to work out custody. She couldn't ask him to uproot and move from Texas. That wasn't fair to Tiffany. Adele would have to move home, and the thought of leaving her friends added another heavy layer to her sadness.

'How do you feel?' Lucy asked. 'You look tired.'

'I am tired. I sleep a lot, and I wake up tired. On the plane here, I read *What to Expect When You're Expecting*, and I guess it's normal.' She'd spent her time the past two days reading and staring at the ultrasound of the babies. 'I have something to show y'all,' she said, and left the kitchen. She grabbed the photo from her dresser, then returned and set the picture on the table. Over the past few days, she'd started to feel a little motherly. The more she stared at the images, the more it felt real, and the more she started to feel protective. She hadn't planned to have children this way, but it wasn't their fault. An unexpected wave of warmth and love washed over her, and she lowered a hand to cover her stomach. It wasn't their fault they looked like little shrimp.

'Well,' Clare said through a smile, 'they're just adorable.'

Lucy laughed. 'They look just like you.'

Maddie leaned forward for a better look. 'Does this one have a penis?'

'Don't joke about that. I'm having girls.' The doorbell rang, and Adele left to answer it. Her friends' laughter followed her as she moved through the living room and opened the door. Immediately she froze in a way that had nothing to do with the snow falling from the sky.

'Dwayne.'

'Hi, Adele.' Her old boyfriend stood on her porch wearing a shearling jean jacket. 'You look good.'

Adele didn't know whether to scream, call the police, or punch Dwayne in the head. For three years he'd left stuff on her porch like he was on some sort of insane reconnaissance mission.

'I'm returning this.' He held up a grocery sack. 'It's that nurse's outfit we bought at The Pleasure Boutique.'

She took it from his hand and crossed her arms over her bulky sweater. 'Why didn't you just leave it on my porch and sneak off like you've been doing for the past three years?'

His cheeks turned a little more pink. ''Cause I wanted to tell you that I'm not going to do that anymore.' His breath hung in front of his face and he shrugged one shoulder. 'I can't explain why I was doing it at all. I just don't know.'

She knew.

'I'd just get this wild hair and . . .'

'Act crazy?' It was the curse.

'Yeah, but I'm over it.' He flashed her a smile that used to make her heart melt. 'You look good,' he repeated.

She wore a bulky sweater, jeans, and fuzzy slippers. Her hair was pulled back in a dreaded scrunchie, and she seriously doubted she looked anything other than complete crap.

'Maybe we can go out for a drink sometime.'

Even if she hadn't been expecting another man's babies, she wouldn't have accepted his invitation. She opened her mouth to let him down gently, but a voice from behind Dwayne said, 'She's not going anywhere with you.'

Adele lifted her gaze from Dwayne's startled face to Zach as he moved within the light of the porch. He wore his dark wool coat, and the porch light caught in the snow on his big shoulders and in his hair. Her stomach lifted and smashed into her heart.

'Who's this?' Dwayne asked.

Dwayne was a big guy, but Zach was bigger. His brown eyes bored into Dwayne like he'd dared to intercept a perfect pass. 'None of your damn business.' Zach stepped in front of Adele's former boyfriend. 'You're out of my sight for two days, and some bozo is asking you out already? If you think I'm going to wait around to catch you between dates again you're crazy.' He pointed behind him with his thumb. 'Did you tell him you're pregnant?'

'It didn't come up.'

He looked hard into her eyes. 'You are still pregnant, aren't you?'

She frowned. 'Of course. Why would you think I'm not?'

'Maybe because you left without talking to me.'

The thought of ending the pregnancy had entered her head and exited very quickly. Maybe if she hadn't seen the ultrasound, she might have given that option more than a passing thought. But she had seen it, and the babies were real to her and becoming more so with each passing hour. 'If I'd decided to end the pregnancy, I would have talked to you.'

'Ahh . . .' Dwayne said, and took a few steps back. 'I guess I'll see you around, Adele.'

'Okay.'

'No, you won't.'

Adele looked into Zach's eyes on the same level as hers. She couldn't quite believe he was actually standing in front of her. 'How did you get here?'

'The usual way. Took a plane. Rented a car with GPS. Here I am.'

'How did you know where I live?'

'Sherilyn.' A puff of warm breath hung between them. 'I went to her house this morning, and she said you'd left. You took off without a word to me about where you were going and when you'd be back.'

'I don't have to check in with you, Zach.'

He rocked back on his heels. 'I'm not going to let you move across the country with two of my children.'

She'd planned on going back, but he didn't need to know that. Not right now, when he was being so bossy. She poked a finger into his chest. 'You don't get to tell me what to do.'

He looked at her hand, then back up into her face. 'It's not just you anymore, Adele. You're having my babies, and you can't just pick up and run away when you feel like it.'

She dropped her hand. 'I wasn't running away.'

'Just like fourteen years ago.'

'I didn't run away. I left.'

'Same thing.'

'No, it isn't.'

'We can argue about this inside.'

She didn't want to argue at all.

'Adele, I'm freezing my balls off out here.'

Even though she wasn't sympathetic to his frozen balls, she took a step back, and Zach followed her inside.

'Hello, ladies,' he said, looking behind her.

With her nurse's costume in one hand, Adele turned and shut the door. Her three friends stood in the middle of the living room, their arms folded beneath their breasts as they eyed Zach. Adele walked around him and set her bag on the chair. 'Zach, these are my very good friends. This is Lucy Rothschild-McIntyre. She writes mystery novels.' Next she pointed to Clare. 'This is Clare Vaughan. She writes historical romance novels, and this is Maddie Jones. She writes true crime.'

'Adele's told me about you ladies, and it's my pleasure to meet you in person.' He unbuttoned his coat and shrugged out of it as if he intended to stay for a while. Beneath the coat he wore a white-and-blue-striped dress shirt tucked into a pair of Levi's. 'Cold enough for y'all?'

'Yes.'

'It's not bad.'

Maddie tilted her head to one side and looked at him. 'It's been colder.'

'I haven't been in a good snowstorm since I lived in Denver. Never thought I'd miss it, but I do.' He smiled and the sudden infusion of testosterone in the room messed with her friends' usually level heads. The tension eased, and they smiled back at Zach. As Adele hung his coat in the closet, they asked about his trip and about flying in through the snow.

Then Maddie got down to business. 'Adele's pregnant. What are your plans?' she asked as if she was Adele's father.

Zach smiled. 'That's between me and Adele.'

Maddie nodded and gathered her things to go. On her way out she put one hand on Adele's shoulders and looked into her eyes. 'Do you have the stun pen I gave you?'

Adele frowned. 'Somewhere.'

'Get it and the Mace.' She looked at Zach. 'If he gets out of line, zap him.'

Adele knew that Maddie was kidding – mostly.

Lucy filed out next. 'If you need anything, call.'

'I will.'

Then it was Clare's turn. 'I love you.'

'I know.' She hugged her good-bye. 'I love you, too.' She waved one last time to her friends, then shut the door behind them and moved back into the living room. Zach stood by the fireplace looking at the photos on the mantel.

'I wasn't running away, Zach. I always planned on going back to Cedar Creek.'

'When?' He set down a picture frame and looked at her.

'I don't know for sure.'

'You don't think you should have talked to me before you left? You don't think you should have mentioned your plans?'

'Maybe.' She scrubbed her face with her hands. 'But I just wanted to get away and think. I'm confused and scared, and I don't know what to do or what I'm doing. I'm thirty-five, and this has never happened to me.' She swallowed back tears when all she really wanted to do was lay her head on Zach's chest and cry. Of course that was impossible. 'I feel so stupid, but I did everything short of abstinence not to get pregnant. I know you don't believe me, but I don't know how this happened.'

He looked at her across the room, and said, 'I believe you.'

Finally. But it wasn't much comfort.

'I should have known better. I *did* know better, but I was too wrapped up in being an ass. I'm sorry.'

The apology shocked her, and her poor deluded heart read too much meaning in it. 'Well,' she said and crossed her arms over her heart. 'You should be.'

'And believe it or not, I didn't come here to fight.'

She frowned. Could have fooled her. 'You came here to see if I ended the pregnancy.'

'While that did enter my head, that's not the reason I'm here either.'

'Then why are you here?' She dropped her hands to her sides. 'And couldn't you have used the phone?'

'Yeah, I could have, but there is something I need to tell you, and you should hear it in person and not over the phone.' He moved across the room toward her. 'You said that in order for a man to be faithful, he has to love his wife. I've been thinking about that, and you're right.

Devon didn't care who I was with, and I didn't love her.' He paused and looked into her eyes. He took a deep breath and said, 'It's different with you. I love you, Adele. That's what I've come all this way to tell you. I love you.'

She looked up into his face, and her heart squeezed like a sponge.

'When you told me you were pregnant, I thought the bottom dropped out of my life, but I was wrong. When I went to your sister's to see you yesterday and you weren't there, that's when the bottom really fell out of my life.' He placed his warm hands on her cheeks. 'I can't imagine you not in my life.' He lowered his face to hers and spoke against her mouth. 'I don't want to imagine you not in my life.'

'I love you, Zach,' she whispered, just before he kissed her, tender and sweet and filled with blistering heat. She wrapped her arms around his neck and kissed him back, deeper, hotter until he lifted his head. His breath rushed fast and hot, and he pulled her against his chest. 'Come home. Live with me,' he said next to her ear. 'Marry me, Adele, and not because you're pregnant. Not because I feel responsible or because you're scared. Marry me because I love you and you love me and we should be together.'

She pulled back and looked up at him. Into his hooded brown eyes. A tear spilled from her lashes and she swallowed past the ache in her chest. 'Yes,' she said. 'And not because I'm scared and pregnant, but because I love you.'

He brushed her tear away with his thumb. 'When you first came back to town, I thought that maybe you'd come back for a reason.' One corner of his mouth lifted in a smile. 'I admit, I thought the reason was purely sexual.'

'I came back to help my sister.'

'You came back to help me.' He gave her a soft kiss that calmed her worries and soothed her heart.

He had helped her, too. He'd helped break the curse, but she figured it was best not to mention it. 'You helped me, and you helped Sherilyn. You put Harris's furniture together.'

'The furniture was an excuse to be with you.'

She wrapped her arms around his chest and pressed herself against his big warm body. 'I started to fall in love with you the day you gave me the tool belt.'

'Ah, you were dazzled by the shiny tools.'

She nodded. 'You have dazzling tools.'

He laughed. 'I remember the day I saw you standing under my portico. You looked like you'd seen a ghost, but you were beautiful.'

'Ah, you were dazzled by my lack of sleep and crazy hair.'

'I've always been dazzled by your crazy hair.' He rubbed his hands up and down her back and somehow got her sweater over her head. 'Before that day, you were just a memory. A memory of a beautiful girl I knew in college who picked me to make love to her for her first time.' He looked into her face and tossed her sweater on the floor. 'I thank God you walked out of my memory and into my life.'

She reached for the button on his shirt. 'What about Tiffany?'

'She'll be fine. I think she's looking forward to having a couple of brothers.' Adele's fingers stilled on the last button and she glanced up. 'Brothers!' He pulled his shirt out of his jeans and looked down at her bare abdomen. 'How are the boys?'

'Girls. The girls are making me nauseous in the morning.'

'Sorry about that.' He shucked the shirt from his arms and pulled her bare belly against his hot skin.

He smiled then lowered his brows. 'Your breasts are bigger.'

'They hurt.'

'Sorry about that.' But he didn't look all that sorry.

She shook her head. 'Twins. You not only get me pregnant, but you get me pregnant with twins.'

'Yeah,' he said through a smile, but this time he didn't bother saying he was sorry about that.

She ran her hands up his sides and over the hard planes of his chest. Who would have thought that she'd find love in the last place she expected? With the man who'd once broken her heart to pieces. Who would have thought Zach Zemaitis would be the man to break the curse she'd been living under?

Not Adele. He'd given her his heart and saved her from a lifetime of bad dates. He'd given her two babies growing beneath her own heart, and she would never be at all sorry about that.

Epilogue

D evon eyed the associate from women's apparel parading around in the new Covington sheath dress. That dress should have been hers, but she'd been body-slammed by the New York socialite. Who would have thought that those girls from the Hamptons knew moves like that?

Devon looked into the case of Maisonette and low-luster pearls. How had she gone from the shoe department at Walmart to the jewelry department at Sears? How was that fair? It just reminded her of all the lovely jewelry she'd once owned. Sears was just a different version of the same Walmart hell.

She stared down at the Black Hills gold that was just so wrong on so many different levels. Sears loved green, pink, and Black Hills gold, when really, if you couldn't afford platinum, why bother?

A few days ago they'd received a shipment of necklaces. All made from the different-colored golds and personalized with the likes of Foxy Lady, and Hot Momma, Nicole, and Veronica. Anyone with an ounce of class knew that wearing personalized anything was vulgar and had socialist undertones.

Just as she reached for an interesting ruby pendant,

the jewelry case wavered and shimmered into nothing. The walls of Sears evaporated, and her skin tingled as she once again stood amongst clouds wearing her Chanel bouclé outfit and Mikimoto pearls. She looked up as Mrs Highbarger suddenly appeared out of nowhere.

'It's a good thing you stayed put this time. I wasn't in the mood to waste time looking for you. I have important things to do.'

Devon wasn't certain, but it hadn't seemed like she'd been in Sears all that long.

Seven months now, her old teacher informed her without speaking. 'You've earned another gift.'

She was shocked and a little confused. 'Is what's-her-name pregnant?'

'Yes, with twin boys.'

Twin boys. 'Yes!' She pumped her fist in the air. 'There is a God.'

Of course there's a God. And He hears you.

Oops.

As one, the two of them moved up the invisible escalator, and she asked, 'What's going on?'

'See for yourself.'

They stopped, the clouds cleared, and Devon looked down into a backyard garden. What's-her-name wore a long white dress and a wreath of roses in her wild hair. Zach stood behind her wearing a dark blue suit. His arms were wrapped around her sides and his hands were on her huge pregnant belly. He looked happy. Happier than she'd ever seen him off the football field. Happier than he'd ever been with her. This wasn't how the curse was supposed to work. It wasn't right. It wasn't right that she had to slave away in

Sears for all eternity selling Cubic Zirconia and faux pearls, and he got to be happy with what's-her-name.

'Are they married then?'

'Just today.'

Anger and hatred swirled and coalesced within her chest. This could not happen. She would not let this happen. 'I've earned another gift?'

'Yes. Use it wisely.'

She put her fingers to her lips and contemplated what to do next. Everything she'd tried so far had backfired. She needed something good. Something foolproof. Something . . .

Within the cloudy vision, Tiffany walked across the yard toward her father. Devon's heart swelled with pride and love. Her baby was getting so grown-up. She wore a light pink silk dress, and her hair was piled up on her head and circled with pink roses. She looked beautiful and just like Devon at that age.

Zach said something that made Tiffany laugh, and she playfully punched him in the arm. Then she bent forward, cupped her hands around her mouth, and spoke to her new stepmomma's belly.

'What's your next gift?' Mrs Highbarger asked.

She opened her mouth and closed it. She hated Zach for not loving her the way he loved his new wife. She hated what's-her-name more . . . but Tiffany looked happy. Really happy. 'I don't know.'

'We don't have eternity.'

She blinked at the image several times. More than she wanted to get back at Zach and his new wife, she wanted her child to be happy. She opened her mouth and heard herself say, 'I guess I'm not going to do anything.' Even if it meant going back to Sears and wearing a personalized Foxy Lady necklace for eternity.

Mrs Highbarger smiled. 'Finally.'

'Finally what?'

The teacher took a step back through heavy gold doors that suddenly appeared. The doors whooshed closed and the gray mist formed solid walls. Even though Devon knew the drill, she was terrified as her skin tingled and she looked down at herself as her beautiful Chanel suit warped and shimmered. 'Where am I this time?' she called out. The suit dissolved and in its place she wore a Carolina Herrera black cocktail dress made of silk. Christian Louboutin pumps appeared on her feet.

She looked around and gasped. Gucci. Fendi. Louis Vuitton. She raised a shaky hand to her lips as she recognized the sights and smells. 'Saks Fifth Avenue,' she whispered. The flagship store. If she could have, she would have wept.

Finally, Devon Hamilton-Zemaitis had died and gone to heaven.

little
black
dress

brings you
fantastic new books like these
every month - find out more at
www.littleblackdressbooks.com

And why not sign up for our
email newsletter to keep
you in the know about
Little Black Dress news!

Pick up a *little black dress* – it's a girl thing.

978 0 7553 3746 0

IT MUST BE LOVE
Rachel Gibson
PB £4.99

Gabriel Breedlove is the sexiest suspect that undercover cop Joe Shanahan has ever had the pleasure of tailing. But when he's assigned to pose as her boyfriend things start to get complicated.

She thinks he's stalking her. He thinks she's a crook. Surely, it must be love?

ONE NIGHT STAND
Julie Cohen
PB £4.99

978 0 7553 3483 4

When popular novelist Estelle Connor finds herself pregnant after an uncharacteristic one-night stand, she enlists the help of sexy neighbour Hugh to help look for the father. But will she find what she really needs?

One of the freshest and funniest voices in romantic fiction

Pick up a *little black dress* – it's a girl thing.

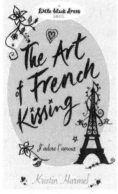

978 0 7553 3828 3

THE ART OF FRENCH KISSING
Kristin Harmel
PB £4.99

When Emma lands her dream job in Paris, she starts to master the art of French kissing: one date, one kiss and onto the next delectable Frenchman. But what happens if you meet someone you want to kiss more than once . . .

A très chic tale of Paris, paparazzi and the pursuit of the perfect kiss

THE CHALET GIRL
Kate Lace
PB £4.99

Being a chalet girl is definitely not all snowy pistes, sexy ski-instructors and a sensational après-ski nightlife, as Millie Braythorpe knows only too well. Then handsome troublemaker Luke comes to stay at her chalet and love rages, but can he be trusted or will her Alpine romance end in wipeout?

978 0 7553 3831 3

Pick up a *little black dress* – it's a girl thing.

978 0 7553 3959 4

TANGLED UP IN YOU
Rachel Gibson
PB £4.99

Sex, lies and tequila slammers

When Maddie Dupree arrives at Hennessy's bar looking for the truth about her past she doesn't want to be distracted by head-turning, heart-stopping owner Mick Hennessy. Especially as he doesn't know why she's really in town . . . .

SPIRIT WILLING, FLESH WEAK
Julie Cohen
PB £4.99

Welcome to the world of Julie Cohen, one of the freshest, funniest voices in romantic fiction!

When fake psychic Rosie meets a gorgeous investigative journalist, she thinks she can trust him not to blow her cover – but is she right?

978 0 7553 3481 0

Pick up a *little black dress* – it's a girl thing.

THE TRUE NAOMI STORY
A.M. Goldsher
PB £4.99

Naomi Braver is catapulted from waiting tables to being the new rock sensation overnight. But stardom isn't all it's cracked up to be . . . Can Naomi master the game of fame before it's too late?

A rock'n'roll romance about one girl's journey to stardom

978 0 7553 3992 1

FORGET ABOUT IT
Caprice Crane
PB £4.99

When Jordan Landeua is hit by a car, she seizes the opportunity to start over and fakes amnesia. But just as she's said goodbye to Jordan the pushover, the unthinkable happens and she has to start over for real. Will she remember in time what truly makes her happy?

978 0 7553 4204 4

You can buy any of these other
Little Black Dress titles from your
bookshop or *direct from the publisher*.

FREE P&P AND UK DELIVERY
(Overseas and Ireland £3.50 per book)

Everything Nice	Ellen Shanman	£4.99
Just Say Yes	Phillipa Ashley	£4.99
Hysterical Blondeness	Suzanne Macpherson	£4.99
Blue Remembered Heels	Nell Dixon	£4.99
Honey Trap	Julie Cohen	£4.99
What's Love Got to do With It?	Lucy Broadbent	£4.99
The Not-So-Perfect Man	Valerie Frankel	£4.99
Lola Carlyle Reveals All	Rachel Gibson	£4.99
The Movie Girl	Kate Lace	£4.99
The Accidental Virgin	Valerie Frankel	£4.99
Reality Check	A.M. Goldsher	£4.99
True Confessions	Rachel Gibson	£4.99
She Woke Up Married	Suzanne Macpherson	£4.99
This Is How It Happened	Jo Barrett	£4.99
The Art of French Kissing	Kristin Harmel	£4.99
One Night Stand	Julie Cohen	£4.99
The True Naomi Story	A.M. Goldsher	£4.99
Smart Vs Pretty	Valerie Frankel	£4.99
The Chalet Girl	Kate Lace	£4.99
True Love (and Other Lies)	Whitney Gaskell	£4.99
Forget About It	Caprice Crane	£4.99
It Must Be Love	Rachel Gibson	£4.99
Chinese Whispers	Marisa Mackle	£4.99

TO ORDER SIMPLY CALL THIS NUMBER

01235 400 414

or visit our website: www.headline.co.uk

Prices and availability subject to change without notice.